The Plan

Susan Klopfer

Copyright © 2013, 2014 Susan Klopfer

Published in the United States by Susan Klopfer, WHO DUNNIT PRESS www.whodunnitpress.com

Contact: publisher@whodunnitpress.com

Development Editor: Frances Hogg Lochow
Development and Copy Editor: Geri Jeter
Cover Designer: Samantha Hensler

ISBN-10: 0982604998

ISBN-13: 978-0-9826049-9-1

Formatted by eBooksMade4You@gmail.com

Readers are saying—

"Klopfer has woven history, fiction, and fantasy into a compelling tale that not only highlights real events, but describes them in a fascinating narrative that pulls the reader along for the ride." — Chris Petersen, author of Methuselah's Secret

"It is such a gift to be able to bring history to life in the form of engaging fiction. Susan Klopfer does this so very well in a gripping, 'edge of your seat' fashion. Bravo!" —Denis Campbell, host and managing editor, World View Show; editor, UK Progressive

"This is a bold and first-rate work that explores very significant social frontiers. Susan Klopfer is a veteran activist of high courage—and a fine writer very well versed in the creative art of suspense." —Hunter Gray, [Hunter Bear/John R. Salter Jr.] Mi'kmaq, author of Jackson Mississippi: An American Chronicle of Struggle and Schism

"Forty-one chapters of conspiracy-filled action, The Plan is tightly based on true fact. Susan Klopfer has written historical nonfiction books for years. This time, she goes a step farther to solve murders that investigators haven't been willing to touch." — Patricia Fua, librarian

"I am not much of a history nut, but I really enjoyed the book. A nicely crafted mix of history, plot, conspiracy, and fun. Well done." — Robert Higgins, M.F.T.

"If you like murder mysteries, suspense, travel, legal topics, mixed with civil rights and fantasy, in an old-fashioned whodunnit that doesn't leave out the FBI, CIA, and COINTELPRO, I know you will like this action-packed read." —Betty Orr, writer

"Filled with information to titillate the most sophisticated conspiracy theorist, Susan Klopfer 's first foray into thriller fiction is thought-provoking fodder and a fun read!" —Frances Hogg Lochow, author, and editor

"'It takes a village to commit atrocities [like JFK's assassination]!' Loved this quote by Sara Mercury, a fired fictional journalist looking for the story of her life (a character in The Plan)!" — Steve Hall, book lover

Other Books by Susan Klopfer

The Emmett Till Book

Who Killed Emmett Till?

Where Rebels Roost: Mississippi Civil Rights Revisited

Abort! Retry! Fail! The PC Answer Book

301 Ways ++ To Get Ahead: Business Success at Home

How Branson Got Started

Internet Success with Fred (with Fred Klopfer)

To Fred, who patiently hears the stories —again and again

Prologue

January 30, 2013
New York University, Department of History

The news came in quickly from Chile on his phone screen. He had to enlarge the display with his index and middle fingers to see it all and read the report, but he loved any technology gadget coming his way, even with their limitations. He'd programmed his phone to receive push notifications and in this case, the story he was analyzing had pushed itself some 5,130 miles north, from Santiago to New York City.

Dr. Dan Bell just learned that Chile's Supreme Court late yesterday had sentenced to prison six former leaders of a torture ring located in a colony hidden in the Andes. A former victim of Colonia Dignidad (a Neo-Nazi camp opened in the mid-1960s by a fanatical German minister) had launched a substantial lawsuit, in the millions of U.S. dollars, against both Chile and Germany, due to their alleged negligence.

"They knew about this and still did nothing about the torture and human rights violations going on there for nearly fifty years," the victim claimed. He was likely correct, Bell thought; the professor was acquainted with a woman who could back up this frightening story, the sister of a deceased colony victim.

Bell returned his phone to the breast pocket of his expensive suit jacket and continued walking down the hallway. He looked up to check his watch against the clock hanging on the wall, reminding himself to call Olga

Weisfeiler and his friend Clinton Moore later that morning. Olga might have something to say about this news event, since her brother, Boris, a presumed Dignidad victim, went missing in the Andes in 1985. Boris, Bell's former colleague at Penn State University, had been camping and hiking alone on a South American expedition when he disappeared. Olga dogged the Chilean government repeatedly over her brother's whereabouts for years, with no success.

Bell now headed into the graduate student conference room toward the small square table set up with coffee and condiments, still considering in the back of his mind the information he'd picked up from his cell phone. He poured himself a cup and laced it with milk and sugar before nodding to his eager graduate students. His call to Clinton, an old law school classmate in the Mississippi Delta who was coming up on his seventy-second birthday, was forgotten. The conversation with Olga took more time than planned, and he simply forgot. By the time he thought about it again, it was too late.

PART I

CHAPTER ONE

My name is Clinton Moore. I am a lawyer born and raised in the Mississippi Delta. I almost made it to my seventy-second birthday—invited over a hundred guests to my party—but a client, and then a stranger, wrecked my plans the day before my cake was to go into the oven.

Mike, who I'd been defending for driving under the influence of drugs and alcohol, was helping me build my new house at the edge of Clarksdale, my hometown, in trade for legal representation on his latest screw-up. I was carrying a lot of money that day—my part of a settlement in a case against a giant Memphis gas company. It was a tough win and having the money on me felt pretty damned good.

"That's a mighty big wad of cash you've got in your wallet, Mister Clinton." Mike grinned as he watched me pull out a couple of bills to pay for construction supplies delivered on site. I smiled back at the kid and returned to work. Didn't want to lecture him, but one day he might grow up and stay out of trouble—at least I'd hoped.

We worked under the blazing Mississippi sun a few more hours, then I looked up at him from my posthole digger, deciding it was time to lay off for the day.

"Hey Mike, it's starting to get late, and we've been moving this dirt for hours. Let's you and me go back to my place and catch a shower," I winked. He was a good-looking young man, old enough to be legal, and we'd already been together.

I liked men more than women. Since junior high, I'd shielded my family and most colleagues from this secret, but my closest friends knew I wasn't straight, including Tom and Karen, my minister and his wife.

In the late 1950s and 60s, you had to keep this hush-hush. Back then, you could be killed for being queer, especially if you were black and lived in Mississippi. But, in my later years, I didn't have to be so careful, and society's change to openness had made life easier.

I thought I knew Mike and looked forward to the next few hours in bed. He was young and firm, with muscles that rippled in the sun, and we should have had a pretty good time together. When we got to my house, I thought Mike followed me upstairs. I was already naked, shedding my clothes on the way up to my bedroom.

I didn't see him grab my 9 mm Glock from a table next to the stairwell. Like all my guns at home, the office, and in the trunk of my car, I kept it locked, loaded, and safety off. I'd reached the top landing, making a quarter-turn of my upper body to the left, to smile down at him. Mike aimed the gun straight at me.

"Oh, God. Don't do this, Mike!" I screamed.

He pulled the trigger, and the bullet entered my left forearm and lodged in my right shoulder, traveling up through my neck. I dropped to the floor, and as my blood spilled onto the white hall carpet, Mike ran up the stairs, found my pants where I'd dropped them off, and reached into the pocket to pull out my fat wallet and take my money.

Then Mike surprised me. He apologized before leaving me there, bleeding. He acted shaken and cried. "Sorry, dude. I didn't really mean it. He made me do it, that man. I didn't want to, but I had to. *Oh, shit!*"

Mike ran back down the stairs, grabbed my keys, and fled out the front door. I heard him drive off in my new

Cadillac. I always knew the kid had no impulse control. This was obvious all along. But who was the man he'd talked about? The man who told him to shoot me?

Once Mike left, everything slowed down and became quiet. I heard my lifeblood draining, and with the little strength I had left, I crawled over to my bedroom door, propped myself up against it, and waited to die. No one would find me; I knew it was over.

Twenty minutes or so later, a strange man slowly opened my front door and crept up the staircase. He found me struggling to breathe. Through the haze I could see he was tall, his body well-toned. Older than I, his steel gray head was closely shaved.

As he bent over to see if I was dead, I noticed his gaunt face, his sharp nose, and his high cheekbones. I tried asking why he wanted to kill me, but could not get my lips to move. The last thing I remember was his strange eyes peering down at me, one green and the other blue. He raised his pistol, and the bullet drove into my left temple, traveling down to my neck. Then my lights went out.

I have no earthly idea how much time passed, but when I tried shaking off the fog, there was nothing left of me to shake. My body was gone. I sensed a slight growing buzz and realized I must be dead, whatever dead was. I began to pay attention to where I'd landed, guessing it was some afterlife I'd constructed for myself.

Would I see my longtime friend and serious lover who was killed two and a half years earlier? Joe's murder had sent me into a sheltered life. I'd been so scared, after seeing that he'd been physically tortured, that I'd quit going to my law office and hung out around my church, where I was the minister, building membership and fixing up the place. I did all of my legal work there and at home instead of my regular office, after Joe's murder.

I could talk about my new state of being for eons, but it's important to look at what was happening back in the physical world shortly after I was killed, since the man who murdered me was still hanging around my house. Perhaps I could figure out who he was!

I hovered over him and watched as he messed up everything, digging through drawers and closets, tearing up cupboards, knocking over a lamp or two, looking for my secrets. All of my important records—including documents showing a racist Mississippi U.S. senator's involvement in assassinations—were stored in the locked safe at my office. Apparently, my killer didn't know this, or he would have gone over there and blown it open, once he finished his work at my house. But he didn't.

When my killer couldn't find what he was looking for, he put my house back in order. That was weird, but I figured he was trying to keep the heat on Mike by cleaning up his own mess and restoring my house to what he thought was normal. This way, it would look like Mike and I'd had a lover's quarrel that ended in a shooting, and nothing else. After killing me, Mike would have had no reason to search my house for anything in particular.

The more I thought about this strange man's actions, the more I believed he probably was the same man who'd told Mike to shoot me. He'd come in behind the kid to make sure Mike did exactly what he'd been told to do.

It was all so crazy, but I followed my murderer around the house while he washed, dried, and stacked my dirty dishes, picked up my dirty underwear and socks, and swept the kitchen floor. I was still wobbly at moving around, but got better as we traveled together. Once, I sat on his shoulders, and he tried to flick me off like a booger, not realizing it was me going along for the ride.

Picking up my magazines and papers from the floor, he neatly placed them on the coffee table—straighter than I'd ever kept them. Later, I'd hear some of my closest friends saying that my house was way too clean when they found me, and that something wasn't right.

When the man who killed me finally put my house back neater than I'd ever kept it, he slipped out the side door and drove off. Curious, I floated along, having no idea where we were going. But I left him at the Jackson-Medgar Wiley Evers International Airport before dispatching myself back north to the Delta.

Morning came, along with my sister Betty, who started knocking at my door at 7:45 a.m. My family always had been nosey about my life, especially after I moved back home in 1971. I'm sure they wondered why I didn't have a wife or date women. They never directly asked me any questions about this, but always seemed to be looking in on me, especially Betty. She had this habit of waking me up in the morning with a phone call to see if I'd left for work. It was silly of her. She didn't need to do this, since I always showed up to work on time, but on this particular morning, I appreciated her usually unwelcome intrusion.

When she couldn't get any response to her wake-up call, she walked a couple of blocks to my house. I heard her knock, trying to get my attention. I was already frustrated because I couldn't answer her earlier phone call and was annoyed that my message machine kept bleeping I wasn't home.

"Clinton! Wake up! It's Betty! You've got to get to work." She pounded hard a couple more times, then opened my front door—that I never locked—and walked inside. Normally, Betty would never have called Chief Jim Billy for help, not on her life. That cracker belonged to the Ku Klux Klan, like so many other white Delta cops. But in this case, after seeing my house abnormally clean, and not being able to wake me up with her yelling, she must have felt terrified, so she dialed 911 from her cell phone.

Within two minutes, Chief Billy raced over in his squad car—siren blaring and lights blazing. It had to be his fastest response to any crime scene, ever. He walked inside and swept the room with his muddy eyes, then bounded upstairs where he tripped over my dead body. I was there on the carpet staring up at him and saw the chief's lip curl into a sneer. I tried to wink, but couldn't. Billy had hated me since junior high school. Years later, he'd spread rumors that I was starting house fires around town so that my legal clients could cash in on their homeowner's insurance.

Billy trotted back down the stairs and lost no time telling Betty I was dead as a doornail. "You'll have to leave the house right now, Missy Betty. I got po'tant work to do, and you'll get yo'sef in the way."

After Billy bum-rushed her out the front door, he did a quick investigation of the crime scene. Three minutes later, Billy dispatched an officer on his two-way radio to haul off what used to be me in the county ambulance while he stayed inside tearing up the floorboards and walls, looking for who knows what! There was nothing hidden in my house, and Billy had to realize this, but he went ahead anyway and tore the hell out of it.

Eventually, Billy walked out to his squad car, carrying a small paper bag, and drove off. He probably didn't want to appear empty-handed when leaving the crime scene, so he placed a few pieces of flooring into his sack. I floated along in his police car to see where he was headed. He stopped off first at the local Rebel's Roost Grill, which we all called "The Grill," where he started spreading gossip that I'd been pushing drugs and child porn. Always was a pitiful little man, that Chief Billy.

I hovered around my friend Walker, owner of the Grill, who after growing disgusted with Billy's mean-spirited talk, sneaked into the kitchen and called up an old white liberal county judge on his cell phone, telling him what Billy was up to. Judge Asher Roy promised he would issue a gag order, while apologizing in advance to Walker that it probably wouldn't do much good. The judge went ahead with the paperwork; to this day, the order has never been lifted.

Later that afternoon, I heard my body drop on a steel table at the state medical examiner's morgue down in Jackson, 172 miles due south of my home. The examiner gets $500 per examined body and knows how to work the system. He's sloppy and slick. He didn't examine the contents of my stomach or look for venous punctures. Didn't check my scalp or feet. He included no ballistics report in his final narrative on me so no one ever questioned the two unique wounds from two distinct weapons delivered by two different people.

I was riding around with the Chief a couple of days later when we caught up with the first shooter, Mike, in another little Delta town forty-five minutes south of Clarksdale. All my money turned up in my Caddy's glove compartment; my Glock, two rifles, and shotgun were still in my trunk.

When the ADA questioned Mike, she bluffed the kid into pleading guilty to first-degree manslaughter. Otherwise, she threatened, Mike would face capital murder charges. When she warned the kid, "You'll get a needle in your arm if you don't agree to this," Mike looked damned frightened. I felt bad for him and disgusted with her. She would do anything to wrap up a case real quick! But I was dead. What could I do?

I tried to defend Mike because he didn't kill me. I heard Mike screaming that a strange man made him shoot me, and that when he left my house, I wasn't dead. But no one listened to him. Floating across the room and waving my phantom arms, I shouted to no avail. No one could hear me, no matter how hard I worked, so I finally gave up.

If none of this makes sense, or if it sounds too ridiculous, it would not be the first time things were screwy in the Magnolia State. I'd been secretly collecting evidence on cold cases—murder and other violent atrocities against black people, and some white folks—for my entire legal life. Obviously, someone wanted me to stop what I was doing, and to steal or destroy my secret files. To keep the documentation I'd collected from causing them problems. Don't bother thinking it was Chief Billy who did this to me, since his radar wasn't usually plugged into the socket, if you know what I mean.

When the Chief left the Grill, I'm sure he was thinking this would be the end of it. And, for most people around Mississippi, especially the white politicians, law enforcement officers, most journalists, and state archival librarians, and even my closest friends and colleagues and family—once I was dead—that WAS the end of it. Except my name still pops up every so often.

CHAPTER TWO

One morning, a couple of weeks after I'd been killed, while hovering over the construction site of my new home that never got finished, I overheard through the open window next door a conversation between a couple of Clarksdale ladies.

If I'd lived to complete my new home, I would have been neighbors with Lucy Bingham Moore, a white female in her late fifties, who wears mid-calf synthetic material dresses and tells others how she hates what she calls homos, carefully getting in both syllables.

Missy Lucy was on the phone with Doris Lee Saylor, a prominent Clarksdale woman, who was gushing. "Lucy, your husband Tom's lovely old home was voted by the Culture Club this morning as the site for our Fall Spectacular Event! We're so happy for both of you! Keep this date open—September 27, 2014. We always plan ahead!"

While Lucy was digesting the call, I noticed Doris, who was off elsewhere on her own mental tangent. I guess Doris was picturing Thomas Moore III's early twentieth-century home as the perfect site for her gala. It would make her look so important, once she inked the deal with Lucy.

Reminiscent of the Old South, the two-story red-brick home was set on a large piece of land at the edge of Clarksdale, just off old Highway 61 going north out of town and known as the Blues Highway. The picture of

Southern hospitality, with its high white Roman columns, tall French windows swinging in to let breezes cool the interior, and forest-green shutters filtering the sunlight, this landmark brought a rich sense of history to the Delta, making it perfect for the event.

Of course it was Lucy's home, too—sort of—but everyone knew about Lucy and Tom's prenuptial agreement; Lucy would never own clear title to Tom's place. Even if Tom died, it would go to his sister. He'd put this in writing, and I knew the lawyer who had prepared it.

But this was to be Clarksdale's 164th annual Culture Club gathering. As Doris spoke to Lucy, I envisioned the fragile ash from her cigarette growing longer until it fell to the floor—that would be so Doris—a slim, anxiety-driven white woman in her late fifties, who liked her jeans tight, her blond hair cropped short, and a martini in her left hand.

Clarksdale was founded by Doris's pioneer relative in 1848, thirteen years before the Civil War began. One year later, he had organized the Culture Club, to give white Clarksdale ladies a focus for their lives. The Club was Doris Lee Saylor's to protect.

"Will there be a story in the Clarksdale newspaper with a photo?" Lucy appeared hesitant in asking about publicity, likely not wanting to make waves and lose this chance for her debut into Clarksdale high society. Doris mentally thought back to their phone conversation and assured Lucy that the local editor would take lots of photos for the society page.

"When can we get together and go over details?"

Doris hesitated. I'm sure she unwittingly concurred it would take more than one meeting for Lucy to grasp her total responsibilities.

"I'll call you very soon."

I heard a loud buzz when Doris placed the phone on its hook, interference that sometimes happens when messages are coming in from my new message board. I was still learning how *dead* works out in these aspects.

Curious, I made it over to Doris's house via the Clarksdale city bus. I found her sitting at her Grandmother Saylor's favorite writing desk, penning a quick note to Lucy. She was outlining Lucy's role as hostess and requesting that she sign a memo of understanding, just to keep everything businesslike; she learned this from her daddy.

Rising from the old mahogany writing table, Doris paused to look out her living room picture window, which was located in back of their plantation home and faced the family's one remaining cotton field.

A warm-colored glow engulfed her body. She probably was thinking about her family's fortunes. Only those with true Delta roots could understand her pride. And *yes*, the "Lee" in Doris Lee Saylor stood for the old general—Robert E.—who was part of her direct blood line.

When I returned to Lucy's house, she was seated at OUR Grandmother Frieda's stained wood dining room table, sipping a fresh cup of tea. I'm sure she was trying to cover every angle of how she would look to the community as hostess of this prestigious event, perhaps figuring that Tom would have time to plant fresh pansies, ornamental cabbage, and dill in the front yard. If Tom's new plants made it through the summer heat to survive the early autumn frosts, all this new foliage would brighten up the event and make Lucy look even better.

I'd been the keeper of family histories since high school, and when Lucy married Tom Moore, I traced her family to the Republican Walkers of Ohio. Her mother's clan had invaded the South after the War, meddling with Reconstruction and making enemies of the losers.

Tom Moore had his own personal complications. Like many small southern towns, nearly all influential residents struggled with two versions of their family trees.

On one side of Tom's family were the white Moores of Clarksdale, and on the other side were the rest of us who held a pinch of the old white planter's blood in our gene pool.

If an outsider was looking for a certain person from an important family in town say, Tim Harper, they'd do best to announce, "I'm looking for the *white* Harpers" or "Anybody know where I can find the *black* Harpers?" Especially if they wanted quick directions to the correct Harper household. Of course, this was the same with finding the black or white Moores of Clarksdale.

Seldom were all families cross-invited to reunions, like Thomas Jefferson's mixed-race kin, but in these post-civil rights movement years, the two Moore families, like some others, were starting to tolerate each other, going so far as to wave hello at the supermarket.

Still, Clarksdale maintained, by everyone's choice, its segregated beauty parlors and funeral homes; the most intimate personal care stayed separated.

Lucy Moore's remarkable rise in this Delta town's white society rested on Tom's three-times great-grandfather, old man Thomas Moore (the first), who because of the South's peculiar institution, and because of his loose genes, was also MY family's old man, Thomas Moore.

Of course, Lucy had no idea that Tom and I shared roots. I sure as hell wasn't going to deliver this news, and neither was he!

The old cotton-planter-turned-banker had earned his money off the backs of my people—his enslaved—and started his business at the end of the Lost Cause, or what some of us call the Civil War. My side of the Moore family never saw any of his money, and there were plenty of us around town, thanks to his virility. Only the white Moores got his money, and they lost most of it in bad investments.

The Moores of Coahoma County represented people from Africa to Ulster. The old white man's pioneer relatives, who first came to the Carolinas in the mid 1700s as descendants of Scots, brought their captive slaves here to work the land. From my genealogical studies, I'd learned the black Moore ancestors were kidnapped from Senegambia, West Africa, but I'm still doing the research. There's a good library where I've landed, with real Mormon archivists.

So, even with his family money mostly spent, Tom Moore still held the old plantation home, a decent job at the bank named after his family, his ancestral Bible brought across the Atlantic, and of course, the Moore surname, making Lucy Bingham Moore a grateful New South woman, despite her being a Buckeye.

Lucy's euphoria appeared interrupted. She sat up in her chair, smacking her fine china teacup on its saucer hard enough to make it rattle, but not crack.

She had to be remembering me! Clinton Moore. A very gay, very black, activist lawyer who almost had been her next door neighbor. I watched her eyes rapidly shift to the left as she peered through the side window of her dining room, then rest on what she frequently called *that damned white rusted-iron fence in front of that mess of a lot next door*.

This was Lucy's description of my specially machined white iron fence, the boundary that would have separated us, had I lived. Its front gate was frozen half-shut and covered with crawling green kudzu.

I'm sure she planned to ask Tom to buy my vacant lot from my sister, so she could rip out my fence, pull up my kudzu, and turn my whole place into a giant flowerbed. Before getting Tom to comply, though, she would have to fix him a nice supper.

At least I was dead. I could hear her clucking about me, while she took a final sip of fresh mint tea, then returned to Tom's parlor, dusting his piano for the third time that day.

CHAPTER THREE

"The best way to describe the Yazoo-Mississippi Delta is that it looks like half a football on the map. Its crescent of small counties hugs the River between Memphis and Vicksburg. We called our home the Delta, and it hasn't changed much at all since the 1800s with its rich soil, cotton fields, wealthy planters, and desperate poverty." *From an oral history interview with Clarksdale attorney Clinton Moore, Spring 2012.*

About a year before a complete stranger murdered me, I was invited by a small private college in Jackson to talk about my part in the modern civil rights movement, first as an activist student and then as a lawyer.

The Millsaps history honors student started out by asking what it was like growing up in the Delta. He seemed envious when I told him I'd been raised near the home towns of B.B. King and Howlin' Jack Wolf, his two favorite bluesmen.

Jim, I'll call him, knew that Clarksdale was the blues capital of the world. He was curious about why I'd left this music oasis, and I told him that by the end of high school. I was ready to fly!

"The old white cotton planters around Clarksdale gave me no reason to stay. I wanted to go out and be part of the modern civil rights movement."

I traveled back in time, telling Jim how I'd helped when the early Freedom Riders came into the city of Jackson.

"I'll never forget these special young and old, black and white, men and women, all brave enough to show up in this violent state to challenge the system. My job was to gather all their vital information before they were hauled off to Parchman Prison in the Delta, where we feared they would disappear.

"So what made you go back home to the Delta? That's quite a change from working in Jackson, isn't it? And then, Chicago?"

I told him a quick story that started out one muggy morning in 1971. While I was preparing for court, the phone rang.

CHAPTER FOUR

May 24, 1971

"You better come home, Clinton. We need your help before somebody else gets killed." Mrs. Fannie Lou Hamer's voice trembled. I cradled the phone between my neck and right ear to talk while hunched over, stuffing case files into my briefcase. She'd caught me off guard.

"What do you mean?"

The civil rights icon spilled out her story. A young girl was murdered the night before in a small cotton ginning town in the heart of the Delta, two and a half hours north of Jackson. Drew was close to where fourteen-year-old Emmett Till was lynched back in August 1955, right after the Supreme Court's Brown II decision to speed up school integration. The place is still known for violence; after a small lynch mob tortured and killed this kid, they drove over to Glendora and threw his body into the Tallahatchie River, weighted down by a heavy circular cotton gin fan.

I was a kid in junior high back when Till was beaten and murdered in a small tool shed owned by a planter. The lynching attracted international media and helped spark the entire modern civil rights movement in the United States. After Rosa Parks heard the story, she decided to go ahead with her plan to sit at the front of a Montgomery city bus.

Nothing about this ugly town ever surprised me, though, including this new shooting of another school-aged child, on her graduation night.

Mrs. Hamer was in tears. "My sweet little Jo Etha was shot and killed, right after she left the high school gym. You know her—she helped register voters for my state legislature campaign." She stopped to catch her breath. Mrs. Hamer—we always called her this out of deep respect—had known this young woman personally. This sudden, malicious act was affecting her deeply. I could tell by the crack in her voice.

"All she was doin' was drinkin' a soda pop with friends in front of the grocery store, showin' off her athletic award, when a pickup truck drove by real slow, and a white kid stuck his gun through the side window. Jo Etha was hit in the neck. They took her to the hospital over in Cleveland, but she was already dead. Too late, they told her mother."

From secret state reports, I later discovered that a 22-caliber pistol "with one bullet missing" was found in the truck along with a 12-gauge Army issue riot gun and a 22-caliber automatic rifle. The information was slipped to me by a friendly Sovereignty Commission secretary, and it looked to me like the truck driver and his two buddies had planned one hell of a night ride throughout the Delta. Like the old days when Klansmen rode through on horses to kill and terrorize black people. Fortunately, the three of them were stopped after the first bullet.

We quit talking—letting silence have its say. I wanted to slam the damned phone down and walk away, but I couldn't do this to Mrs. Hamer. So I eased back into the conversation.

"Sounds like Greenville, doesn't it?"

Two years earlier, Flora Jean Smith died violently in this river town; shot to death and her body thrown into a stagnant *bogue* north of town. A white man first lured this teenage girl into his car to babysit his child. But he lied.

He had no children and later confessed he wanted to see how it felt to kill a black girl.

Mrs. Hamer was twenty-four years older than me. We'd grown up hearing rumors about dead bodies at the bottom of the Delta's small lakes or caught in the rushes of slow-moving bayous. Most folks could direct you to *Whore's Lake*—a large gray body of still water outside of Drew, tucked between the cotton fields. Filled with bodies of black women killed by Klanswomen for sleeping with their men, the white women claimed.

"He was arrested and jailed the same night as he killed her," Mrs. Hamer explained. "He and the other two didn't even know her, except as a black girl who didn't matter. This won't be the end, Clinton. More violence is coming. Hundreds of Jo Etha's family and friends are demanding to march through downtown Drew in her memory, tomorrow night. That's why I'm calling. You've got to come help me keep everyone calm."

The mayor was refusing their request. He wouldn't allow a candlelight march in her honor. Wouldn't give out a permit and said he would arrest anyone in the streets.

"We have a right to honor her. Can you help?"

Gulping down the last of my coffee after closing my attaché—I was due in court in twenty minutes—I kept the phone to my ear while looking around my desk to make sure I'd gathered up everything I'd need.

"Can you believe this?" she asked. "The sheriff told reporters Jo Etha's murder was a crime with no motive."

I stopped my juggling act and leaned forward in my chair, as if she were in the same room talking to me. "So how about the color of her skin, Mrs. Hamer?" I half-whispered this into the telephone. "Was it a contributing factor?"

She let my question slide. We needed this moment of silence. The conversation already had ended, and I rose from my chair, straightened my tie, and brushed lint from my suit. I always looked good in court. I didn't want Mrs.

Hamer to feel dismissed, but time was running out, and I had to leave. I began to close the conversation.

"Look, I've got to go to court. I will take off for Ruleville when I'm done. Don't worry, I'll get to your house before nightfall. I know—don't travel alone after five."

This was the rule for any black person wanting to survive in the most turbulent years. If you had to go somewhere, it had better not be alone at night. Safer to do your work before the sun goes down. Mrs. Hamer, and all those who'd lived through the worst of times, still held by this mandate. And they were still alive!

"Love you, Clinton."

"Same to you, Mrs. Hamer."

After taking a final look in the mirror, I headed out to meet my client. Later that afternoon, I took off for the Delta to help my old friend with the memorial march and funeral. We succeeded in calming the Drew community, but after I'd returned to Jackson a month later, I packed my bags and moved back to the Delta. My community needed me.

CHAPTER FIVE

Mollie found me in Clarksdale late that summer. I was sitting behind a desk piled high with stacks of case files. A little heavier, up perhaps twenty pounds since high school, with my hair shaped into a moderate Afro and my face showing added creases. It's always been a kind face, people tell me, but now more temperate. My body still strong and well-toned—no longer the frame of an athletic teenage male, but a physique of substance.

She discovered me working on contract language for a client, and when Mollie Johnson found me on that hot late-August morning, she walked right into my life and broke my concentration with her silly fake Southern twang:

"Hey, old man. I *ha'ir* you've come back home to the *Miss'sippi* Delta to set up a new law practice, bringing us some *jaystice*." She slurred over the second syllable of Mississippi like butter melting on warm biscuits, her way of announcing she'd returned home, poking fun at Delta speak.

I looked up from my work, amazed to hear her voice, then quickly jumped up to cross the room and embrace her.

"I can't believe it's you, Mollie. My God, where have you been since high school? You're looking younger and more beautiful than ever."

For a moment, all I could do was stand there and look at my old friend. I never thought we'd see each other again. We had been tight before she disappeared the day after high school graduation. You can't explain away so many years of absence in a moment, and I didn't expect this from Mollie, but hoped she would fill in some of the gaps—maybe later, over lunch.

She was clearly on a mission, and it was as if the past twelve years apart didn't matter. It was so like her to skip what she considered minutiae.

"Hey, Mister Clinton Moore. I see you've got an ad in the newspaper for a legal assistant." She held up the newspaper's classified section and angled it next to her cheek, pointing her finger at my small help wanted ad buried midway down the page. The announcement in *The Clarksdale Press Register* must have come out early.

"I want to come back home to Clarksdale. My parents are getting old, and they need me. I need a job, Clinton. So, when do I start?"

Of course I needed help running my new practice in Clarksdale, after deciding to come home and open a solo practice. My lover, Joe Means, and I had not been getting along. He was younger than me, still in law school at the time, and not entirely certain he was gay. But I wanted him to move to Clarksdale and join my law practice when he graduated. He didn't like the idea.

"So you are asking me to come home and stay tucked away in the closet?" Joe's neck had turned red, before telling me that he would not spend one more day in "that rat hole of Clarksdale."

"I did everything you told me to do, Clinton. I always respected you like you were my big brother. You taught me everything—how to stay safe, keep the jocks off my back, and suck up to teachers. You weren't there with me when I was in high school, but it didn't matter. You still told me what to do every step of the way by telephone, and on any weekend that you came home. Like I couldn't figure out anything for myself?"

He needed to blow off steam, so I said nothing and let him continue. Didn't counter any of Joe's remarks, including the deepest insults, and he was harsh.

"You said to find a beard, someone like Mollie, so I could attend school dances and everyone would think I was straight. You laid it all out, handed me your personal roadmap, and I followed that map so damned close that by the time I left home for college, I didn't know who I was. Even at Jackson State, I was damned careful, and once again, thanks to you my big brother, I lied through another four years of my life."

The discussion was over. I made no ground. Deep down, I knew that Joe deserved time to try out life on his own. Someday we would be together, but this would come later. I would honor Joe's request for freedom. We kept our alternate weekends calendared, with an understanding this was to be an open relationship. I always believed one day he would move home to Clarksdale to live with me.

So here I was. Alone, single, and practicing law in my home town, the hub of the cotton center of the world, a real back end of civilization. But the place honored good music and was home to the Delta blues. With the possibility of Mollie coming home to Clarksdale, my life suddenly looked a hundred percent better, even if Joe lived elsewhere.

She was a beautiful woman. Her face accented by her fuller lips, big eyes, and well-shaped eyebrows. Her high cheekbones and blemish-free completely black skin almost made me quiver. Mollie was exotic, a standout with very short hair that framed her face. She had a tall and slender body. Important to me, she knew I was gay. Had known it clear back since junior high.

We'd talked a lot about this when we were teenagers. She was always there when I needed her—not only for artificial reasons like accompanying me as my "date" on Prom night—but when I really needed to talk to someone about being different, and trying to sort out if something was wrong with me—my deepest fear.

"Does it show?" I would ask. I'd been made fun of a couple of times because I didn't always go to dances or parties with a girl. It frightened me to think I might look gay. I never got beaten up, like some other gay kids, but I was still insecure about who knew, since my brother and sisters didn't—at least I believed. I could trust Mollie to help me out with these and other issues like no one else. She was my best friend.

We'd tried sex once. It was her suggestion, and it didn't work. I'd been afraid of physical intimacy and apologized. She said she was sorry for asking me to do this. She was beautiful afterward, in her unconditional love and understanding of who I was. Nevertheless, she disappeared the day after high school graduation, with no warning. I never heard from her until that day she showed up at my office.

I begged her parents and friends to tell me where she'd gone. Either they didn't know, or they weren't telling me. She'd had a boyfriend in high school. He'd gone on after graduation to work in Jackson; occasionally, I'd see him on the street when I was at Jackson State.

Had he heard from Mollie? He would stare away before saying no to my question. I didn't trust his answers. I imagined she was pregnant and had moved far away. Maybe she was married with a family.

Years passed. My feelings for her lessened, but I didn't quit thinking about her. I'd see an old friend at a party and ask if he had heard from Mollie. Always the answer was no. Coming back home to Clarksdale with these memories had not been easy.

And here she stood at my desk. Demanding a job. Banking on the newspaper advertisement, my messy office, and our friendship. Mollie assumed this job was hers to lose, and she started flirting to win it—just like the old days. She returned to *Delta-speak*, with its soft accent and pseudo formalities: using *Miss* and *Mister* before first or surnames, whether the conversation was serious or light. Missy was reserved for snotty black or uppity white women and was used by blacks and whites both.

"You know you need me, Mister Clinton Moore. Someone's got to clean up this big fat law office mess of yours. You go ask your sis'tuh Miss Betty, and she'll say it's so, you ha'ir?"

I joked. "She put that ad in the pa'puh, herse'f, hoping some nice young belle like you would come ovu'h and h'ep me out."

Mollie swept her right arm across the clutter, shaking her head side to side and making clicking sounds of disapproval. She got down on both hands and knees to attack the hundreds of small paper file tabs stuck in my carpet.

"When's the last time you filed something? Sent out bills? Or cleaned up this floor?" She reached out for paper clips, also stuck in the carpet weave. "Don't you ever answer your phone before the third ring? I don't think so. I tried calling you this morning to let you know I'd be coming ha'ir for the job."

I thought I should help her out and took to the floor, perhaps a little too quickly. Mollie back-crawled a couple of inches to look me square in the face.

"Now you don't want to mess up those good suit pants, Mister Clinton. Let me do this for you." She followed me with her big dark-brown eyes as I eased back up from the floor to a standing position, lifting each foot in the air and pretending to shake wrinkles from my trouser legs.

"Nice dress suit." She looked into my face. "Armani?

"Not quite. I'd have to go to N'awlins for that. Tough to get the good Italian stuff here in Miss-sippi, you know."

"Nice trimmed mustache. Cool Afro—maybe too short," she continued her assessment. I laughed and waggled my finger at her face.

Out of the blue, I started singing Mississippi Goddam, a wild 1964 protest song actually banned across the state after Nina Simone sang it to the world. Mollie started dancing, and I found myself scanning her trim black body from her head on down. Had I changed? I didn't think so, but I had to wonder.

A couple of minutes, and I returned to checking over clauses I'd established for Harry Stork's contract, still watching Mollie from the corner of my eye. She'd gone back to picking up paperclips. Her short yellow jersey wrap dress hugged her ass and her breasts dropped forward into the soft cloth. Mollie's perfectly shaped legs were accented by black heels with thin straps buckled across her small ankles. She'd topped off her summer look with a low-pocketed jacket and carried a bulky leather purse, giving her a 70s urban look.

My reactions surprised me, and I began to wonder what would have happened between us if she hadn't left home? If I weren't gay? If I hadn't loved Joe? I shook my head a couple of times to clear it before going back to the Stork contract.

"I think you can skip the typing test," I called to Mollie.

I sensed fleeting pragmatism. While Mollie had been out of my life, I'd done time in some of the grimmest years of the civil rights movement, before and after becoming a lawyer, often diminishing my sense of humor. Was I too quickly growing old? Becoming an old fart? I hoped not. But another good reason for having Mollie back around the office; she'd always liked to flirt and have fun! She would keep me young.

Finished with the carpet mess, my old school friend sat there with her legs crossed, watching me work. I needed a legal assistant—someone with brains—and here she was in my Delta office, playing cat and mouse.

Mollie had been one of the brightest people I'd known. As Clarksdale High's 1959 class valedictorian, she balanced calculus, chemistry, and cheerleading without a hitch. Why did she leave home the day after graduation? Without saying goodbye? Or calling me on the phone? I deserved answers to the questions now filling my head once again, but all of this could wait. I couldn't let Mollie slip away. It had been too long since I'd last seen her, and I needed her help.

"You're so smart, Miss Mollie, you could have been a lawyer yourself. You should be offering me a job," I kidded her while mentally calculating what I could afford to pay. I knew I had to get Stork's legal work done; it meant an extra fifteen dollars. I had to get back to business. But there'd been a spark of pleasure in watching her move around my office in that tight-ass dress and those spiked heels.

"I'll need to buy an extra desk and office chair by tomorrow," I called out to her, then went back to work.

Noon approached, and my white shirt collar was getting moist—my forehead dripping. The six-blade metal fan used to cool the office whirred, but didn't help much except to recirculate the hot air. By the end of April, unbearable heat moves into the Delta. Most folks wilt. Mollie's face stayed dry, as drops fell onto my pressed shirt. She glowed in the Delta humidity.

"How about some lunch? Forget walking on the hot pavement. We'll take my car! Say, do you remember that day we walked down to the sandbars? When it was so damned hot?"

I'd had this memory while the temperature moved up. Everyone around here says don't go down to the Mississippi River sandbars after April, unless you leave by nine in the morning. The river is low, and it may look like fun, but walking there in the heat is dangerous.

"Yeah! I was wearing gym shoes with socks, and you had those dumb rubber thongs on your feet," Mollie laughed. "Two hours later you could barely pull your naked feet up and out of the sinking, hot sand on our way back to the car. Remember? You had to crawl on all fours when your thongs broke!"

Mollie's eyes shined. She wasn't about to forget our senior sneak-out to the Mississippi River's hot sand banks. I closed my eyes, and her cheerleader voice came back: "Come on Clinton. You can do it!"

"I could have had a stinking heat stroke and died! Buried in the hot, sucking sand for all you cared, Mollie."

We'd reached the cool interior of Jim's Eat Place, where our conversation moved beyond my humiliating senior trip to talk over Mollie's new responsibilities and celebrate her homecoming. I'd finally stopped sweating like an ox, once the cool air hit. Mollie, of course, kept her jacket tightly wrapped around her shoulders, complaining it was too cold. She surprised me by not making Jim turn up the heat, or turn down the air conditioning in the restaurant.

The next day, Mollie came to work ten minutes early. She started answering the phone on the first ring, and by Friday she'd caught up my entire client billing and put it in the mail. Including a bill for fifteen dollars to Harry Storks. Since Mollie found me, things were definitely looking up.

CHAPTER SIX

I loved my scales of justice—a small desk toy that Joe purchased for me in a Jackson antique shop. It reminded me of the gadgets that Grandpa Willie kept in his tool shed.

I would drive Mollie nuts with my scales, dropping paperclips on the Truth or Fairness side, depending on how I'd fared that day in court. The scales are supposed to remain in balance for justice to prevail. But for black people in Mississippi, this rarely happened. The Magnolia state could use a third scale, for Ludicrous. One day the Coahoma County assistant district attorney wanted to put my young client in Parchman prison for stealing aspirin for his sick baby. Even the old white judge appeared disgusted with the ADA and dismissed the case.

I took my win that day with grace. Did my usual thing behind the ADA's back and returned to the office, ready to load up the Fairness side. I called out for Mollie to open a new box of paperclips and join me, but she appeared busy. As I walked through the front door, she yelled from down the hallway, "Can we get rid of some of these messy cardboard boxes, Mister Clinton?"

"What's the problem, Mollie?" I was hanging up my suit coat, first giving it a quick brush while listening. Mollie could get overly excited over silly stuff, so I wasn't tuning in to what she had to say—at first.

"One of your boxes back here in the storage room fell over and spilled its guts into the hallway. Those boxes are creeping out of their places, and I'm afraid more of them are about to flop over and burst open."

I was a meticulous man who brushed lint from my blue serge suit, picked my short Afro, and shined my shoes to military standards—always going into court with a handkerchief in my breast pocket, so any mess in my office normally concerned me. These boxes held papers I'd been collecting for years. They were important to me, and I didn't consider them to be a problem. Each box held documents that might one day solve a crime—or send someone to prison. I knew they created a space problem, but I had already warned Mollie she never was to touch or even go near them.

I sensed she knew on a deeper level to leave the boxes alone. She probably did have some idea of what I was doing, but we didn't talk about it at first. I didn't feel it was safe for her to have this knowledge. My attitude eventually changed; in later years, I shared some of what I was doing. But not in these early years of my law career.

Joe, over in Montgomery, Alabama, was one of two people who knew about my collection. Joe had his own assemblage stored in his back office. The other person, Ann, was a kind woman from Jackson who'd helped me gather a good share of what I'd collected, in the first place. Ann was head secretary of the Mississippi Sovereignty Commission and handled plenty of secret documents and reports that she slipped to me on the qt. But even she didn't know about Joe's collection. I thought it my responsibility to keep quiet about my own growing boxes of secret papers. Everyone would be safer, I rationalized.

Ann helped me put my hands on some of my very best and most secret materials that could shed light on dozens of cold cases, things like horrid beatings and murders. The Commission was formed after Emmett Till's murder in reaction to visits from the feds who started snooping around Mississippi, asking questions, and rattling a few cages for a short time. By 1977, the state closed the Commission's doors, and its secret files gathered by former FBI and military intelligence spies were sealed for the next fifty years. After a lawsuit in 1989, a federal judge ordered the records opened, with some exceptions for still-living people. I wasn't surprised to hear from Ann that my name was on their list.

"Mr. Clinton, if you don't do something soon about this mess, we could have mice trapped in one of those cardboard containers, and they could have babies, and their babies could have babies until kingdom come." Mollie was carrying on, close to shouting by now as she stared down at the files and papers strewn across the hallway floor.

I didn't get to load my justice scales that day—something I liked doing right after a solid win—but had to walk down the hallway, get down on my hands and knees, and scoop up the mess of papers. But I didn't mind.

"Don't worry, Miss Mollie, I'll get to the rest of this over the weekend." I looked down and noticed her tapping foot next to my face.

"Sure I can't help?"

"Yes."

Molly returned to her desk.

As I finished picking up the papers, Mollie called out, "How'd it go in court today with Missy Zooey? Uh, you didn't—"

"Course not, Mollie. I promised you I wasn't going to do that again."

"Well, your sister said if you do, I should call her, and she'll tell your mama."

Now, there's a conversation that floats through the galaxy. Mollie was always saying I treated Missy Zooey like a sixth grade boy in heat. Because if I beat her in court, I'd do something before leaving the courtroom that Mollie called pathetic. I just thought it was fun.

"Come on, Molly. Cut me some slack. You know it's funny."

"Mister Clinton, I promise if you do THAT again, I will tell the judge. And then, your mama."

Mollie carried on like this because out of the judge's sight, and believe me I didn't let the old peckerwood see me do this, I'd stick out my tongue at Missy Zooey's small white rear end as she bent over in a tight cotton skirt, stuffing her court documents into her girly-looking briefcase. And then—I'd waggle it.

That's all it was. Real simple. But the first time Mollie caught me, she nearly had an asthma attack. She'd come to help in court that day, and once we got back to the office, she ratted me out to my sister!

"He could be arrested for this, Miss Betty. You have to tell him to quit. He won't listen to me, and Sheridan's old man will freaking kill him." She was almost crying on the telephone.

Mollie was right about Missy Zooey Sheridan's daddy. He was a mean old SOB who looked over his dark-haired brown-eyed limited-brain-power daughter like a Mississippi buzzard. Everyone knew she owed her law degree from the Senator James O. Eastland School of Law solely to her daddy's gifts to the university foundation— earmarked for white students only.

"Now, Mister Clinton. You know her daddy is mighty pow'ful. She might be stupid, but—"

We'd had this conversation many times. She knew Sheridan's daddy had people murdered and so did his daddy, and his daddy's daddy. Growing up in the Delta, most black folks see ghosts and smell evil rising from the vapors of its steaming alluvial soil. Sheridan's family had a lot to do with this.

William Faulkner, this state's literary genius, knew the Delta's heritage well when he said that in Mississippi, "The past is never dead. It's not even past."

The Sheridans, and others like them, weren't about to dissolve into the steamy cotton haze as the years rolled by. They'd been hanging on for too long to disappear; their past would never dissolve, but would only melt into the present. Faulkner would have appreciated this, I am sure.

One of my coveted paper-filled boxes held highly confidential documents signed by witnesses who claimed Sheridan's daddy and a couple of his cronies helped kidnap and kill fourteen-year-old Till.

It wasn't until 2004, forty-nine years later, that the Justice Department reopened the murder case that brought international news coverage to the Delta. I held secret papers I'd been collecting for years suggesting the Sheridans, and others involved in the murder, were still alive and could be held accountable.

I believed that I also could tie the old planter to a murder in Bloody Belzoni—a white public defender killed by Klansmen for doing his job. They took him out one night and beat him to death. Then they cut off his limbs and buried his body under a small earthen dam. There'd been only a limited investigation because one of Sheridan's friends said the young lawyer had left the Delta. "He's somewhere in New York with his family," this man told state investigators. And that was good enough for the officers, back then.

Personal stories and other documents, all stored away in my cardboard cartons, were waiting for the right day to see light. Waiting for Mississippi to shed its destructive roots—waiting until the U.S. Department of Justice grew gonads and sent FBI teams here to kick butt—which never happens in this state. Frankly, I was surprised by the DOJ's decision, years later, to take an honest look at Till's lynching.

Mollie knew that I was looking into this cold case. It was a crime that anyone of our age who lived in the Delta would never forget.

"Why did Emmett Till's mother call you on the phone," she quizzed me one day after I ended a call with Mamie Till Mobley. I had to admit that Emmett's mother and I spoke frequently on the telephone about her son. Our calls carried on until she died in 2003.

"She knows that I was born in the same year as Emmett, and she's counting on me to find everyone involved in the murder of her son. You know that I went to law school because of Emmett," I told Mollie.

Sadly, Mrs. Mobley was still living in Chicago when she died at the age of eighty-one, one year before the DOJ finally decided to do something about it.

What data I'd collected over the years didn't stop with Sheridan and his friends. I had even more names, and some of the crimes I'd investigated were rooted far away from Mississippi, taking place in Alabama, Louisiana, Texas, and Tennessee. I thought I was keeping most of this secret from Mollie.

I kept the most important of my provocative papers in the locked safe at the back of my office. Ann's husband was a liberal white Baptist minister in Jackson who had no idea that she was helping me. Ann insisted he remain protected by leaving him out of the loop. Like I'd insisted on doing with Mollie.

If Mollie thought sticking out my tongue at Missy Zooey Sheridan was my biggest problem, so be it. I didn't want her involved in my highly secret snooping; it could be extremely dangerous for her, just as it could be for Ann's husband.

I'd meant to keep things operating this way. No one knew what mysteries were stored in my boxes, or what surprises were locked up in my safe. Or what Joe was hiding in his collection of documents. Only Joe and I shared this clandestine information when we got together on weekends.

I always hoped that someday everything we'd collected would make a difference—would cause justice to be served. This was what I had been working for.

CHAPTER SEVEN

"You'll make a fine minister, Clinton." Betty gave me a warm hug and patted my back. My own minister, Tom, stood by her. He'd helped me get here—spending extra hours at night with me and my studies, sharing his thoughts and encouragement. Karen, his wife, edited my papers. All three had been my support team.

I'd been the first family member to finish high school and then go to college and law school. Now my sister, with all my family members, were shaking my hand and calling me the Rev. Clinton Moore—our family's first preacher.

"It's going to be tough to balance the two careers, but I'll work three or four extra hours two evenings a week at church, then be with congregation members all day Sunday," I told Betty. She was concerned about how I was going to manage both roles. Our parents had passed on years ago—after I'd returned home to the Delta. I was sorry they'd missed this important day in my life.

Small black-run churches and funeral homes have remained popular Southern enterprises—good ways to make money as small businesses—but I'd opened Holy Trinity for other reasons. I had gone through a period of self-reflection grounded in resentment and depression following the modern civil rights movement of the 1960s.

Becoming a minister turned out to be a good decision, and my depression actually faded when I finally began to grow my congregation. Holy Trinity was housed in a white stucco former car dealership that I'd personally purchased. Over the years, some of the stucco had fallen off the front of the building, leaving several gaping holes in the façade, and the large show windows were cracked. Most of the building was tagged with graffiti. It would take a great effort on everyone's part to turn this into a viable church, yet I had faith this would happen, in time.

Most evenings, church members dropped by for help with personal and family problems, requests for prayers, or to help out with church chores—doing everything from rehabbing the building to scrubbing floors or mending torn pages of hymnals.

On Sunday mornings and throughout the holy day, Trinity came alive with laughter and cheers as our members danced, screamed, shouted, and clapped—behaviors that would embarrass or wake up most straight-laced Presbyterians or liberal Episcopalians.

I pledged to church members, "This church will be a reminder of the kindness and cruelty, struggles and successes, the love, bitterness, and biases that make up our lives."

By now growing older, I thought this church would provide a good way to ease out of my law practice. My plan was working out, and my own life improved significantly as Holy Trinity kept taking new form, amazing all of us who came together to worship.

CHAPTER EIGHT

The first Tuesday in November 2010 started off with no problems. Mollie came in to work around eight and made a pot of coffee—warm and weak. I headed out the door for the Rebel's Roost Grill with my mug hooked over my second finger, expecting Walker to solve my problem. He did, and then a banker friend and I spent the next fifteen minutes talking over the state's newly announced school appropriations plan, while we drank a couple cups each of Walker's black bean roast before I went back to the office.

Warden Roy Bolton of Parchman Prison was sitting out in the front reception area waiting for our scheduled monthly talk. Mollie had just poured him some coffee, which he had set on the table to cool. He picked it up to bring with him as I invited him to follow me into my office.

"You can hang your jacket over there, Roy." I pointed to a wooden coat rack. After placing his fringed coat on the hook, Bolton walked over to the conference table and put his mug on a coaster. He allowed me to talk first. New to Mississippi and the Delta, the lanky West Texan was unnerved over an upcoming scheduled investigation of his prison farm, situated thirty miles due south of Clarksdale.

"So you're here today for some quick education?" I smiled, trying to put him at ease.

"Thanks for your offer to bring me up to snuff on Parchman, Mr. Moore. I really do need to know more about its past and current culture before this big meeting coming up."

Bolton unfolded his crossed arms and started to look a little more relaxed, leaning back in his chair. I was surprised that he was comfortable seeking the advice of a black man. But he had a lot to lose if Parchman didn't pass this inspection.

"Please call me Clinton."

I'd met Bolton the week before at a prison board meeting. As the first black person appointed to a local prison board in the state's history, this had been a surprising honor for me, coming from the state's first liberal governor. What a change for Mississippi—a black state board member, and I was it!

Not much else had changed at Parchman since it first opened in 1901 as a brutal four-stockades prison farm. The old wooden structures had been replaced with prefab metal buildings, making the place hotter than hell during most of the year and freezing cold in the winter.

We had a productive talk that day, and I believe I'd helped Bolton get through the dreaded visit. Close to the end of our meeting, the phone rang, and Mollie put the caller on hold. Bolton stood from his chair, noting he was going over to the Grill for lunch. "Care to join me?"

"Sorry, but I'll have to take a rain check. I'm due in court."

We shook hands, and he left.

Joe Means' wife Tara was holding on the phone, Mollie informed me. I picked up the call. Then Tara delivered the blow.

"Joe killed himself Friday night."

She said it twice before I registered that the man I'd known since grade school, and had been lovers with on and off since high school, was dead. By his own hand.

I clenched my fists and closed my eyes. I could see Joe. A medium-sized very black man with short, tight curly hair and sharp black eyes that could pierce a soul, inherited from his half-Chickasaw great-grandfather. He'd carried himself with precision, always standing proud "like a Marine," I used to tease.

It did not make sense! The last time we'd seen each other, he hadn't acted or looked depressed, anxious, angry, or even happier than usual. He was simply Joe that night.

We'd been through so much together. Civil rights battles that moved into Vietnam protests. Later, searching for answers to cold cases. This report of his death was a lie; it had to be a mean trick. I wondered for a moment if Tara was trying to punish me for sleeping with her husband.

For over thirty years, I never tried persuading Joe to move home. He loved Montgomery and was always telling me about a new opera or play when we got together. Rarely, I visited him on his turf, not wanting to invade the privacy he'd won after college. But one weekend, less than five years ago, on our regularly scheduled visit, did I get a surprise!

Joe had pulled into my drive and I could see him from my front window. I walked out to greet him. He didn't leave his car, but looked straight ahead, saying, "Let's go for a spin." His eyes were red and puffy. I wondered why he wanted to go somewhere after driving hundreds of miles to get to Clarksdale. Quietly, I walked over to the other side of his car and took my seat. We headed for Rosedale, where he parked along the river near a quiet place where we'd often picnicked. Silently, I opened my car door, got out, and walked over to a wooden picnic table.

I felt a cold separation between us as I waited for him to leave his car. He walked over to the table and sat on the opposite side. My eyes landed on a small heart that had been carved into the wood, and I started tracing the design with my thumbnail, hoping Joe would talk first.

"I need a life, Clint. You know I can't help the people who need me if the higher ups who manage most social agencies and public organizations think I am gay. I'll never have a chance, even with some liberal groups."

I wanted to jump in and say we should go ahead and get married, even if it was still not legal. He must have already considered this because he talked about going to San Francisco.

"We could pass the California state bar and live an openly gay life. But you would have to start out all over finding new clients, and I don't have the kind of money it would take to build a private practice out there, Clinton. I don't know if—"

"Stop talking, Joe." I took his hand and looked him in the eyes. "We live in strange times. We're black. We're gay. We're liberal, and we've pissed off a lot of people over the years, haven't we? I'd say we've done a damned good job."

Some of the stress left Joe's face. Maybe I saw a small grin.

"We've needed each other every step of the way to get as far as we've come," I said, "maybe even to stay alive. I am okay with this life of complex privacy, but you are not, and you don't have to say another word."

I wondered what he really was trying to say, or if he had a plan of some kind. Any celibacy plan made no sense. He told me a sad story about a recent job interview he'd experienced, trying to demonstrate what he was going through emotionally.

"I'd made it to the end and was invited to dinner with the director and board chairman of a large social service agency. The chairman greeted me alone, before the director arrived. He said he liked my resume and experience, but then asked to meet my wife. When I said that I wasn't married, he apologized for his agency not being 'progressive enough' to hire me at this time."

41

Joe said he'd walked out of the restaurant. "I didn't have anything to say. It hit me too hard in the gut."

He said that he had a new plan. I was totally unprepared to hear it.

"I have to try something different. There is this woman, Clinton. We work together. We're good friends, and we're getting married."

What could I could say ? I had no big brother lecture to deliver; I let him carry on and listened as he revealed his plan.

"I had another interview with the region's ACLU office. He wants to help my career, but he laid it out to me, real damned clear. Said if I want to go somewhere, have the right cases, sit on the right committees and boards, I'd better make it clear that I only date women. Too many of these organizations are backed by religious money and are not ready for lesbians and gays, let alone someone who might be transgendered. At least I don't have that problem," Joe said, as he managed to give a small smile.

Joe knew that he'd hurt me. It was a stab in my heart, but I remained quiet.

"Look, we can still get together. Same time, same place, every two weeks. But the rest of the month, I have to be seen with Tara—that's her name."

Still tracing the carved heart in the table, I moved my finger around and down, up and over to the top, then back up again. It felt good on my thumbnail, so I pressed down harder and made a couple of swerves on a nearby set of carved initials.

It was my turn to talk.

"Okay, Joe. You tell me that you are going to pretend you're straight. Marry a lady and take her on your arm to dinner and the theater. Do you have any particular Greek tragedy in mind?"

He smirked. That little brat who I'd cared for like a brother and screwed all of my adult life like a mink—a precious little mink—was about to legally hook up with a beard. I had to let him have it.

"Hey Joe, I think I just invented a new form for you. You're going on the up low. See, guys on the down low are seriously heterosexual. If you are going this direction—you know, up to pretend you have straight genes—this means you're really a homo who needs some serious woman ass on the side –"

"Stop! Don't do this, Clint. Tara is a fine woman, and I'll go a hell of a lot farther in life with her at my side, than I'd ever go with you!"

Joe and Tara were married one month later. I didn't go to the wedding, and I didn't see that little cocksucker—as I was calling him by then in my dreams—until one month after the honeymoon. And damn it was good.

"He killed himself, Clint." Tara said this on the phone again, and I went numb. The panic started in my chest; my lungs worked hard to suck in each breath. Why would she wait four days to tell me this? Why hadn't she screamed for Mollie to put her call straight through to me? What in the hell was wrong with this woman? Had she lost her frigging mind?

I moved into a place of silence, half-listening as Tara's words flowed into a description that sounded rehearsed. She talked of a private service planned for Wednesday afternoon. But I didn't want to hear anything about a funeral. I wanted to know what happened to Joe!

"Please call Tom and ask him to come to the funeral," Tara requested. Joe and Tom, my minister, had been close friends. I promised Tara I would give him the news plus her invitation to the service. The conversation was over as far as I was concerned. I said goodbye, after assuring her I would leave in the next few minutes for Montgomery.

Mollie had come into my office. Her eyes caught mine as I ran through the conversation with her before she stopped me midsentence.

"Four days? What does she mean it happened four days ago? And why would she wait until now to call you?" Mollie beat me to the logical question, "What do you think is going on?"

"I have no idea, Mollie. Nothing about this sounds right, and I have no idea why she would wait four days to call. But cancel my appointments for this afternoon and tomorrow. I'm leaving for Montgomery in ten minutes."

CHAPTER NINE

Suburbia Montgomery.

I drove into one of the city's few upscale neighborhoods that opened its arms to a mixed-race couple, rolling my car to a stop in Tara's driveway. I noticed there was no crime tape around the scene. Why should this surprise me? Everything about Joe's death had been fishy so far. Even if this was a suspected suicide, surely there would be some evidence of a criminal investigation, unless it really did happen four days earlier, and the forensic team was already finished with their work.

She took her time answering the doorbell. I wasn't in the mood to see her anyway, rarely was. She'd done her best to keep Joe and me apart. That, I could understand. It had to be difficult having a gay husband who appeared straight in public.

Tara and I never got along, but I'd always faked it for Joe's sake. He'd met her when occasionally working short contracts for a legal group in Montgomery; she was the trophy receptionist. He was lonesome when her boss introduced them. The tall, thin blond was a knockout, and it seemed a good match unless you knew her. Unless you knew him.

Inviting me into their home, Tara looked pale and elegant. She leaned forward to accept my kiss, her thick hair spilling down over her shoulders. I followed her to the coat-tree in the stone and art glass foyer where she took my jacket, then silently motioned me ahead into the formal living room.

Tara sat in a stuffed black chair across from me, her green eyes refusing to connect as we spent the first twenty minutes talking about Joe—his strengths and how we both would miss him terribly.

"So, you're doing okay, Tara?"

What a dumb thing for me to ask. Her husband was dead, and she was a widow. How could she be doing okay? Tara looked like she'd been crying. I'd notice her frozen smile when she first greeted me. It was a strange grin limited to her mouth, staying a moment longer than expected, then stopping abruptly. This phony smile could be a sign of deception, but I wrote it off the first time, since she was under stress.

"Yes, I am doing fine," she sniffed, pulling a lace-edged handkerchief from the side pocket of her tight black dress. She'd poured herself into the outfit, so I was surprised it had room for the pocket.

"Let me get my glasses," she said, squinting as she dabbed her eyes.

"I was doing some close needlework on a memory blanket for Joe just as you drove up and don't need them when I'm sewing."

Memory blanket? Needlework? I guess this didn't surprise me. She was a Southern lady so it was likely that she was crafty.

She read my thoughts, offering further clarification. "It's an old family custom to send off dead people with a small hand-stitched blanket displaying special dates in their lives sewn onto each quilt block. Do you have a date you'd like me to stitch on Joe's blanket?"

Specific dates jumped into my head, and for a moment I felt embarrassingly horny for Joe.

"Uh, no. That's okay, Tara. Nice idea, though."

She left the room to look for her glasses on the sewing table, giving me time to gaze around the handsomely decorated area. Over the fireplace mantle were two burning candles set on each side of Joe's framed photograph taken on the day he passed the Alabama bar, showing him shaking hands with a smiling judge. When she returned, I asked Tara about her family.

"Will anyone be attending the service? Your mom or dad?"

She kept looking down at her lap, fidgeting with the handkerchief before responding.

"I'm the only child, and my parents are old. But as soon as the funeral is over, I'm flying out to their home in Upstate New York. I've already booked my flight. They live way out in the countryside, Clint, and they're hard to reach. So don't try."

I moved in closer with my questions, thinking about her odd reply—that I shouldn't try to reach her.

"About Joe's suicide. Was he upset about anything you can think of?" I waited for her answer, closely following her eyes and body movement while looking for twists and jerks.

"Really, nothing. Joe had his moments, but nothing out of the ordinary." She kept her arms and hands close to her sides, as if trying to stay in the smallest space possible while answering my new questions.

I was going to start digging and see what she had to say—how she reacted to this new pace. Had he fought with anyone at work? Did he have bitter clients? Was he receiving phone calls at odd hours?

"No, No, No," On the second no her right hand had moved to her cheek, then over to her lips and down, resting on her throat by the third no.

Oh, Tara, you're a damned liar and not very good at it, I thought. Every hand or facial motion she made or omitted was giving her away. I deliberately increased my pace.

"How about medical problems? Did you talk to his doctor? Perhaps Joe had a health issue?"

Her hand reached up to her head, grabbing a strand of hair that she started to twist as she spoke. "No. Uh, the nurse said the doctor was out of the country."

"So, you did call his office?"

"No. I mean, yes." She released the strand of hair and moved her left hand up to scratch behind her ear. Her hand never made it down to touching her heart, a place on the body where the open hand of a liar rarely goes, something I'd learned from years of observation.

"Has the autopsy been completed?"

"I couldn't do that to Joe's body. He was so handsome. Let him rest in peace, Clint." She returned to twisting her hair.

"Who found him?"

Tara avoided my question and walked over to the bar. "Let me fix you a gin and tonic before I finish up in the kitchen with dinner."

As I eased off and watched Tara at work, I noticed tenderness in her eyes. Something that I hadn't picked up on before this trip. She handed me the drink and headed into the kitchen as I settled back on the couch, soon thinking about the last time Joe and I were together.

It was only a couple of weeks earlier when he came over to Clarksdale. We'd talked about our work, and he told me he was picking up new clients. When he had the time, he was spending evenings on the Dr. King assassination. Neither one of us would ever let this go. We knew there was far more to his murder, and interesting new information had come to light. Joe said he had learned about an Alabama Klansman who claimed he was involved in both the Kennedy and King assassinations.

Back in the mid-sixties, this man had first bragged about his participation in one of Jim Garrison's investigations when the New Orleans prosecutor was preparing to try local businessman Clay Shaw for his involvement as a CIA agent in the JFK conspiracy.

"Have you talked to this man, Joe? Do you have a name? Have you been able to locate him?" I remembered asking Joe these questions.

"Not yet," Joe had told me, "but I'm on the trail. I could be meeting with him, soon."

"Well, keep me informed," I'd instructed him, "and give me copies of any notes you have. I'll lock them up in my safe."

Joe never spoke about this man again. And I never asked any more questions. But the topic of Dr. King's slaying never went away. We often spoke about it:

"James Earl Ray was scapegoated, just like Lee Harvey Oswald," Joe used to assert. We both heard from an FBI friend that Ray was grilled for days, with no rest and under intense lights. Joe had been picking up on his own that the entire King investigation was a ridiculous mess, an embarrassment that finally blew up in the FBI's face as more documents slowly were declassified.

Conspiracy theorists had started writing and talking of involvement by others early on, and Joe was gathering what names he could find as more people talked. Whenever he came to see me, he'd have a name or two or other information that I'd lock up in my office safe. A sizeable group of conspiracy theorists had been digging through this new information—he wasn't acting alone. I devoured each new assassination book or report as it was published, keeping my eyes open for newly declassified documents.

"Not many journalists do their job," Joe would say, but he remained impressed with several lawyers outside of Mississippi who stayed on the trail of King's assassin, writing books, and speaking out as they learned and collected more stories and evidence. Then, in 1993, a man named Loyd Jowers (one "L") appeared on national television and related details alleging the Mafia and the U.S. government worked together to kill Dr. King.

"Jowers said that a Memphis police officer fired the fatal shot," I remember Joe saying. He'd promised to bring me copies of any new records he'd received through the Freedom of Information Act or from direct interviews, the next time we got together. He never followed through.

Had Joe learned something new and purposely kept me out of the loop? Had he simply run out of time before getting back? I wondered.

CHAPTER TEN

Tara invited me into the dining area where she'd set out a light meal. I unfolded my dinner napkin, put it on my lap, then took a bite before picking up where we'd left off.

"Who found Joe?"

She swirled her wine before answering me. "I heard him drive into the garage, so I went out to greet him. When I saw him hanging from a ladder, I started screaming and ran back into the house."

"Who did you call?"

"Uh, 911. They sent someone over right away. The funeral home man came and knocked on the door, and I pointed to the garage. He went in and took Joe's body."

"Did any officers talk to you?"

"No, Clint. I said his body was taken away. He will be cremated before tomorrow's service."

I took a few more bites of dinner, and then looked directly at her.

"Tara, I don't believe that Joe killed himself. He wouldn't take his own life."

She placed her fork down on her plate, wiped her lips with the napkin, then folded her hands on her lap.

"I don't know why you'd say something like that, Clinton." Tara stared ahead, once looking into my face and giving me one of her longer-than-normal, frozen-mouth-only smiles followed by a blank stare.

Dinner over and seated back in the living room, we spoke several more moments before she added a new twist to her story. I think she was trying to convince me there was a reason behind Joe's suicide.

"I told them Joe was worried about having enough money for retirement. He really was concerned about this and talked about it all the time. Oh, a police ambulance took his body to the black funeral home that's close to here, Ivers and Smith."

Her story was inconsistent and heading south. Earlier, she'd claimed not speaking to any police officers, that the funeral home man took the body away, not a police ambulance. But at least I'd learned something concrete—that Joe was worried over money and where I could find his body. I believed the latter, but not the former. Joe and I shared investment strategies, and our portfolios were sound when I'd checked last week.

It was clear that I needed to see Joe's body. I might have a better idea of what really happened to him if I took a close look. I still did not believe he'd killed himself.

"When can I see him?"

"You can't. It is a closed casket."

Tara was firm about the casket. I hadn't mentioned a casket and wondered why she'd ordered one if she had arranged for his body was to be cremated? That made no sense!

"I need to see him, Tara, for closure. I need to look at Joe's face one last time." I'd decided to push hard on her, while playing to her emotions, hoping she'd give in and let me see Joe's body.

"Well, you just can't." Tara got a smirky look on her face as she turned me down. "Yes. I know you'd like to see his body. But you can't. I can't allow it, and remember I AM Joe's wife, Clinton."

With that, I knew nothing more would come from talking with Joe's widow. I stayed twenty minutes more, long enough to be polite.

"Will you be okay?" I asked her this from the front steps of her home, almost feeling a little sorry for Tara, even if she was a lying bitch. I owed it to Joe to be civil with her.

"I'll be fine," she sniffed, then smiled for a second or two in that funny, frozen way.

I kissed Joe's woman goodbye, then walked away from his home forever, thoroughly convinced that Tara was deceiving me. I had to discover why.

CHAPTER ELEVEN

I needed time to digest what I had not learned from Tara. I was too tired to drive home that evening; the five-hour trip from Clarksdale to Montgomery had taken its toll on my old body. I was drained, angry, and needed a break, so when I saw signs for a city botanical garden, I turned my car into the lot, parked it, and shut off the ignition, allowing me time to think.

Crime scenes are like puzzles. The pieces have to be collected so that whatever took place is recreated. Something in Joe's garage might have helped me decide if he'd committed suicide. I might have discovered a piece to this puzzle, had I been allowed to look! When I'd asked Tara for permission to walk through the garage, she'd refused.

"You're just being morbid," she claimed.

Someone must have assessed the scene before Joe's body was hauled off and reported as a suicide. That would be the usual way. But now, it looked like no public officials were ever involved.

I'd really screwed up. There were so many questions I should have asked her, so much I should have investigated. Were there signs of forced entry into the garage? Did anything look out of place? A box of spilled tools? Anything suggesting a fight or struggle? Blood on the floor or pieces of fiber stuck to any objects? Shoe tracks?

My list of questions went on forever, and I damned well should have been cagier in getting answers. But if I'd asked Tara anything, she wouldn't have cooperated. That's how the entire evening had gone. Still, I should have tried.

I didn't believe any law enforcement officials—local police or sheriff—ever came to Joe's house to question Tara, or to do the rest of their job. Anyone could have carted off his body and dropped it anywhere. No one had collected evidence or protected the possible crime scene, from what I saw.

Tara didn't have her own story straight—her answers to my questions changed nearly every time she opened her mouth. Her twisted body language confirmed deceit. With no crime tape around the scene and no reason to believe there had been any sort of investigation—no fibers collected, no search for prints, no chemical or any other analyses, as far as Tara's recollections and her answers went—I had no answers.

What happened to Joe that night? What did Tara know, and what was she hiding? I wasn't about to call any law enforcement agency on the telephone to ask for help, since they weren't doing their jobs in the first place—or they didn't know they had a job to do, if no one called them.

Three simple question came to me that yielded a yes or no response: Did Joe kill himself? Did Tara kill Joe? Did someone else kill Joe? I couldn't come up with any answers, but at least I had three solid questions!

There was one thing I did know: Joe's body was either at the funeral home or somewhere else in the world by now. After five minutes going through all of this self-talk, the air in my car was getting stuffy. I felt tightness in my chest and discomfort in my legs. It had been a long drive, and at my age, sitting for a long time was hard on my circulation.

I got out of my car, closed the door, and walked over to a neat pile of fall leaves that some poorly paid city worker had probably spent hours raking or blowing together. I kicked the first pile of dry maple leaves hard, sending them flying into the air. Another pile became my target, then another, and another. I must have kicked every pile of foliage around me until they were all spread across the grass.

Someone killed my best friend. I didn't believe what his wife told me—what little information she'd given— and I knew that some sort of a cover-up was underway. Leaf-kicking calmed me for the moment, and afterward I returned to my car and stayed there, sitting in my own sweat and forcing my mind to rest until the sky turned black.

Tara had instructed the funeral home director to allow no visitations. No one was to see her dead husband before the service. Joe's body was to be cremated in the morning. But I had other ideas.

Finding Joe would not be hard to do, although I was not comfortable with breaking into private property. I took my law degree seriously and normally would avoid doing something that caused disbarment. After I'd passed the white Mississippi exam, I'd still had to fight the bar's redneck officials for the right to practice law. Nothing ever came easy.

But if my lover was laid out on a cold basement shelf of a funeral home, and if I had to break into the place before his body was cremated to learn how he died, then that's the way it would go. I would help Joe solve his last crime—figuring out who in the hell killed him and why— one way or another.

CHAPTER TWELVE

The only solid information I'd gotten from Tara was the name of the funeral home where Joe's body was sent. It wasn't hard to find, after locating it on my car GPS.

I pulled in next to the red brick Italianate structure and sat for a moment steeped in Montgomery history— the first capital of the Confederacy in the War between the States and known for its bus boycott and civil rights marches.

After a moment of silence, I left my car and walked up the wrap-around porch with its square cupola bordered by two large white wood Roman columns. My eye caught the mahogany doors and their immense brass doorknobs, sculpted into the shape of hunting dog heads. I stifled a laugh. How much more "Alabama" could a fine funeral home be? I had to give Tara credit for her choice in parlors. The Ivers and Smith home represented the Southern charm Joe always loved about this midsized city.

"Looks like you're getting a very Sutherin send off, Joe," I whispered.

About a dozen cars were parked in the side lot. I'd hoped for this, since evening visitations remain a popular social activity in the South. My plan was to walk through the front door as a visitor, then quietly sneak off to find Joe's body. If caught, I'd just say I was looking for the bathroom.

In the parlor lay Miss Elsie Lee Dorn, tucked away in a faux-marble casket surrounded by white lilies; her thin, long black hands with their pearly nails were folded across her chest, and she hugged a white-and-gold-bordered King James Bible.

In the far corner next to an heirloom square piano, I spotted a doorway lit by a red exit sign. I zigzagged over, nodding and smiling to family members as I headed that way to slip through the door. I found myself in a dark narrow hallway.

To my right, I could make out a slanted stairwell heading into the basement. Conscious of the creaks coming from the ancient wooden floors, I tried leaning on the unsteady handrail to keep off my direct weight. Once at the bottom of the steps, it took little time to find a small preparation room at the end of the short hallway. I wasn't surprised to find it unlocked.

Ivers and Smith was a small operation, its owner not terribly concerned with security or privacy. Easily getting into the room, I was prepared for the initial smell of antiseptic cleaning products that hit my nose. As a one-time, small county coroner, I'd used a menthol ointment under my nostrils to mask the smell of rot, but I didn't think to bring any with me. I was careful to fight attempts to breathe shallow or hold my breath.

In my training, I'd learned to see the human body as purely anatomical, understanding why it works and why it stops working. I learned not to perceive the work as morbid, but helpful to families who needed answers. I hoped if Joe's body was stored here, I could maintain objectivity and learn answers for myself, if for no one else. Tara appeared satisfied with whatever it was that she knew.

I made this quick, since I didn't want to get caught and end up explaining my presence to the police! My eyes moved across the room to the shiny, two-body stainless steel walk-in refrigeration unit. Joe would be there, I believed. I found it locked with a deadbolt key/padlock, but it only took a few minutes of searching around to find the key under paperwork in the bottom drawer of the only desk.

I unlocked the padlock, opened the refrigerator door, and found a body wrapped in plastic and laid out on a stainless steel shelf. The plastic bag was not bound by rope, signaling the body had not been autopsied. Hence, the true cause and manner of death was not officially established, just as I expected. The body arrived here, likely bypassing all required investigations from crime scene to pathology. This was incredible, nearly unbelievable, unless the funeral home was in cahoots with some other organization. Higher ups had to be involved. Had to be—to make this work.

Of course, I doubted Tara's story of when and how Joe died. From the start, it never sounded right. Someone must have figured that Tara would need to believe that Joe's death was legitimate, and that his body was disposed of appropriately. They'd concocted a suicide story, I guessed, but it didn't take long to see all of this was a lie. But, I could not stop and think about this now. I had to make the best use of my time so I prepared myself mentally to look over Joe's body.

First, I unwrapped the plastic sheet to see if it was really him. There he was, underneath the wrapping, lying on his back. The blood had settled in the lower part of his semi-rigid body. Joe's skin was paler than normal, and his face had relaxed. He was past the maximum rigidity that arrives about twelve hours after death, so I figured he'd been dead for perhaps twenty hours, judging from the stiffness in his muscles. This meant he might have been killed several hours before midnight, but not the four days ago that Tara claimed.

My eyes focused on a large bruise on his upper right arm. It looked as if someone had come at him with a six- or seven-pound sub-gun and hammered at him, probably slamming him against a wall. He must have tried to block the blows.

Looking down his body, I saw that all the fingers on his right hand were badly bruised and crushed. The bones were coming out of his skin. Most likely, whoever did this to Joe had used a large mallet. On his left hand, only two fingers appeared in this condition, so they got the information they'd come after. Did he give them my name?

Who did this to Joe? The crude hammering and crushing could have been the work of an ignorant jerk, or of someone who wanted Joe's murder to look as such. I presumed his killer was more sophisticated and had tried to make it look as if organized crime or KKK had done their usual crude job.

I wanted to know how Joe actually died. There were no bullet holes in his body that I could find. Tara said he'd hanged himself, according to the "agent" who came to her door, but there were no contusions or discoloration around his neck. And no one tortures himself before committing suicide! My best guess was that Joe finally was killed by some type of injection, after he was beaten and tortured to an unconscious state. Maybe the killer used air or poison, perhaps a home chemical. This would be a sophisticated way of ending his life, suggesting a contract killer, but for whom?

I had been away from the visitation area for at least ten minutes and was becoming uneasy. I took several quick photos of Joe's bruises and broken and smashed fingers with my small digital camera before rewrapping his body in the plastic bag, leaving him face up on the shelf, where he would remain until cremation. There wasn't anything else that I could do.

Before shutting the refrigerator door, I stopped to look at the bag holding my dear friend. I gave him a military salute, turning away to wipe my tears. I re-padlocked the unit, put the key back in the bottom desk drawer, quietly left the building, and walked to my car without ever looking back. Now I had to go back home to the Mississippi Delta and decide what to do next.

CHAPTER THIRTEEN

Joe collected Asian art. Its steep black and white mountains and waterfalls expressed the flow of life, dark and light, in collaboration. He would describe his collection to me, and I'd tease him—say he'd tripped on too many mushrooms instead of studying his contract law books. But I admired his sophistication, his seeming knowledge of life and how it works. The yin and yang of it all.

I'd left my lover's body in a locked stainless steel refrigerator pending cremation. His cool naked corpse, once warm and shining, now was pale and gray, death removing his life force and distorting mine.

The drive back to Clarksdale went more slowly than my earlier race to Montgomery. For seven hours in the dark of night, unnerved and scared, I guided my car along the winding rural landscape, wondering if the darkness that encased me would remain forever.

At two in the morning, I walked into my house and immediately called Tom to let him know I'd met with Joe's widow. Didn't tell him I'd seen Joe's body, or broken into the funeral home, and didn't disclose I'd found bruises on the body or broken fingers.

Tom assured me that he would leave at daybreak for Joe's funeral, asking once again if I wanted to ride along with him for the service, but I said no. I had seen enough and couldn't do anything more about Joe, except to secretly wait and find out if his killer would come after me. It was a fear that gnawed in the back of my mind, after facing the reality of Joe's death—seeing him there in the funeral home. He must have known enough to get him into trouble. The problem was that I knew a lot of what he knew. And maybe more.

Had he given his killer my name? Joe was brave. But brave enough to endure blinding pain? I expected someone to come after me, even if Joe hadn't revealed me to his attacker. I would be easy to find, and it could happen at any time. I'd already started to think about this on my drive home.

When Tom came back to Clarksdale late that night from Joe's service, he called and invited me over to his home to talk. "You might not believe this, Clint, but no one showed up for Joe's funeral except me."

I was surprised at this, but said nothing—listening to what else he had to say.

"It was embarrassing. Even Tara wasn't there. She had already left for her parents' home in New York, the chaplain told me. He said she called him early in the morning, asking him to give me her best wishes. It was all pretty weird, Clinton."

"Did you look to see if a death notice was published in the Montgomery newspaper?"

"Yeah. A small paragraph saying it was a private service for the immediate family only and giving no details."

What could I say, sitting there on Tom's couch? I had no idea why Tara wouldn't show up to her own husband's funeral. This was appalling. Most of his Alabama friends probably had no idea that he was dead, or they abided by the private service request. I wondered if any of them would be curious enough to probe further. Everything had happened so fast.

Tom looked down at the Indian rug on his living room floor as I wove my story. Didn't interrupt me, ask questions, or pry. Once a funk musician in Michigan, he'd left Detroit for the Delta to open a church and preach, bringing his calm with him. Nothing ever seemed to shock or surprise him. I'm sure he'd seen it all in Motown.

I decided to trust him. Tom listened as I spilled out my story, still careful what I chose exactly to reveal. I'd had all day to think about it. I knew that I had to confide in someone, and Tom was the only logical choice. But I didn't want Mollie to have this knowledge. I feared she might be a target; anyone looking for me could easily find her, then figure she also knew too much.

About what? I still had no idea.

I talked late into the night and early morning. Explained that Joe and I had information about dozens of unsolved murders that had happened in Mississippi and around the South, but I didn't give Tom names or specifics. I told him about my collection of secret boxes filled with pieces of potentially incriminating information I'd been collecting since the late 1960s.

I also told Tom how Joe had followed in my footsteps—that between us we had collected sufficient information about past crimes to easily get either one of us killed. We had enough information to make a number of people uncomfortable; this almost sounded like a brag. But, in fact, we had enough to send some very rich and well-known men to prison for life.

There was only one problem: Whoever murdered Joe will come for me next. I was sure of this.

Joe was smart, and so was I. We'd poked around in dangerous places for a long time. The more I thought about it, someone could be out there looking for me, maybe waiting in the bushes in front of my house, just like they'd stalked and killed Medgar Evers.

Tom sat quietly in his chair and listened. That was all that I'd wanted him to do. I didn't need a two-way conversation, or need his advice. I just needed to talk and suck it up, then decide what to do—take action or forget it.

I said what I'd come to say. We prayed together for Joe's soul, and then I drove back home and went to bed, where I stayed awake five more hours, going over cold cases in my head. By the time I finally got up, put on clean clothes, and went to work, I'd decided to completely change my life. Sure, I was being irrational. No argument.

But from then on, I would work from my church, building my congregation and practicing law. I was going home to Jesus! I was also making sure that Mollie would never be in the line of fire, should the worst occur. Client matters would be taken care of at the church, or Mollie could handle them from my office, calling me on the telephone when she had questions. I knew she would do this for me, and if I asked her not to question why this happened, I wanted to know she would honor my request.

If I needed to sign a pleading or other papers, Mollie could bring them by the church. I'd still make court appearances when necessary, but avoid my office. My new way of doing things would work. It had to, and it did—for the next couple of years.

CHAPTER FOURTEEN

Trinity remained my fortress, my tight-fitting cocoon in the two and a half years following Joe's murder. It was the only place where I felt comfortable and where I knew that I should be. Usually, I arrived at work by seven in the morning, staying until nine or ten at night rebuilding walls, replacing cracked windows, plastering, painting, and plumbing bathrooms and the kitchen. And, of course, helping people find the Lord.

I couldn't complain, since fixing up Trinity and ministering to my parishioners turned out to be the best therapy after losing Joe, even though it meant managing my law practice from a distance.

It might seem odd, but I think I enjoyed fixing up the kitchen shelves for our new dishes more than anything else. I would drift off, feeling the happiness church dinners would someday bring, even if I no longer was around to lead the prayers.

"Hey, I miss you," Mollie announced one afternoon as we neared the end of a phone call. She was sitting at her desk in my old office across town, and as usual, she had been dinging me about the piles of boxes still tipping on their edges, a topic she couldn't suppress. Of course, she wanted everything cleaned up, or better—gone!

"Hey, I could shove a few of those boxes into my car trunk and bring a load over to the church for you to sort through," she offered this time.

I ignored her offer, focusing on her earlier nostalgia.

"Me, too, Mollie—I miss you a lot. Miss your rusty coffee—choke, choke—your smile, and even your sporadic fits."

Our tête- à-tête was forcing me to ask myself—not for the first time—why I'd left my law office to turn a dilapidated car dealership, set in the middle of Clarksdale's mostly abandoned downtown, into a successful church. Even before Joe's murder, I'd spent large parts of my week rehabbing the graffiti-covered building, with its leaking roof, into a decent place for my congregation. Turning this banged-up building with structural weaknesses into a church seemed crazy, whenever I stopped to think about it, before going back to painting or taking a break to write Sunday's sermon.

Mollie was doing her best with her attempts to lure me back to the practice, this time promising fresh coffee after giving up on the boxes. She had to be kidding.

"You ever coming back to the office, Mister Clinton? I've got your favorite coffee cup washed up and ready and waiting on your desk."

Just the thought of her lukewarm brown sludge jolted me back into reality. Occasionally, she'd half-threaten me with what could happen if I didn't return. Today she was out trolling again and landed on this:

"You know, Mister Clinton Moore, I could get in a heap of serious trouble doin' all this legal work for you without bein' a real lie'yer."

I caught her intended distortion. "A liar, you say?" I stopped to laugh. "I've already explained that I am not being unethical, Mollie; the law practice carries on. We conference by phone at least once, maybe twice, a day. I write the documents here, you come and get them, or I send them over by email. You bring papers to the church for my signature before filing or putting them in the mail."

I had to take a breath before I finished my thoughts.

"And you know that I defend clients in court, meet them in the courthouse law library before and after—I just prefer not to use my law office. I still attend state bar functions. I meet new clients at the church office, so I am still practicing law—just differently, while keeping the client numbers low."

I'd said my piece, and Mollie was quiet, but only for a moment. No quitter, she struck again with an entirely new topic.

"Say Mr. Clint—one more thing before I go back to work—have you ever heard from Missy Tara? I was just thinking about her today."

Funny she brought up Joe's widow several years after Tara had left Montgomery without saying goodbye to any of us, even skipping out on her own husband's funeral. We'd never really talked about her before today, and I'd assumed that Tara was still living in upstate New York, maybe somewhere in the Catskills.

"Nope. Haven't heard a word from Blondie. I'd guess she's still with her parents. You haven't gotten wind of anything different, have you?"

"Nothing. Nada. Zip."

I really didn't care if I ever saw that woman again. It would have helped had she given me access to Joe's cold case files—okay, so I didn't directly ask her for this—but she'd been so hard to work with, refusing or unable to answer questions about Joe's death, even calling it a suicide when it clearly wasn't, there'd been no reason to track her down.

I never believed Tara killed Joe or set him up to be murdered. Tara wasn't that bright and easily could have been lied to, even manipulated into lying to me about Joe's death. This was a possibility I'd been considering as time passed. But I knew that she loved Joe, in her own way.

Mollie's phone call ended, and I took a moment to reflect. I could go back to working at my law practice office, maybe save my own neck, if I could learn the truth. I still believed I might be in danger, despite receiving no threats thus far. Maybe I'd overreacted at Joe's strange death, but I really didn't think so. More than likely, I'd been left to live because of my quick withdrawal to semi-isolation, immediately after Joe was killed.

Mollie's offer of bringing over boxes for me to sort through at the church sounded like a good idea. I'd been collecting files that held statements, court documents, newspaper clippings, personal interviews, and photos documenting atrocities occurring for decades, and I honestly didn't know what all I had stored away over the years.

I needed to go through the mess and see what was there. I could bring over a few boxes at a time, sort through the clutter, and build a list of people who might have a reasonable motive and means for killing Joe, and maybe me.

Tom and his wife were my closest friends, and I'd finally started sharing with them what I had been going through and what I believed might have happened to Joe. One day, Karen quickly framed the problem I faced as we sat down over lunch. Placing on the table a wood block cutting board containing bowls of hot lentil soup, she sat down to join us. She looked tense as she unfolded her napkin.

"Tom and I've been wondering if you or Joe put someone in prison who might have been paroled and decided to get back at either of you?"

"Could either of you be a target for cleanup on an old crime? Something that was covered up for years, maybe the wrong person was convicted in the first place? Or maybe one of you learned something you weren't supposed to know?" Tom injected.

Their ideas represented some of mine. There were plenty of boxes waiting for me to open and check out along these lines. One particular carton involved leads Joe had been following over the King assassination. I'd remembered hearing him talk about possible links to the Kennedy murder.

We'd finished lunch when a thought came to me— one I hadn't shared—that my own name once appeared on a hit list just below Medgar Evers's name, not long before he was killed. I'd learned this from a prison guard at Parchman, Walker's older brother. Our names had been circulated around the state on a Ku Klux Klan flyer. Tom and Karen were surprised.

"Sounds like something else to look into," Karen noted.

Back at my Trinity office, I was thinking about our lunch conversation when a knock on my door turned out to be the kind of interlude I liked:

"Rev. Moore, we need your help." A volunteer peeked through the door. She was holding a can of paint and a small brush.

I rose to walk down the hallway with her, putting my arm around her shoulder, and asking, "Now you're sure you want me? You know how bad I drip."

"Oh, I'll do the painting, Reverend. You steady the ladder."

We both laughed. At least the extra pounds I'd gained over the past few years were worth something. Searching through messy boxes could wait another day. Now I had something more important to do, and I'd better get on with it!

CHAPTER FIFTEEN

Several days following the lunch with Tom and Karen, I slipped away from Trinity for a couple of hours to drive over to my law office and dig through some boxes. Mollie was surprised to see me on her turf—elated, in fact.

"Why Mister Clinton Moore. What are y'all doing here?" Mollie looked up from her desk, her deep brown eyes always hard to resist.

I'd left her with a giant mess, never explaining what had happened in Montgomery, or why I'd been staying away. Of course, she knew I was building the church, and she surely picked up on some of my fear. Mollie would not have understood its source or recognized my fear of putting her in danger should Joe's murderer come looking for me inside my law office. She was a loyal friend, a dedicated legal assistant, a kind-hearted woman, and I felt guilty over the deception I'd created. Still, I didn't tell her. I also knew her quite well and sincerely wondered just how many of my boxes she had already gone through.

"I'm ha'ir on a mission," I fake-drawled, sounding just as silly as she did. "Ah've been missing you, Miss Mollie, and thought I'd jes drop by and chat."

Truthfully, the moment I walked through the door, I realized how much I'd missed my law practice, the way it used to be—Mollie, my clients, my scales of justice, and even Mollie's pathetic coffee.

"I see you've got the scales all polished and in balance." My paralegal of over thirty years had carefully meted out enough paperclips and thumbtacks to balance Truth and Justice.

We chatted about nothing important while I signed some papers. Then I confided I was here to finally do something about cleaning up the boxes.

"So you got your horse sense back, Mister Clinton?"

I looked at her and smiled, wishing I could be honest.

"I'm only here to do a little paperwork. Got to thinking about some old cases, and I thought I'd come by and pull records. But is there anything I can do for you, before I get started?"

She signaled me with her crooked index finger to follow her back to the conference room, where we spent the next hour going over a couple of tricky billing issues. It felt good working together. It had been over forty years since the day Mollie found me, answering my frantic help wanted ad in the Clarksdale newspaper

She had aged beautifully. I could not keep my eyes away from her sweet neck as she bent over paperwork, remembering how she had come back into my life and made a difference. After a second attempted sexual relationship soon after she'd started working, an endeavor that went absolutely nowhere, she'd finally given up on me, realizing that I still was gay, and knowing we could never be lovers. She married a good man, a farmer who supported her as well as he could. Together they raised two sons, but I always wondered what if.

Afterward working on the bills, I headed to the storage room, taking several more hours to go through twenty specific boxes I'd decided to examine first. Flipping through old records, time slowed. Each paper I viewed brought memories of people and atrocities I'd almost forgotten. Soon I drifted into thinking of Joe, running into cases we'd worked on together.

Many were local crimes—like the shooting of a Glendora service station attendant and the "accidental" drowning of his wife—and carried little weight. But how in the hell could so many black people have been killed in so many accidents in Mississippi? No wonder this state was called the belly of the beast by civil rights advocates around the country.

Joe had come to Clarksdale frequently to work on cold cases. I remembered one Saturday morning as he bent over papers, reading every word, how he'd looked up at me for answers. Because I was four years older than him, I know he thought I'd have them.

"Why are journalists and historians so gullible in accepting these pitiful official excuses over and over again? Where in the hell is the Department of Justice?" he'd ask. I could not give him any answers.

We'd spent years looking for clues in the murder of Dr. King, refusing to leave his assassination alone, after the government and countless well-known journalists caved to the lone assassin theory instead of doing their jobs—finding every person who was a part of it—just as they'd given up on tracking down the murderers of JFK and his brother, Robert Kennedy. I recalled many of those conversations:

"In Dr. King's case, the very FBI agents who hated his guts were the same ones assigned to investigate his murder. See this?" Joe held up a newly declassified Department of Justice document, an internal report that supported what he said, despite numerous redaction marks on the page. DOJ easily could shed light on the mystery of Dr. King's assassination, and we both knew it.

"Hell, Joe. With modern equipment, investigators could now be running all of the fingerprints," I remembered saying.

"You're right! They've collected prints over the years, and it would be so easy to do. Don't think it hasn't been suggested to them by sophisticated investigative writers and others! DOJ has to fear that some old FBI cracker agent's prints would come up. Now that would stir things up real good, wouldn't it?" Joe snickered.

"They must be pretty damned afraid of a surprise match that would throw their sloppy investigation into a tailspin. But who in the hell knows what they're thinking?"

Even many media experts were unaware that in the late 1970s, the House Select Committee on Assassinations examined a $50,000 bounty on King's head, and I'd mentioned this to Joe:

"Oh, you mean the reward issued by a St. Louis businessman who belonged to Mississippi's White Knights of the Ku Klux Klan? You mean that one?" Joe used his best facetious voice.

We both knew the Klan also promised a separate $100,000 bounty that James Earl Ray heard about and reported while he was in prison in Missouri. Nothing was done about it, as shown in later released FBI documents I'd acquired.

"Remember, the house committee agreed that Ray shot King," I'd reminded Joe. The committee also reported it was likely a conspiracy existed to kill King— that more people than Ray were involved."

"You are kidding me!" Joe dead panned, never looking up from his notepad, while trying to act surprised. Of course this information was old, and we'd both known about it for years. Yet devoid of verifiable information, too many people still believed Ray acted alone.

Regretfully, the House Committee's surprising conclusions in 1978 were mostly ignored by the national media. Much of its evidence was sealed for fifty years under Congressional rules. But then in 1992, Congress passed legislation to collect and open up all the evidence relating to Kennedy's death, creating the Assassination Records Review Board to further that goal. I'd been able to collect thousands more declassified records, and so had Joe.

The wrongful death lawsuit filed by the King family in 1998 didn't receive much media attention. A jury quickly found a local restaurant owner, Loyd Jowers, guilty of conspiracy. The jury also decided the assassination plot involved governmental agencies and organized crime as unknown coconspirators.

"And only two reporters attended that trial!" I remember Joe saying, as he slammed down the pen he'd been using to write notes on his yellow legal pad. He'd become so angry over the lack of media coverage that he'd left the room to get calm—returning with a ham and cheese sandwich and a cold beer. I'd heard him fooling around in the kitchen for five minutes.

Both of us were on the lookout for the other coconspirators alluded to by Jowers—the criminal and government connections. I never got very far. But had Joe? Could he have uncovered information that he couldn't share?

Finished with my first round of investigation, I waved goodbye to Mollie who was working at her desk, while carting out to my car three full boxes of selected documents I'd gathered from the original twenty boxes involving the King assassination.

"Okay, I'm heading back to the church," I called to her. She rose from her desk to open the front door.

"Later!" she waved.

Back at Trinity, I started digging through my files and searching my memories. I almost sensed that Joe was hanging around my office in spirit. It was a warm and comforting thought, and that night I hated turning off the light and going home.

CHAPTER SIXTEEN

Lopsided.

My piles of boxes were decreasing at the law office, while they grew higher at Trinity. I was now making regular trips between these two locations to sort through each one of my stuffed, worn-out cardboard containers, glomming onto anything that looked important.

Late at night, parishioners found me going through stacks of papers and writing notes. "What's with your office? Are you trying to start a storage business to help us make money?" one church member kidded me. She was rightfully curious; my small office was filled with boxes stacked in every corner. I locked the door whenever I left, not wanting anyone looking at these documents.

Some whispered about my mess as they headed home at night, looking back the next morning to see containers stacked higher than before. "Just some old legal work that I need to catch up with," I would lie.

Shuffling through papers one afternoon, I recalled Joe and I joking about what would happen to our glorious collection once we were finally dead and gone, assuming we passed away naturally, of old age.

"A family member might get a tax break by donating them to a special historical archive," he joked.

"So let's make sure this mess is sent to archives outside of Mississippi or Alabama or it could take hundreds of years for some white supremacist archival assistant to scrub files intended for the public eye," I'd suggested.

We both had heard stories about the literal miles of documents donated to the University of Mississippi from the estate of U.S. Senator James O. Eastland. Friends teaching at Ole Miss described how Eastland's files were looked after by a censor, an old employee of the racist senator who'd been assigned a quiet office in the basement of the law school to do his important work.

Deep down in the quiet underground space, the Eastland crony meticulously went over each scrap of paper to remove any word or sentence that made the foghorn senator look good. The censor kept his school-supplied paper shredder busy.

It took a dozen years or so before any of Eastland's files were made available to researchers, and by then what was left of his special collection consisted mostly of news releases and other feel-good documents, making the old fart look almost virtuous.

A law professor later told me that few of the secret memos Eastland sent or received to or from the Mississippi Sovereignty Commission—papers that I had received copies of, and that were stored in my personal collection—made it into the Ole Miss Archives. I knew some of what should have been in Eastland's public collection, because I had my own set of copies thanks to Ann at the Sovereignty Commission.

"And for this, somebody got a big fat tax break," Joe laughed over a glass of wine while sharing what we'd learned, during a quick break in the early morning hours. Neither the finely aged cheese I'd bitten into nor the merlot I swallowed that weekend could remove the foul taste from my mouth.

CHAPTER SEVENTEEN

I close my eyes and pull up images of Big Jim Eastland. He's standing on a flag-draped bandstand in a little Delta cotton town, giving a rousing Fourth of July speech, his ignorant words peppered with racial slurs. Kids sit around the stage as white parents stand behind them, arms folded across their chests.

William Faulkner never came close to developing a character that looked and behaved like the real Senator James O. Eastland. Faulkner didn't have the guts. Even without such a mythical image to spark my imagination, I'll always remember this power-hungry man—how he looked, talked, and smelled.

The senator's two-thousand-acre Doddsville plantation, south of Parchman prison, wasn't far from Clarksdale. Occasionally we would see each other—even shake hands—at government meetings or similar occasions when he was home to pump up voters and keep tabs on his family business. The old goat was practically my neighbor until he died of pneumonia in 1986.

It was Mollie's relationship with Eastland's plantation secretary that proved lucrative in discovering one of the senator's deepest secrets. Mollie, June Grey, and I had gone to high school together. One day, the two women accidentally bumped into each other at the Drew Town Bank where Eastland was a member of the board. Though a powerful U.S. senator, he remained on the decision-making body of this small community institution. Eastland had a time-honored reputation of keeping his fingers in every pot—and this included Drew.

Mollie's chance meeting with June led me to some of the most vital information I held, bless her heart! My secret Eastland files became more voluminous than any others over the years, mostly because of Mollie's sleuthing.

"You won't guess who I ran into," she informed me one Monday morning, after plugging in the coffee pot, ready to give it a go. "Remember June Grey? The nice girl at Clarksdale High?"

Few other kids had shown kindness to black students back then, as Brown I and Brown II threw public schools into full integration. June tried making up for the hatred that often confronted us as most, but not all, white kids left for the private academies named after civil war generals. June's family was poor, and she was stuck attending school with us! In this rare case, poverty was the equalizer—June was humble enough to accept half a sandwich from my lunch sack when her family was struggling to survive.

"Sure, I remember her. So how is she doing?" Mollie poured herself a cup of coffee, before it percolated, and came into my office to fill me in on her meeting.

"Where's mine?" I asked, before she sat down.

"You always pour it out and then go begging to Walker with your empty cup. Why should I waste this good coffee on you?"

That sounded fair enough, so I motioned for Molly to take a seat and continue with her story. She was right about Walker, and I planned to walk over to The Grill in the next ten minutes—cup in hand.

"I was in the Drew Bank Saturday morning to make a deposit," said Mollie, "and June walked in. After twenty years, I still recognized her! Same short brown hair and tiny figure! She was delivering bank records for the

Eastland plantation. And get this—she's the old man's private secretary when he comes home from Washington. Her daddy started managing the Eastland plantation after we graduated from high school, and he got her the job. We recognized each other right away, and we went out for coffee after she finished her bank business."

This was interesting news. I began to see how I might profit from it, as Mollie continued with her story.

"You won't believe this: June says Eastland calls her in for important meetings. She takes notes, and when the visitor leaves she reads her notes to Eastland, and he recites them back. Once he has them memorized, he tells June to burn the notes!"

That was amazing. The old man was too shrewd.

"Listen Clint, I think June will be our friend," Mollie continued. "She already knew you were back in Clarksdale. She followed what went on with Jo Etha's murder, but said she never approached you when you were in Drew. She knew the situation was bad and felt it was best to stay away. She didn't want to cause you any more problems than you already faced. But working for Eastland, she has to know what goes on in Mississippi. Maybe she'll help with our cold cases."

I did a double take when I heard Mollie mention cold cases.

"Our cold cases?" I stopped her right there and cautioned her to be careful about getting into matters over her head. I wasn't specific, but I'd seen that cheerleading gleam in her eyes and should have known she'd been going through my boxes.

I guessed it was time to let her in on more of what I'd been doing. We worked closely together on everything else. She was a smart woman, and I trusted her. It wasn't appropriate or fair to keep her in the dark, so we talked for another hour.

I ended up telling Mollie even more than I'd planned to reveal, details on some of the evidence I'd already collected on the murders of Emmett Till and others. I told her, for instance, about a murdered service station attendant, Clinton Melton, and his wife, Beulah, from Glendora, the same town where Till's body was dumped into the Tallahatchie River four months earlier. Both were killed when a relative of one of Till's murderers went into a rage over the amount of gas that Melton had pumped into his car.

"You can't get involved in these cold cases Mollie. It's dangerous for you to know what I am doing, and what I've collected. But we can work together in a small way, and I do trust you to know about what I am doing. It is critical that you spend most of your efforts with my day-to-day practice. This frees me to work on church projects and all of this other stuff."

I knew that she understood what I was revealing about my work on cold cases, and she likely saw through my attempt to guilt induce her to keep on task. But it also was evident to me that Mollie already had been working in my boxes. Mostly because I'd discovered color tabs and detailed file notes in several of my files—and in her handwriting! Not in every box, but I was seeing more and more clues of her involvement in the Eastland and Till files, especially after she began visiting with our old friend, June. Mollie's attention to Till's murder in a plantation shed outside of Drew made sense, because Eastland, of course, had collected intel on this internationally reported murder that occurred in his own backyard.

Mollie and I had a lengthy visit that day. I thanked her for the organization skill that I'd discovered in these files, and we agreed that it helped me tremendously. But I said nothing about Joe or my conclusion that he'd been murdered. I still believed that could be dangerous information for Mollie to have.

We developed an open understanding of my secret records collection from this discussion and defined her limited role in what I was doing. Eventually, I told her about Ann at the Sovereignty Commission.

"Don't ever ask for a detailed message from Ann—she calls herself Sharon, by the way. If she calls, give her the church number, and if I'm not there, let her know I will get back to her."

The Eastland files became voluminous and were giving me plenty of documents to sort through. The senator exercised vast control over the Mississippi Delta and the U.S. Senate—and regions of the world—for over four decades. Eastland knew people in every agency of government and used them as personal spies. Schooled as a lawyer, Eastland served fewer years than the state's junior senator, but was still known as Mississippi's senior senator because he held the most power—as chair of the United States Senate Committee on the Judiciary for over twenty years, then President Pro Tempore of the senate during his last six years of office.

More than once in my Texas law school days professors would refer to the records of my state's senators when picking out the worst civil rights case examples. Usually, I wanted to dive under my desk. Each had pushed embarrassing legislative agendas.

In my first pass through these files, I found a small intriguing article clipped from the New Orleans Times-Picayune. I couldn't remember clipping this myself and had never read it before. It had to be something Mollie received from June. The date stamp was hard to read, but I noticed the news article was dated 1956, seven years before President Kennedy was assassinated in Dallas. The gist was that a former chief counsel for Sen. Joseph McCarthy's House Un-American Activities Committee, HUAC, accompanied by a private detective, had traveled to Eastland's district office in Greenwood to confer with the senator for more than three hours. Afterward, Eastland's counsel described the conference as "completely satisfactory."

This meeting might not sound like much, but here was the kicker: the detective turned out to be Guy Banister, a former FBI agent who personally knew Lee Harvey Oswald—JFK's supposed assassin. Banister and the chief counsel had worked together through Eastland's very secret Senate Internal Security Subcommittee or SISS, sometimes called SISSY.

Recently declassified documents show that Oswald did intelligence work for this committee, as well as for the office of Naval Intelligence, or ONI. Banister would later be associated with Oswald and the assassination through his New Orleans detective agency and SISSY.

I had interesting confirmation of this from an old law school classmate of mine, now a full professor at NYU. Dr. Dan Bell sent me a packet of papers from what he called a recent successful mining expedition. Included were declassified FBI documents showing both Oswald and Banister had contracted to do intelligence work for SISSY clear back in the late 1950s, and with the knowledge of the special counsel, Bobby Kennedy.

This revealed much about Oswald—who he really was—and perhaps could lead to the identity of the secret planners of the president's assassination. It definitely was worth digging through the rest of my Eastland files to see what else was there.

If this newspaper clipping was a fascinating find, later, after digging some more, I found a whopper. Whenever the senator made short visits home to Mississippi, he often brought powerful friends with him. In a buried folder, I came across a typewritten note from Mollie about a confidence shared between herself and June.

I read it once quickly and went over it again. It was one hell of a note. I don't know why Mollie didn't come to me and talk about what she'd learned from this conversation. Maybe she was uncomfortable in telling me she had been cleaning up these files, although we'd agreed she could organize the Eastland stuff. That was so like her, to quietly do her job and protect my back. But Mollie also had a stubborn streak, and once she got started working on anything, it was best to keep out of her way and let her do her thing.

Meeting with Mollie for lunch, several months after Eastland died, June had shared this story about her old boss and J. Edgar Hoover. According to Mollie's note:

"June said that she believed Eastland carried critical information about the JFK assassination to his grave, 'but he wasn't directly involved'—June's quote."

June told Mollie that Eastland liked inviting important people as plantation guests. One weekend in Fall of 1963, a week before Kennedy was assassinated, Eastland was hosting a visit by FBI director, J. Edgar Hoover. June overheard them talking as they sat on the veranda, according to Mollie's note:

"Hoover told Eastland what was about to happen— the president was going to be killed. June told me that she witnessed this conversation from a close distance. She said the FBI director said there was nothing that he could do to stop the assassination. June heard him say it was already in motion. We'll have to sit back and watch, were Hoover's exact words."

It was terrifying to hear that Eastland and Hoover knew what was about to take place, yet did nothing to stop it. There was no reason why June would have made up such a story.

By now, thanks to Mollie, I'd sorted into a pile at least one hundred Eastland-generated documents, with topics ranging from the murders of Emmett Till and Medgar Evers to the presidential assassination, the killing of the three Freedom Summer civil rights volunteers, and the assassination of Dr. King. This put the senator at the top of my A-list.

It hadn't been long since he'd died, and there could be someone lurking in the Delta, or possibly in

Washington D.C., who needed to protect the old man's secrets and his questionable reputation.

Did Joe get in the way with important Eastland information he'd kept to himself? I couldn't answer my own question. But, I had more boxes to search.

CHAPTER EIGHTEEN

I was watching the weather reports one Saturday morning while reviewing cases. There's not much winter that comes to Mississippi. In late fall, we enter our most severe season, as the television weatherman calls it, when temperatures sometimes drop by twenty or thirty degrees, bringing arctic winds with ice storms.

The house had cooled down, so I got up from my desk chair to find a sweater. By now, even my church office was stacked with collapsing boxes, finally forcing me to move the entire mess over to my house. I had moved my most secret papers to the locked safe in my law office. This had been a good idea. If I got tired from working, I could take a rest. If I got hungry, I could make a sandwich and then go back to work, or pick up a book and read, if I needed a break.

"Mr. Clinton. Here are your slippers. You'd better put them on now, you hear? A storm is moving in."

My neighbor, Gladys, heard I had a cold and had come over to check in on me and deliver a large bowl of hot soup. Gladys was good company and gave me kind attention when she thought I needed some. I know she wanted to be my housekeeper—she had been almost pushy in asking me for the job—but I wanted my privacy, even if it meant my house was usually a mess.

Besides, I liked padding around in my bathrobe and slippers. I was getting older and starting to feel more aches during the winter months, but I hadn't given up on what I was doing—no way. I appreciated this new flexibility in maintaining my search for Joe's possible killer, now that Trinity's rehab projects were mostly done.

After making a first pass through my entire collection of documents from Mississippi's pathetic senior senator from years back, and waiting for a possibly severe storm to pass through Clarksdale, I began browsing through random reports I'd collected on various crimes over the years, looking for anything that jumped off the page.

All of it was fascinating reading, especially from my history junkie perspective. I found that some of what I'd gathered years earlier was now making sense. Added time and subsequent events gave me new perspective.

If I were going to get anywhere in reasonable time, I knew I'd need a better system for evaluating the importance of my collected information. This led me to build a list of the most serious crimes Joe and I'd had studied. Here was my first cut:

1. Lynching of Emmett Till, 1955 (the Delta)
2. Assassination of Medgar Evers, 1963 (Jackson)
3. Assassination of President John F. Kennedy, 1963 (Dallas)
4. Murders of Michael Schwerner, James Chaney, and Andrew Goodman, 1964 (Philadelphia, Miss.)
5. Probable murders/mutilation of Birdia Keglar and Adlena Hamlet; possible murder of James Keglar, 1965 (the Delta)
6. Probable murder of former FBI agent John D. Sullivan, 1966 (Vicksburg)
7. Assassination of Dr. Martin Luther King Jr., 1968 (Memphis)

I had a big job ahead. As a public defender, former county judge, once-coroner, and armchair historian, I knew that many people must have participated in at least several of these assassinations or murders, making longer periods of cover-up, with even more killing, necessary and wide-spread, to keep the material witnesses quiet. With respect to Kennedy and King, the lone assassin theory had never done much for me, or for Joe. We knew from our research that effective assassinations require great planning and the involvement of at least a handful of personnel.

With the modern civil rights movement winding down, I'd seen justice occasionally meted out when a brave prosecutor would march some stooped, white-haired defendant in shackles before the media, trying to get a conviction in one of the above or related murders. Occasionally this worked; an old Klansman was shown heading off for prison while leaving his network of cronies behind. This is exactly what happened in 1994, on the third and successful attempt to convict Byron De La Beckwith of killing my mentor and civil rights leader, Medgar Evers. But even after De La Beckwith was locked up in prison—thirty-one years after Evers' 1963 murder—it never felt quite right to me, or to some other Delta people, who would occasionally talk to me about his conviction.

"We've got rumors floating around this place about Medgar's murder again. Still not sure they're looking at the right guy. What do you think, Clint?"

A Parchman prison guard asked me this one Saturday morning, about nine years ago, over a cup of coffee at the Grill. This was the week before De La Beckwith's third trial opened down in Jackson.

"Honestly, Jim, I never believed just one person was involved in killing Medgar," I explained. "He had too many enemies. There wasn't an eye witness, and De La Beckwith was reportedly seen in Greenwood close to the time of the murder—Jackson and Greenwood are two hours apart. And I think the timing of Medgar's murder speaks volumes."

Walking Jim through it, I continued. "You might not remember, but one day before Medgar was shot, Governor George Wallace, in an effort to block the integration of the University of Alabama, made his futile 'stand at the schoolhouse door.' That same day, President Kennedy announced the National Guard peacefully had enrolled two black students at the University of Alabama over Wallace's racist objections."

Kennedy's speech had been more than a mere recap of what occurred in Alabama. He'd asked for unity behind what he, for the first time, called a "moral issue." His remarks came when many white Americans still saw civil rights as a regional, largely political, question. And here was Kennedy, asking all Americans to "stop and examine" their conscience.

"Wasn't this the centennial year of the Emancipation Proclamation?" Jim asked as he sugared up his coffee. I pulled the bowl over to my side of the table, then motioned to Walker for extra cream.

"Yes, and until then, Kennedy had ignored this anniversary. But that night, he made up for this, insisting that none of us we will be free until all of our citizens are free. I remember him asking Americans of all backgrounds to engage in bringing about change, in a peaceful and constructive way."

Jim was looking down, slowly stirring his coffee.

"That was some speech. It had to make Kennedy some enemies."

I nodded, remembering Kennedy's brave words that night. He'd introduced comprehensive civil rights legislation and spurred school desegregation beyond its current slow pace, making this his most historic civil rights address.

Of course, we both knew what had happened next. In the early morning hours of June 12, Medgar Evers pulled into his driveway, returning from a meeting with NAACP lawyers. As he stepped from his car, carrying a load of NAACP T-shirts that read Jim Crow Must Go, a bullet struck him in the back.

Jim took a drink of coffee, then paused.

"I remember reading the police reports. The bullet was fired from an Enfield 1917 rifle; it ricocheted into his home. He staggered thirty feet before collapsing and died at a local hospital fifty minutes later."

He stood up, and we shook hands. "Gotta get back to work, Clint."

He slowly left the Grill, his shoulders hunched as he walked out the door.

Some folks would call people like Joe and me conspiracy nuts and ridicule us. That's a big reason why we'd kept quiet about our cold case research. Also, considering where we lived, it could be perilous speaking out in public. Besides, this was a part-time obsession. We both had regular legal work to do—work that supported what we called our addiction.

"Do you think De La Beckwith could have planned this all on his own?"

I'd asked Joe this question after the first De La Beckwith trial—the one that resulted in a hung jury. In 1964, the state of Mississippi again attempted to prosecute this white supremacist Klansman for Medgar's murder, still with no success. The jurors were all male and all white.

"De La Beckwith didn't have the resources to pull it off. It's the same with Lee Harvey Oswald and James Earl Ray," Joe would start in.

And here's something about Joe: if I found something tasty to feed him fast—as soon as he stepped from the car door—he could go on for hours nonstop on a topic like De La Beckwith. I knew exactly when it was time to pick up barbecue. All I ever had to do was ply him with a grilled turkey sandwich as soon as he pulled into my driveway after the long trip from Montgomery. I knew what Joe loved and how to please him. This was his favorite food, and once his stomach was full, he would answer all of my questions. As long as the sauce was good, and there was plenty of it.

He was right on Oswald and Ray. Neither had the resources to do something so dramatic as slow down Secret Service cars or call for auxiliary military guardsman to stand down, as had been done in Oswald's case. Or delay the Memphis police response to the crime scene, as with Ray. Joe could go on forever with his impressive list of activities that neither Ray nor Oswald could have accomplished on their own.

I had my own questions about Medgar's murder. I'd heard once from a deep source in the state prosecutor's office that it might have been an entirely different gunman, not De La Beckwith, who killed Medgar because, "We needed to convict someone!"

Even the state's key witness in the final trial secretly admitted to me years later she always wondered about the conviction.

"He was a frightening man, and I think DEE-Lay might have been trying to scare us at the time he confessed in the car."

Later, Joe and I learned independently that De La Beckwith had questionable associates. I first learned this from a friend, Andy, a jailer in Jackson. Several weeks after De La Beckwith's first arrest for Medgar's murder, Andy said the new prisoner often was visited by Maj. Gen. Edwin Anderson Walker.

"Wait a minute," I said. "You're telling me that the same famous general who was forced into resignation by President Kennedy for calling Eleanor Roosevelt and Harry S. Truman pink—in print—and telling his troops how to vote—right wing, ultraconservative—is visiting De La Beckwith in jail?" I was astonished.

"Yep. Walker's the guy," said Andy. "Comes in to see him like clockwork."

"How do they know each other?"

"Don't know. Maybe when Walker was leading the riots at Ole Miss in 1962, or maybe at a Minuteman meeting."

I wanted answers and asked Andy to keep his eyes and ears open.

"Let me know if Walker comes again, and see if you can pick up any of the conversation."

"I'll do my best, Clint," he promised.

Joe firmly believed the assassinations of Evers, both Kennedys, and King were linked.

"We just need to find the right people to question, and we'll eventually get answers," he would say.

The right-wing militia assassination trail intrigued me, as I worked to find connections between the KKK and other extremist groups, like the Minutemen and White Citizens' Councils. In my secret boxes filled with documents, memos, old photos, and notes, I had placed dozens of items showing links I'd discovered.

For one more hour, I dug through the last cardboard box of the day. Then I ran into a legal pad filled with my handwriting. The notes came from an interview with a Ku Klux Klan leader. I'd almost forgotten about this encounter; the frightening man from Greenwood had given me something new to consider about Medgar, and possibly JFK's murder. Thank God I found those notes!

CHAPTER NINETEEN

Bankers, doctors, lawyers and other professionals, making up Mississippi's White Citizens' Councils typically viewed themselves as "too polite" to belong to the ill-reputed Ku Klux Klan. Financially backing the Klan to do their dirty work—undercover and mostly at night—these respectable men attended church on Sundays without losing sleep.

A well-known Pulitzer Prize-winning Mississippi journalist, Hodding Carter Jr. of Greenville didn't buy it. He once came up with the moniker Uptown Klan to describe these model citizens—and it stuck.

A hefty pock-marked pharmacist, Robby Slaughter, headed the Greenwood Citizens' Councils. He was a good Episcopalian who also led the local White Knights of the Ku Klux Klan, a fact lost on most of his family members, neighbors, and customers. Slaughter ruled this region of the Delta; he was a powerful man, and nothing went on that he didn't know about or plan.

After more than twenty years in existence, the White Knights, begun in the early 1960s, still didn't hold public demonstrations or release information to the masses. Similar to the United Klans of America (UKA), Slaughter's group was secretive. Members once had numbered as high as six thousand, with klaverns in over half of the counties in Mississippi. But the number of active members who called themselves Christian militants, had by this time shrunk to around four hundred. Still, according to the FBI, they were considered the most violent and clandestine of all Ku Klux Klan groups in the South.

I wanted to talk to Slaughter, meet him face-to-face, and ask questions about Medgar's murder. See if I could learn who'd been after me. I knew Slaughter would be tough to approach, but I needed to try. I was closing in on middle age, but still young at heart and brazen.

"Say Molly, I'm going over to visit with Mis'tuh Robby Slaughter Thursday afternoon at four. So calendar it. Okay?"

I paused for her reaction, knowing full well what was coming, and it took less than a second for her to deliver.

"Mister Clinton! What are you telling me? You don't mean that old SOB over in Greenwood who runs the Klan? You don't need more clients, do you?"

"Listen up, Miss Mollie," I said. "I need to get some specifics about business regulations over in Greenwood and was referred to him by the Chamber."

Of course, I was lying, and she knew it.

"It's your neck," Mollie quietly said as she jotted the appointment in her book, and then slammed it shut.

Trying to talk face-to-face with Slaughter was a brave thing for a black man to do back then, but I thought that Medgar's killer would never be convicted. Slaughter was Byron De La Beckwith's closest friend, so maybe he could fill me in. At this time, De; La Beckwith was still a free man, living somewhere off in the mountains of Tennessee, so I wasn't afraid of asking Slaughter a few questions about him, knowing De La Beckwith wouldn't be around to harass me.

I never called to make the appointment, but dropped by his pharmacy on that set day. Giving Slaughter a moment to properly ignore me, a black customer, I greeted him while looking down at my shoes, not wanting to appear uppity—still a problem in post-Jim Crow years.

"Good afternoon, Mr. Slaughter. Glad to catch you at work," I quietly said. He gave me a grunt. I figured I might as well jump in and start asking about the trials and De La Beckwith, after introducing myself. "My name is Clinton Moore, and I'm—"

"Yeah. I know who you are and what you do. Why are you here?" Slaughter glared, cutting me off mid-sentence. I forged ahead, thinking it might help to start with a little praise:

"Since you know more about what goes on in the Delta than most other folks, I want to ask your opinion about the murder of Medgar Evers. And by the way, I don't think your friend De La Beckwith did it."

He was too seasoned to show emotion, but there it was. I'd laid out my thoughts on his dark-stained drugstore counter. He could have called in some of his thugs and had me hauled off and beaten, but he didn't. It was a big risk on my part; some might call it stupid, but I was lucky enough to catch him in a civil mood.

Slaughter stood behind his counter and kept working at filling a prescription. Afternoon winds were blowing dark clouds across the Delta sky. Walking out from behind his work station, he pulled up the window shades, trying to coax a little more sunlight into his drugstore before the day turned black, perhaps so his store wouldn't look like he'd closed up and gone home early due to the weather.

Slaughter started talking about quail hunting, but minutes later he appeared to relax, and surprised me by inviting me into his back room where we could "talk more private." Hidden behind the pills and other pharmaceutical supplies was a small area where he could take a smoke break and still see approaching customers through its open shelving. He pointed toward a wooden chair, followed me as I sat down, then anchored his right foot on my chair rung. Slaughter lit a cigarette and looked down at the top of my head, before blowing a fat smoke ring above it.

"Interesting we agree on DEE-Lay, you being a nigrah and all," he said.

I could tell that he was feigning politeness, using a distinctly Southern white word for Negro. But he acted pleased that someone was asking for his expert opinion, even if that someone was black.

"Well, you're right on this one. My friend didn't do it, and that jackass state prosecutor will get his one of these days, count my smoke rings."

When I look back, it was not too long after De La Beckwith's conviction that the prosecutor was sent to state prison on charges of obstruction of justice. Slaughter did wield enormous power.

Blowing another circle into the air, he took his foot down from my chair rung and walked over to a small cabinet set off in a corner and pulled the knob. He grabbed a bottle of bourbon and two small glasses.

"Care for a drink?"

I hadn't expected any suthrin hospitality on this visit, but nodded yes. He handed me a glass, then sat down in the chair across from me, holding the bottle of bourbon. Poured himself a shot first and downed it. Then poured one for me and drank his second shot in a gulp while I drank mine slowly.

Slaughter leaned forward and stared.

"Why Big Jim Eastland and his rich friend from New York City, Draper—you know who they are, don't you, Clint? They planned the whole damned thing. DEE-Lay was just a pawn. But mind you, someone had to kill that fanatic fool, Medger Evers."

I held my tongue. My mind strayed for only a moment to a national magazine interview Medgar had given shortly before he was killed. Asked why he didn't simply move away from Mississippi, he said, "I live here so I can try and change the things I don't like."

Had Medgar really believed he could survive a man like Slaughter? Turn him around? I said a silent prayer for my slain brother before returning my attention to this Klansman.

Slaughter already had confirmed my hunch that De La Beckwith or DEE-Lay didn't work alone. There was big money behind Medgar's assassination, and Slaughter had linked the trail to a man named Wickliffe Draper, a multimillionaire textile machinery heir and virulent racist. He also was an ardent eugenicist, anti-Semite, and pro-Nazi. I had Sovereignty Commission records showing Draper played a major financial role in Mississippi's fight to keep segregation intact, including copies of his checks that had been laundered by the state treasurer and sent on to private organizations fighting civil rights legislation.

Draper, now dead, once gained national notoriety for embarrassing a handful of lily-white Ivy League professors who'd received grants from his racist foundation to do heredity research. When an East Coast news reporter discovered their funding source and wrote how Draper had once traveled to Berlin to attend a science conference hosted by Nazi Germany, the prestigious professors were chagrined. But they kept Draper's money.

"That Draper! You know he paid for segregated schools in Mississippi. We even got some of his money right here in Greenwood for our private Gen'ral Nathan Bedford Forrest Academy, where kids learn real Civil War history—the truth," Slaughter said.

I nodded along as he spoke, feigning continued interest. I knew that Draper's Pioneer Fund held a special place among The John Birch Society, The Shickshinny Knights of Malta (a mysterious secret, right-wing Catholic group), and The American Security Council—all blatantly pro-Fascist and anti-Semitic groups that all could have played a role in the plot to murder President Kennedy.

Near the bottom of my special Draper box, I had found a copy of a memo to the Sovereignty Commission's director from the commission's accountant showing

Draper had funded most of Mississippi's fight to halt the 1964 Civil Rights Act. But here was the big ticket item, and I wasn't sure if Slaughter even knew entirely what this pro-Nazi veteran had been up to. My records showed that Draper used Mississippi as a financial pass-through for handing out big chunks of money meant for various persons at suspicious times.

I had in my files state accounting records showing successive six-figure installment payments to the Mississippi Sovereignty Commission from this financier not only before Medgar's assassination, but also around the times of the bombing deaths of the Birmingham Choir Girls, the Kennedy assassination, and the murders of the Freedom Summer CORE volunteers.

New documents I'd recently acquired showed links to Eastland who'd been Draper's longtime Chairman of his special Eugenics Committee, part of the Pioneer Fund, that supported dozens of controversial research projects whose goal was to demonstrate scientific support for segregation.

Ann once gave me copies of the cancelled checks made out from Draper's personal New York banker to the state of Mississippi.

"Even the state got embarrassed over this and decided it wasn't a good idea to be passing Draper's money through the state treasury," she'd said.

The funny part about my special meeting with Slaughter was that it turned out I knew a hell of a lot more about Draper than he could ever imagine, including where Draper's money had gone and Eastland's involvement in Draper's "projects." I also had a strong idea that Beckwith knew about this circle of friends. Slaughter's big mouth, backed up by his big ego, confirmed it:

"You do know that DEE-lay was Senator Eastland's relative?" Slaughter taunted me.

He had to be thinking this was new information for me. I'd hoped he would puff up and tell me more, but I already knew that Beckwith's nephew by marriage had written a critical book about his famous uncle, the U.S. Senator. There'd been no book reviews by the Mississippi press, so the story stayed local.

The sky was turning black by now, and the temperature was dropping. as the Delta prepared for one of its heavy rainstorms. The air had been hot and muggy earlier in the day, but it rapidly changed. I heard a bang of thunder roll across the flat cotton fields, and Slaughter's words became harder to hear. When lightning raced across the sky and thunder again boomed, I closed my eyes. I really didn't want to hear more of Slaughter's sick words, yet I'd come here for information, and I needed to take note of what he was saying. So I moved my chair in closer.

"They wanted this to be a knock-out blow, something big to upset his friends," Slaughter said. "Kill the leader and they'd throw in the civil rights towel. Hey, it worked—didn't it?"

Slaughter spit out his words and watched for my reaction. I was determined not to show surprise. I heard more thunder claps in the distance and didn't flinch. No way would I let him see he'd struck a nerve. Their plan to crush the civil rights movement didn't work, and Slaughter had to know this in his heart—if he had one.

"So, who put my name on a hit list—the same list that Medgar topped?"

I'd made it this far and wanted to know why I was on that hit list.

"How would I know?"

"So you do know what I'm talking about?"

The pharmacist stared into my eyes.

"If you really want the answer to who wanted you dead, look to the FBI and that COINTELPRO crap they were dishing out back then—"

"And still do," I quietly said of the controversial domestic spy program that had done so much harm to the movement. An acronym for COunter INTELligence PROgram, this had been a series of covert, and at times illegal, projects conducted by the FBI aimed at surveying, infiltrating, discrediting, and disrupting domestic political organizations. Targets included leading Americans who criticized the Vietnam War—people like Senators Frank Church and Howard Baker, civil rights leaders including Dr. King, journalists and athletes—besides campus activists, like I had been while in Texas.

Imagine Slaughter and me coming to agreement over government intrusions. I'd wondered if the FBI had anything to do with Medgar's murder. And here was Slaughter, possibly answering my question!

Was it worth my trip to Greenwood? I thought so after hearing from Slaughter that both Medgar and me had been targeted by the FBI, possibly resulting in the Klan's go-ahead to kill Medgar. For some reason, I'd been spared. At least in that round.

After taking Slaughter up on his offer for a Cuban cigar, I left his pharmacy and headed back to my office.

CHAPTER TWENTY

Back home, memories flowed while going through my boxes. In 1965, two older Charleston women, Birdia Keglar and Adlena Hamlett, both well-known and admired in Tallahatchie County for their voting rights activism, died in a suspicious car crash on their way home from Jackson after being honored by the U.S. Commission on Civil Rights. I don't want them to be forgotten, I thought, as I looked through what I'd collected on this cold case. Keglar had been a successful businesswoman and Hamlett, a teacher.

I say "died" because that's the official story from all the law enforcement agencies. Both Joe and I strongly believed they were tortured and then murdered by Klansmen after their car was run off the road. The brutal treatment they'd reportedly received was an important clue. Two family members, interviewed years later, claimed both women had limbs cut off, which were sewn back on by the funeral home attendant. Klansmen were known to viciously play with their prey before killing it.

"It was horrible what I saw at the funeral," Mrs. Keglar's granddaughter told me. "I screamed. Others took me outdoors, told me to stop, and they never listened to what I was saying. I'm sure my mother and father didn't want me to cause more trouble for their families. They had to keep living in Charleston, after we went back home, and wanted to be safe."

It was a pity no one would pay for the exhumation of their bodies. I'd gone through these particular files, keeping in mind how the years 1964 and 1965 had been particularly dangerous for activists. It was a time of increased Klan activities in the Delta, particularly those of the White Knights as they reached their pinnacle.

"You need more clues?"

The FBI agent, visiting my office at my request, held the papers he read from, as we walked through the case. I knew he was disgusted with me, as he tried to convince me that the two women hadn't been murdered, but were unfortunate victims of a head-on collision caused by the drunk son of a wealthy Delta cotton planter. A dozen sheriff's deputies and state highway patrolmen working in the specific area of Sidon were later publicly outed as members of the Klan, and the small town outside of Greenwood where the women were killed was known to be a klavern, a place where there had been increased Klan activities. I thought these were good enough clues, but none of this seemed to matter to the agent.

Sadly, these women lost their lives one day before the opening of the federal investigations of the Mississippi Klan. In all regions across the country, as similar state investigations opened, crosses were burned, and black people in each state were terrorized and/or murdered. The FBI agent still tried to convince me that Mississippi was different—even though this state was known to be the belly of the beast, the state with the worst documented civil rights atrocities.

This agent didn't like me and probably wanted me to go away. But I remember pressing on, unconcerned whether his own possible racism might cause me grief.

"And what about James Keglar, Mrs. Keglar's son? Are you at least going to investigate his murder?"

"He was a damned drunk!"

Yes. James was an alcoholic, I admitted, and yes, he died during a house fire three months after his mother was killed. But I'd been told he'd gotten out of the military early, to try and learn more about how his mother had died. Then he expired in a questionable fire when a lamp was turned over after he'd passed out on the floor. I'd also been told that the fire occurred subsequent to his attempt to set up a meeting with the FBI in Clarksdale.

"But now you're telling me you have no records of his contact with the Bureau?"

"Look, Mr. Moore, this is a cold case, and we're doing our best," was the only answer I ever got.

I expected no perp walks would ever occur in any of these cases, including the Emmett Till lynching—a mystery to this day. Others had to have been involved in this young man's murder, besides Roy Bryant and J. W. Milam, who were both tried and acquitted in fall 1955. The trial drew media representatives from around the world, and today, dozens of different stories circulate around the Delta about this murder of a black child from Chicago who may have whistled at a white woman in a grocery store, and who paid the ultimate price for his transgression.

Years later, I could only watch as the tri-county black female district attorney half-heartedly advocated for this murdered child. She was expected to get a few convictions with help from the FBI, but her agency rejected the Bureau's serious offer of support, even though the FBI had actually done months of competent research. The ADA took the case before the grand jury, using none of the information that had been assembled. Guess what? The ADA came out empty-handed! Big surprise.

CHAPTER TWENTY-ONE

Each time I opened and sorted through another packed box of documents, my emotions ranged from anger to worry. But then I started looking into the papers I'd collected on a dead Vicksburg private detective, and I confess feeling a smidgen of amusement. John D. Sullivan, a racist, white member of the Citizens' Councils, had worked occasional spy jobs for the Sovereignty Commission. For a few bucks and a small per diem covering his gasoline and lunch, Sullivan would set up civil rights leaders and perform other despicable chores.

One day in 1967, Sullivan reportedly shot himself in the nuts while sitting on the corner of his bed cleaning his rifle. It happened soon after Sullivan came home from a dove hunt with friends. According to the report that I later received from my good friend, Ann, he bled to death,

After I came to believe there might be ties to JFK's assassination. I'd spent time looking at Sullivan's death as a cold case, Sullivan had worked for a former FBI boss on a special job in New Orleans during late spring and early summer 1963. But I didn't arrive at my insight until a number of years after Sullivan's death. Eventually, Joe became intrigued by Sullivan's "accident," after I'd taken a second look.

Going through these papers spread out on my dining room table, I wondered if Joe had learned something more about Sullivan and didn't let me in on it, or simply forgot to tell me. I picked up a yellow, tattered copy of the detective's obituary, which had been scissored out of the Vicksburg daily newspaper, years ago. As I started reading the article, it brought me back to the late 1960s when Ann, my dedicated Sovereignty Commission snitch, sent it to me for the first time—soon after I'd opened my Jackson law practice. I'd glanced at the story before tossing it into a file, not thinking about it, until years later, when she again reminded me of his death.

"Sullivan's accident—if you want to call it that—was never given its due diligence," Ann said. "I've always wondered why no one took a second look at this, Clinton."

This resurrected my interest. Ann wasn't one to give up!

I didn't ignore the clipping, but this time shared it with Joe, along with some other papers Ann had sent. I became more interested in Sullivan, as it overlapped an important trial in New Orleans, when in 1966 a brave prosecutor tried to convict a local businessman of conspiring to kill President Kennedy. Sullivan worked in that city until a few months before the assassination, and he had connections with some of the people mentioned by the prosecutor.

I remember Joe's first observation that the mere idea of a trained marksman shooting himself in the balls by accident was hard to accept "unless he'd been drinking." I looked through the official toxicology report, and there was nothing indicating Sullivan was impaired by drugs or alcohol when he died. Later, from his daughter, I learned that Sullivan's children didn't believe the story about their father's accidental gun death, either.

Ann's packet had included notes she'd taken while speaking to Sullivan's widow on the telephone not long after the "gun accident." She had been directed by her boss at the Sovereignty Commission to contact Sullivan's widow because he wanted to "get his hands on" Sullivan's entire set of detective files and his personal library. Mrs.

Sullivan apparently agreed to make this donation to the state, but when Ann called to make arrangements for someone to come pick it all up, the widow said that some men dressed in dark suits had come to Vicksburg and swooped up all of her late husband's materials. She'd thought the men were from the Sovereignty Commission, but it turned out they were not.

Who were these secretive men? No one from the Commission had a clue.

"My boss was furious, and I thought it was pretty strange," Ann told me.

Ann's notes on Sullivan also mentioned that his widow reported her late husband had been quite upset after returning home from working in New Orleans with Guy Banister, his old FBI boss from Chicago. The Big Easy is about 220 miles due south of Vicksburg, so Sullivan came home to visit three or four times before returning for good.

"Mrs. Sullivan said that her husband was nervous," Ann said. "He spent a lot of time talking with a family friend, a retired judge, Ben Guider, about the experience he'd had working with Banister, but she never knew why he was so agitated."

Ann also learned that Sullivan made a chilling statement to his son.

"The information was so big, I did not know where to go with it."

What information—picked up in New Orleans—could Sullivan have been talking about? What was "so big" to this small-town detective that it scared him, causing him to confide in a retired judge and not his wife? I wanted answers, and by now Joe seemed interested, too, even though he saved his hardest efforts researching the assassination of Dr. King. Had Joe found something more about Sullivan and kept it from me?

Just last year, I read a book by a woman named Judyth Vary Baker. She described the New Orleans assassination staging area, and I thought she might be of help in learning more about Sullivan. With a friend's help, I contacted her outside of the United States, where she was living. She told me she had moved around because she had received death threats. Her story was that she had been Oswald's girlfriend while he lived in New Orleans before the assassination. I never found any notes on Baker in my Sovereignty Commission, DOJ, or FBI materials, but she insisted that Oswald was set up to be the lone assassin. He actually had admired JFK, she told me, and wanted to try and abort the assassination plan; he may have successfully foiled an earlier attempt to kill Kennedy in Chicago, shortly before the president's trip to Dallas, she also said.

But I wanted more proof. Had Baker had met Sullivan? She told me that David Ferrie, a strange-looking pilot with bushy eyebrows, who was alleged to have been involved in the conspiracy, knew Sullivan and had spoken of him in a derisive manner. Ferrie once told Baker that Sullivan was a member of the militia and not too bright. When Banister applied to be director of the Sovereignty Commission following the assassination, Sullivan misspelled Banister's name with two n's in a letter of recommendation, and Ferrie said Banister was furious about this mistake. I later found this letter in my Commission files, complete with the spelling error. Baker did a good job of describing Sullivan's personality and politics, so I believed her.

I was impressed with Baker. She was a brilliant woman, who'd been a scientist, a rising star in her early years before she was pulled into this mess, initially by the National Science Foundation. Her professional career and a later marriage were both destroyed because of it. It was an intriguing story.

Sullivan may have crossed paths with Carlos Marcello, boss of the New Orleans crime family. Marcello was no stranger to anyone working in or around law enforcement, including me. The detective's death certainly had suspicious overtones—shooting himself in the nuts and then bleeding to death! But it was messy. Amateurish. Too substandard for the mob!

I took a third look at Sullivan and New Orleans when the film JFK was released in 1991. This movie, directed by Oliver Stone, made the point that the planning of Kennedy's assassination took place in New Orleans, a place known for its jambalaya, jazz, and organized crime.

Sullivan was never mentioned in Stone's movie. I found this peculiar, and even disappointing. Regardless, the movie turned up new evidence supporting what the New Orleans prosecutor, Jim Garrison, had said all along—that the JFK assassination planning definitely occurred in his city. If Garrison was correct, then it looked to Joe and me that Sullivan's death was no accident. New Orleans, in fact, was a dangerous place for several of the potential witnesses for the prosecution.

Two typed suicide notes were found at the scene of David Ferrie's death; neither note was signed. Baker confirmed that the last time she saw Ferrie, he said he was afraid for his life. He had warned her to leave New Orleans.

Joe drove over to Clarksdale on the weekend of JFK's release to work through some of his cases while I worked on mine. I was curious if he'd caught any mention of Sullivan, since I hadn't. I don't know why I would ask Joe if he remembered anything. He was an excellent research guy who always had data at his fingertips and easily could answer most any questions about a cold case. Especially if I plied him with a barbecued turkey sandwich.

Joe had noticed this omission, too. Regardless of whether or not Garrison knew of Baker or Sullivan, this famous prosecutor initiated what many conspiracy writers, researchers, and serious historians would see later as the most critical investigation into the JFK assassination. And to think, a despicable little man from the Mississippi Delta might have played a secondary role.

Another suspicious set of occurrences surrounded the 1969 trial of New Orleans businessman, Clay Shaw. Fascinating to me, was that Banister, Sullivan, and Ferrie—all three potential witnesses for the prosecution— were dead before the Shaw trial opened. Banister died of coronary thrombosis at the age of 64, six months after the president's assassination. Sullivan died in October 1966 from his strange gunshot wound, five months before Garrison arrested Shaw. David Ferrie's suspicious death came four months after Sullivan's in February of 1967, only one month before Shaw's arrest. Shaw was acquitted less than one hour after the case went to the jury.

"Spooky!" Joe was finishing his sandwich, as I walked him through these critical dates. "Damn, that's good barbecue. Abe's?"

Of course it was Abe's. The dumpy little shack of a restaurant was located south of the Crossroads sign of U.S. 61 and U.S. 49, on the Blues Highway, the spot where bluesman Robert Johnson allegedly sold his soul to the devil to achieve musical fame. The bluesman along with the region's extra-long staple cotton had made Clarksdale famous. But so had Abes's Bar-B-Que.

Joe only stayed for the weekend when we had these twice-monthly get-togethers. He returned to Montgomery on Sunday afternoon, and not every hour was spent working. So we had to use our time well.

Taking his final bite from the fat turkey-filled bun, Joe scanned the dining room table to see if there was any more food. I realized I would have to make another run over to the Crossroads to keep him fueled for the rest of the weekend.

CHAPTER TWENTY-TWO

Sullivan's fearful remark to his son—"something so big I don't know where to go with it"—kept rolling around my head. I looked back through his documents and papers and tried recalling conversations I'd had with Joe about Sullivan's death, and what this detective might have been doing in New Orleans that was cause for his murder.

I needed Joe's full attention so that I could get the Sullivan story straight in my mind. Joe's elephant memory was a great benefit, and I was happy he'd become involved with my Sullivan interests, since his heart was in solving who killed Dr. King.

We'd finally decided that Sullivan must have found himself in the thick of assassination plotting while working in New Orleans, but I never believed that he was on the planning team. "He probably saw secret papers lying around on Banister's desk and got scared."

I told Joe: "Even if he was an embittered racist, perhaps Sullivan still had enough integrity that the prospect of a presidential assassination might have shaken him up. I'd sure love to dig through his friend Judge Guider's notes! I wonder who has them?"

Banister's coronary thrombosis was another death we had questioned. Perhaps it was a natural passing—he had some history of heart problems—but likely not. I had learned from reading some especially captivating reports, that the CIA long ago developed special weaponry to make a death look like heart failure, using a cyanide gun glove or shooter that leaves no traces. Was this how the former FBI bureau chief's life ended?

"So when did Sullivan actually work for Banister?" Joe asked me out of the blue one weekend. I was standing in the kitchen, looking through cupboards trying to decide on what to cook that night for dinner.

"Late spring and early summer of 1963," I called out, while thumbing through Southern recipes ripped off from black grandmas who'd taught white Southern women how to cook. The cookbook was published by a famous female chef who gave no credit to these old black ladies, and this hacked me off—especially when I thought of how hard my mom and grandma worked in the kitchen to make their meals taste so good. But I did like her recipes. I wiped my hands on a dish towel and went out to the living room to hear what Joe had to say.

"Wasn't that about the time Lee Oswald was supposed to be in New Orleans, before leaving for Dallas? Have you tried the beef brisket recipe?"

I didn't have to wonder where Joe was going with this, and his mention of brisket sounded good. Banister, Ferrie, Shaw, and Oswald—if Sullivan had seen them all together, in the same place, at the same time—it would not have been good for this small-town detective. Especially if he were called by Garrison to testify against Clay Shaw. The Warren Commission wanted the lone gunman theory to stick, and so did the assassination architects. Both Sullivan and Baker, vis-à-vis Garrison, would have put a kink in their plans.

"I have everything in my cupboards but the rosemary. The brisket takes three and a half hours to cook, so I've got to get started. While I go to the store, why don't you call and see if Tom and Karen can come over for dinner?"

These two long-time friends were always good company, and it would help to run by them some of the theories we'd been tossing around all day.

I later tried to learn if Garrison's papers included any mention of Sullivan and was told by the archivist that there were no such files. He was not familiar with Sullivan's name and didn't sound interested. Once I thought I'd found a file on the Internet that connected Sullivan with some Banister files. But I wasn't careful and could not retrieve it on a later search.

At a JFK Conspiracy convention I attended in Dallas, a moderately known author confronted me and asked about Sullivan, saying that he knew I was from the Delta. I'd decided to attend the weekend event, which attracted both serious researchers and fan geek types, and was surprised to be baited by him.

"No one takes John D. Sullivan seriously," he asserted.

I found him strangely irritating and later learned from another researcher that he was "probably CIA," and was trying to learn any gossip floating around on Sullivan, as well as any other stories heard around the convention.

"We always have spooks hanging around, whenever we meet," the researcher laughed and then looked around to see if anyone was watching him!

I did learn from this man that some of Garrison's staffers were compromised and knew all along about Sullivan. They also feared that the Vicksburg detective, as well as David Ferrie, might wreck Shaw's defense. Garrison later admitted in his book that he didn't know what he was up against, including CIA plants, at the start of his own investigation.

After struggling through all of these cold case murders—Till, Evers, Schwerner, Chaney, and Goodman, along with those of the Keglars, Hamlett, Kennedy, Sullivan, and King—I took off a full week to think about what I had learned, all the papers I'd read, and the conversations I had recalled.

When I went back to work, I narrowed my search to three assassination victims: Evers, John Kennedy, and King. These three civil rights leaders were known internationally, and the stories of their murders would not fade into history. There was strong reason to keep quiet—for good—anyone who didn't swallow the official stories offered by the government and the compromised media. These leaders had become martyrs and had the power of influence beyond their graves.

In the case of President Kennedy, the growing list of dead witnesses, including Sullivan, gave me more reason to head in this direction. These records of names, by now on the Internet, continued to increase in number each year, while the stained Warren Commission report had all but faded. Historians and assassination researchers kept writing volumes about the president's murder—and about the possibility of the involvement of an array of individuals and groups, from public to private.

Eventually, even the U.S. government came up with a new explanation for President Kennedy's assassination, at least something more believable than Oswald and their lone gunman theory. The House Select Committee on Assassinations reported in 1978 that Kennedy's death was probably a conspiracy, and that the Secret Service could take some of the blame, along with the organized crime. This was one giant step forward.

One fall day, while rooting through my files and preparing to refocus on my three final choices, my eyes caught a wrinkled handwritten note in one of Joe's legal notepads. When I pulled this sheet from the thick manila folder, I was puzzled. Joe carefully had printed out the name Kimble in red ink. I recalled this name from earlier research, but I didn't have time at the moment to look further, and put this aside. I'd decided the night before it was time to look into my King files. I only had scratched the surface of this collection and couldn't put it off any longer.

But there was something else I could not put off, as well. Telling Mollie the truth about Joe, and that I was trying to find his killer. The opportunity came about one day when she called me from the office—angry.

"I needed to buy supplies yesterday. I couldn't track you down to get money! Now I'm out of staples for the stapler," she fussed as I walked in the door of my law office. Mollie was on a roll.

"Do you think Della had to go to Perry every time she needed paperclips?"

Mollie might have been joking when she brought up Perry Mason and his brilliant legal secretary, but she wasn't kidding about the inconvenience of being financially dependent on me when it came to managing the office. When we'd worked together, this hadn't been a problem. She would give me a list of supplies to pick up, or I would hand her a blank check, and she'd do the shopping.

"I can't even buy toilet tissue without consulting you first, " she complained, "and then I have to wait for the money."

This was easy to solve. I walked over to my friendly banker and made arrangements for Mollie to have a debit card and a business credit card. "Just sign these papers, and they'll mail them to you this week," I told her when I returned to the office.

She smiled as I handed over the signature card and application. But she looked tired, and I was concerned.

"You okay?"

"Sure," she answered, turning her eyes away.

Mollie's behavior bothered me that evening. It made me start to think about keeping her in the dark on Joe's murder, and I felt guilty. We were friends—better than friends. She was the best and only legal assistant I'd ever worked with; she was my old high school chum, and my twice-attempt lover!

My drift to the past took me to a pleasant place for the moment. But here I was, trusting this wonderful friend to manage my law practice, without lettering her know what I'd really been doing and why.

Now that I had narrowed my focus on where I would be spending the next months of my investigative time, I couldn't keep Mollie sheltered any longer from all of this; she deserved the truth.

The next morning, after I arrived at Trinity, I called her on the phone.

"Say, we haven't been spending much time together," I said.

"I just called Walker and asked him to sack up some sandwiches and a couple of pieces of his apple pie. I'll drive by and pick it up at noon. Let's have lunch at the office."

Mollie's voice picked up, as she agreed to the idea.

When I arrived for lunch, I grabbed some paper and a marker and printed up a "Closed for Lunch" sign for the front window. We went back to my old office where we enjoyed the food that Walker had prepared.

"I've got something serious to tell you, Mollie," I said, while finishing my last bite of pie. She quietly listened as I told her the whole story of my trip to Montgomery—Tara's behavior, my trip to the funeral parlor, and how I discovered Joe was murdered. She didn't act terribly surprised.

"Well, I always knew there had to be more to the story. Now that you explain it, Joe's murder fits, I am afraid to say."

I told her that I was trying my best to learn who killed Joe. I said I'd been afraid for my own life, as well.

"I don't think that anything is going to happen to me, now. I have stayed low, and it has been too long since Joe was killed. See! I am still alive and kicking." I smiled, wanting to put Mollie at ease.

"Why won't you let me help you?" Mollie asked. It was the first thing she said, when I finished my story.

"We could work together like we've been doing with Eastland and Emmett."

I quietly said no.

Of course she was worried and told me so. Mollie also knew, by now, that the contents of my boxes spelled potential danger. It was one thing to solve cold cases, but quite another to prevent a future murder.

Then Mollie admitted she had an idea that there was more to what I'd been up to when going through the boxes. She'd been looking at more than the Eastland and Till collections.

"Okay, I admit it," she said. "I didn't keep my activities limited to those boxes. You know me, Clinton. I had to look! There were so many cases. And I saw Joe's notes, so I naturally began to wonder if Joe had discovered something that got him killed. I was worried about you, too, but I was afraid to ask you what was going on. I think I was afraid to know the answer, quite honestly."

Mollie started to cry, and I realized how awful these couple of years had been for her. I'd treated her badly and hadn't trusted her. She was a sharp, caring woman whose help I could use. I walked over to her chair and looked down at my friend, then gave her a hug.

"Please forgive me. I should have told you this, but I was afraid, too."

Mollie promised she would stay focused on managing the practice. and would not try to solve Joe's murder. I told her that I would let her know more about what I was doing.

"But some things must remain secret," I said.

I finally got Mollie to laugh when I forced her to take an ad hoc loyalty oath that started: "I Mollie, swear not to sleuth."

By now, most of the boxes were in my possession, anyway. I'd carted nearly all of them home and put other critical papers in my office safe. And I wasn't going to give her a key! Once again, I agreed that if something came up that she should know, I would share it.

"But you're just going to have to trust me," I told her.

"Will you tell me if you find Joe's murderer?" she asked.

"Sure. Once he's locked away for life."

Mollie wadded up her paper napkin and tossed it at my face. I went back to the church, removing the "Closed" sign on my way out the door.

CHAPTER TWENTY-THREE

I will never forget the moment Dr. Martin Luther King Jr. entered the Southern Christian Leadership Conference training room in Chicago. We were new employees, and this was our first day of work. He stood in the doorway at first and slowly looked around, his piercing eyes taking in everything in his view. I was stunned by his deep stillness.

The meeting lasted less than an hour. Initially, he said nothing while our supervisor introduced each of us to him with a short bio. So still, so silent—we gave him our complete attention when he finally began to speak, telling us the history of the SCLC and its important role in the modern civil rights movement.

His words were lyrical, the pace was slow. His presence moved me deeper to my commitment. He shared with all of us in the room that all men, women, and children are equal and must demand to be treated as equals.

"You are not doing this for yourselves," he'd told us, "but for generations yet unborn."

I had wondered about this man of medium height, with a dark-brown complexion like mine, who carried himself with such power and grace. Where did he find his energy? Where was this movement going? Would it end too soon?

Of course, many years have passed since then, and I think even more of Dr. King, about who he was, and what he stood for. While working in the Windy City, I also met one of Dr. King's most trusted confidants, Stanley D. Levison, an intriguing New York lawyer and businessman. Later, I'd talked about Levison with a fellow intern, Dan Bell.

Dan and I became close friends in law school, then moved on together as SCLC interns in Chicago. Dan later decided to go for a PhD in history and first taught at Penn State before moving on to New York University. We'd maintained limited contact over the years; occasionally, as Dan ran into juicy political information, he sent me copies, knowing about some of my cold case endeavors. As Dan rose through the academic ranks, the quality of his secret stuff got better.

"Did you know Levison was a Communist?" he asked me one day. We were still interning for the SCLC at the time.

"I don't think he is a Communist now—he just used to be one." Levison was one of the few people with whom Dr. King could speak his mind. It was said that they talked almost daily by phone or in person.

"I don't know, Clinton," he questioned. "Even if Levison quit the CPUSA, the FBI and the CIA are probably using his membership as an excuse to monitor Dr. King. It's possible they're listening in on their phone conversations and reading their correspondence vis-à-vis Levison files. I'm pretty sure they are doing this, but I'd have to prove it."

Dan was dead-on, as it turned out, and one day many years later, after Joe's death, he called me. I had been sorting through my boxes when he caught me at Trinity, after Mollie redirected his call. I'd received a sympathy card from him when Joe died, and he had accepted at face value the story of Joe's suicide. I chose not to talk about what I'd learned in Montgomery to Dan or anyone else, keeping quiet about my suspicions with everyone except Tom and Karen. It still hurt to talk, and I felt it was best to maintain secrecy while I was trying to learn the truth.

Our conversation started out relaxed, as we chit-chatted about the old days. Then Dan moved into the reason for the surprise call.

"We've been lucky with our FOIA's." I felt his smile over the phone. FOIAs are formal requests under the Freedom of Information Act. Originally signed by President Johnson back in 1966, the Act lets anyone ask to view federal documents, but this can be a complicated process.

This was always good news to hear from Dan. He was a meticulous researcher who knew how to wrestle documents from powerful government administrators and uncover paper trails showing the FBI's inclusive spying habits during the civil rights era, much of it done through COINTELPRO. Dan that knew I always was interested in what he had to share, and this time he had uncovered a pile of Levison and King-related documents.

"So, tell me more," I said. "You know what a kick I got looking through the last batch of secrets that you mailed me. I wonder how many copies the post office sent over to the NSA?" We both laughed.

Both Dan and I had started early using this investigative tool, having a heyday filing FOIAs to gain access to records and reports hidden by the FBI, CIA, DOJ, NSA, USDA, and several other secretive government agencies.

Dan was much better at filing these requests than I. After working in Chicago, he'd gone back to graduate school and turned filing FOIAs into an art form—going after various agencies to see what they'd tried to suppress about the civil rights movement. As a full professor, he now had a cadre of eager-beaver graduate students helping him with his work, and they loved every moment of what they were doing.

"My students come from the post-assassinations years," he once told me, "landing into this crazy world just before the '92 Los Angeles Riots—you know, the Rodney King era. But, they recognize that I've seen it all, and they fight to be in my pack. They hang around while I drink my coffee, and beg me to tell war stories."

I'd laughed at the thought of students pleading to take Dan's class.

"And I'll bet you tell them some real whoppers," I'd teased. Dan admitted embellishing a story or two, "just for the hell of it."

We got back to the reason for his call.

"Remember how at first the CIA claimed they'd collected nothing on Dr. King?" he asked. "Well, not so long ago, we discovered that twenty-seven million formerly sensitive CIA documents were declassified, thanks to former President Bill Clinton.

"Did you say million? I asked.

"Uh, huh. That's right. Not surprisingly, we found quite a few interesting CIA reports buried in this mess. Guess who the spooks were spying on? Dr. Martin Luther King Jr.! Reports on him were hidden among everything else."

Dan was not kidding me.

"The CIA hadn't limited itself to overseas spying, running roughshod over foreign governments and killing democratic leaders," I said. "That was old hat. They had their hands in our own country's civil rights movement, too," I shared.

He blew past my sarcasm. I could sense amusement mixed with tension in Dan's voice. He'd found these new records, not through the Department of Justice, as one might expect.

"We caught the CIA red-handed," he told me, "holding big bunches of files on King they'd hidden away. Get this—in their very own Cuba/Castro stash! I'm guessing they figured King was a communist, because of

Levison's communist past. You remember him, don't you, Clint?"

"Sure. We talked about him when we were back in Chicago—interns at SCLC."

"Well, they must have seen King as a potential threat to all of Western civilization because of his relationship with Levison. The CIA claims that their suspicions gave them a legitimate right to set up a vast spy network on King, within this country, and inside the SCLC.

I swear I heard Dan rubbing his hands together over his newest cache.

"So how'd you make this happen, Dan? Couldn't have been that easy."

"One of my eager-beavers got creative and FOIA'd for records on Levison," he said, "including what the CIA might have on him from his Ecuador operations, Hundreds of reports popped up."

"Ecuador? What are you talking about? Levison was from New York."

Dan back-tracked to explain that he'd seen Levison one day at Chicago O'Hare International while he was still working for SCLC.

"He was on his way to South America," he said. "Told me that his parents owned several dry-cleaning operations in Quito and Guayaquil. Then after I left Chicago and started teaching for the Universidad del Azuay in Cuenca, I ran into Levison again, walking into a local credit union. It was quite a surprise! He told me that he was there to check on his Ecuadorian businesses. We had lunch together."

How had Levison coped with living in Ecuador, I wondered, a country with few Jewish people.

"It had to be a little strange, maybe tough for him to be doing business. Hadn't some Nazis settled there from Germany after the Second World War?" I asked.

Thousands of Nazis had established themselves in South America, mostly in Argentina, Bolivia, Uruguay,

Brazil, Chile, and Paraguay, but later, Dan confirmed, some moved to Ecuador. Many made their new homes in Quito, and a few others in the smaller city of Cuenca, about ten hours south of the capital. Dan had been working on a South American economics history research project, when he ran into Dr. King's trusted advisor.

"Someday, I'll have to tell you more about that project," he said. "But real quick—we actually found that Hitler's chief economist, Martin Borman, escaped Berlin and spent time in several South American countries. Borman sightings were even reported in northern Ecuador, near the Colombian border, by a Colombian newspaper. But that's another story."

"How can you remember all of this crap? It was so long ago, Dan."

"I never thought much more about South America, until long after I returned home. Then a strange thing happened while I was teaching at Penn State."

Dan slowed down, and I knew another good story was about to come. He didn't disappoint me. He'd had a colleague in Pennsylvania, a math professor named Boris Weisfeiler, who in 1985 disappeared on a camping trip in the Southern Andes of Chile. Weisfeiler, a Russian Jew, went there alone and never returned.

"His sister, Olga Weisfeiler, and I made several trips to Chile to look for Boris," Dan said. "Then last summer, a Chilean judge ordered the arrest of eight retired police and military officers in connection with Boris's kidnapping and disappearance. According to court filings, they will all be prosecuted for aggravated kidnapping and complicity in his disappearance. But the ruling made no mention of where Boris was taken after his detention or whatever happened to him afterward. I am sure that he is dead."

I was stunned by Dan's story and kept listening.

"So out of the blue, Olga calls me one day. She's trying to get the U.S. State Department involved and asks me to help keep the heat on them. Our campus American

Association of University Professors group got interested, and even petitioned the Chilean government to try and find him, even if it takes investigating the entire colony where Boris may have disappeared."

I couldn't imagine what it would be like to lose a sibling in this way, to have to worry for the rest of your life, even if you've done everything possible to rescue the person.

"The colony is a strange place, Clinton. Started by an old Nazi reject. The name of the compound is Colonia Dignidad, and there were rumors for years of pedophilia and torture going on there, especially during the Pinochet years in Chile. Chile finally has taken some control of this place, but not when Boris first disappeared. The fate of Weisfeiler, though, remains a mystery—his sister's conversations with local officials and the U.S. State Department, the findings of a private investigator she hired in Chile, and bits of the official record that Olga has pried out of U.S. agency declassified files have not answered key questions. Chile has been little or no help, either."

Did Olga Weisfeiler think that her brother might have stumbled upon a compound of escaped Nazis? Was he killed immediately or kept prisoner for a long time? Could he possibly still be alive? I asked Dan.

"Well, I can't answer any of your questions," Dan continued. "It's still a strange place, and we're learning more as historians are gathering World War II documents about where the Nazis fled, who assisted their escape—who ran the rat lines—and the economic impact that was triggered when the Germans settled in South America. German money still circulates in most of those countries, including Ecuador."

Had I ever visited any South American countries? Dan asked. I hadn't, but the side comments he'd added in about Ecuador—the Galapagos Islands, the jungle, and the Andes—made it sound like a place I wanted to visit, and maybe would if I ever retired.

"Thousands of retired Americans are moving there as expats," he told me. "My wife wants us to retire in Cuenca, and I think I'll check it out. Cuenca's climate is the best."

We'd gotten seriously off track, and while I found his comments on South American history, economics, and the plight of his friend fascinating, I wanted to learn more about his recent CIA document find. Maybe there would be something useful for my own research.

"It's all fascinating, Dan, but even if you find in some of these new papers proof that the CIA set up Dr. King, giving a helping hand to the FBI by smearing his reputation—calling him a communist—you can't leave out the Klan factor or the extreme Right element."

Involvement of the Klan in King's assassination was uppermost in my mind at that time.

"Joe and I always thought with the Mississippi Delta so geographically close to Memphis," I said, "that there could have been local KKK involved in King's assassination. The White Knights were still highly influential and active in Mississippi back then. I've been working on his assassination lately and even found some new stuff."

When I paused, Dan said something that surprised me.

"And so had Joe."

Those four words slowly tumbled from his mouth, before I could ask if he knew anything about Kimble. His mention of Joe left me speechless.

"What are you talking about, Dan?" I finally asked.

"Why, Joe's trip up to Canada, you know, to find that Kimble guy. Remember when Joe took his trip to Montreal and—?"

I stopped Dan midsentence. "Did Joe ever find Kimble? Talk to him?"

I'd casually been sorting through papers while talking on the phone. But now I pushed everything aside on my desk and waited to hear Dan's response. First I was angry—thinking that Joe had gone off on his own to talk to Kimble, without telling me.

"You didn't know? Joe eventually found Ron Jules Kimble living close by in Yonkers! Relocated courtesy of the federal witness protection program. Kimble got out of prison early and was rushed there sometime in 2010. Joe tracked him down, and I guess that Kimble agreed to talk. So Joe met him in New York. I thought you knew all of this. Joe and I had lunch together while he was here, before he had his meeting with Kimble, but I never got back with him. I don't know what he learned."

Of course, I didn't know a damned thing about this meeting between Joe and Kimble. Joe hadn't said one word to me about his trip and now that he was dead, I had to hear about it second-hand from Dan—someone who hardly knew him.

"When did Joe go to New York?"

"I'd say about a month before he died. Honestly, I assumed that he'd told you about this trip."

"Did Joe ever talk to you? Report back what he'd learned?"

"I never heard from Joe again. Assumed he and Kimble got together. I was busy with my graduate students while he was here, and I didn't think to check back. Then I heard Joe killed himself. I sent you a sympathy card, didn't I?"

"Yes you did, Dan."

Dan was quiet. I didn't say anything else to lead him to believe anything different about Joe's death; the two had not known each other very well. But in the back of my mind, I began to see what might have happened, or at least why Joe left me out of the loop. He was fiercely competitive. And I could easily imagine Joe going out on his own, trying to find Kimble, not telling me anything, and then surprising me at the end with a good story, backed by solid evidence. But someone killed him first.

Dan and I had had been visiting for over thirty minutes, when he had to leave for a faculty meeting. I would have to reexamine everything I'd collected on King's assassination and Joe's few materials he'd left me, and look for anything that might stand out. I had more questions for Dan, but saved them for later.

CHAPTER TWENTY-FOUR

My opinion.

Anyone spending an ounce of time investigating the April 4, 1968, Martin Luther King Jr. assassination soon realizes it was not the strange little man, James Earl Ray, who did it. Even though he'd agreed to accept final responsibility for the act.

Had Ray been found guilty by jury trial, he would have been eligible for the death penalty. He was sentenced to ninety-nine years in prison, but later recanted his confession and tried unsuccessfully to gain a new trial. Thirty years later he died in prison of Hepatitis C.

Joe and I always knew that Ray didn't fit the bill of a cold-blooded sociopath. However, the documented stories of his mistreatment by jailers and lawyers didn't look good for the government. You can get a person to admit to anything when you keep them sleepless for days and nights, under shining lights.

Ray didn't have the ability to place military snipers on a nearby roof, slow down the arrival of the police and ambulance to King's side, trim the bushes in front of the sniper's nest after a reporter showed how they blocked the sniper's view, delay his own chase, and so on.

It was looking more and more like Ray was set up like Oswald—a patsy—but in Ray's case, a patsy with fewer assassination skills than Lee Harvey Oswald, and without

Oswald's military intelligence experience. But Ray may have had government links.

As I continued patching together what I'd gathered over the years on the King assassination, I remembered how Joe and I both talked about the crime, recalling clearly how some of our conversations played out.

"Say Clint, ever hear of a guy named Raoul? Ray always claimed this mystery man set him up and dropped the incriminating bundle with the hunting rifle and radio used later to identify and locate Ray at the scene."

Joe had recited this litany so many times, he could have said it backward or with a mouthful of barbeque."

But Joe shared few details beyond this.

I took a day off to drive to Jackson to do some more research on Raoul at the university library and learned that in 1989, Jules Ron Kimble, serving time in a federal prison in Oklahoma as a convicted murderer, admitted to British filmmakers that he was this Raoul. Kimble—a name that I knew—went on to say that he was intimately involved in a widespread conspiracy to kill King, along with FBI and CIA agents, elements of the "mob," as well as Ray.

The librarian helped me locate a copy of this British television documentary, and I spent the next hour listening to the confession of this shadowy figure who corroborated much of Ray's self-serving story.

Kimble clearly alleged that Ray, though involved in the plot, did not shoot King.

"He was set up," Kimble said, "to take the fall for the assassination."

This convinced me that Joe must have been looking for Kimble for quite some time. Did Joe find him?

Joe had collected another strange side story about the King assassination. One that I almost forgot about until I opened a small folder containing notes I'd taken on a Saturday afternoon, not that many years ago. He learned that those who planned the King assassination might have met in a log cabin in rural Mississippi near the Tennessee border. In fact, the sniper may have been there three months before the event.

I found notes I'd written when I talked with Joe about this. A Klansman told Joe that a black family was run out of their home and forced to live with their relatives, while three strange men took over their house several months before King was killed.

Joe spoke to this family's son, probably by accidental design on the young man's part, when he sought out Joe for advice on getting into law school. Later, I would find more notes.

Jules Rico Kimble. I'd never been able to find him. But had Joe tracked him down and learned something about King's assassination? Had Joe run into evidence that put him in peril?

I knew that Garrison independently had established links among Kimble, Shaw, and Ferrie. Together they traveled to Canada before the JFK assassination, where they allegedly picked up a fourth man in Montreal who spoke broken English.

This confusing conversation came back to me. Joe believed this additional man was Christian David [pronounced Dah-veed], a member of the old French Connection heroin network and a leader of the Corsican drug trafficking network in South America known as the Latin Connection. If Joe had found and talked to Kimble, he certainly would have asked him about David, seeking confirmation of this story.

As I went back through my notes, I searched for other mentions of Kimble, spending another day going through this box to see if I'd passed over any other scraps of papers. And then I found a captivating note on a small piece of legal notepad paper, in Joe's printing:

"IMPORTANT" was underlined twice—along with three questions.

- Why didn't Garrison call Kimble to testify in Shaw's trial?
- Was Kimble still working as an asset for the CIA?
- Was he embedded in the militia or Klan?

Kimble remained a real mystery man. I never could find any solid records on him or any photographs. All that I had to work with were notes from the Garrison archives and several declassified FBI documents, plus Joe's sketchy notes. Who had Dan hooked Joe up with to find Kimble? How did this person know where Kimble was stashed away? I would have to ask Dan. I made myself a note.

By the end of the day, I was tired and couldn't quit yawning. I knew that I should be shutting down my computer and turning on the news or finding a movie to watch. I stretched my mouth wide open. Took in oxygen, then found myself doing this several more times. I gave up and went to bed. Learning more about Kimble would be waiting for me the next day. I turned off the light and went to sleep.

PART II

CHAPTER TWENTY-FIVE

I woke up at dawn, exhausted and fighting a headache from the burning fields that circled Clarksville. The smoke was everywhere. Following an unusually warm spell at the end of a winter that left too much nitrogen in the soil, Delta wheat farmers tilled the ground early due to explosion of upward shoot growth. They were now turning on their irrigation pivots as fire protection, while burning their newly tilled fields to get rid of the grass.

Groggy from the haze and not ready to start a fresh new week, I took more time than usual preparing and enjoying my breakfast, thinking this might boost my energy. I would have to live with the headaches until the burning ended, or at least subsided. I brewed a fresh pot of coffee, spread peanut butter and marmalade on my toasted homemade bread, courtesy of my sister Betty, and then sat down to read the morning newspaper. The daybreak sun beamed through my kitchen window, and I thought how I could use a couple of days respite from my work—all of my work—from the few church property renovations still not completed, to my digging through boxes and sorting of papers. None of this had required particularly hard physical labor, but it had taken its toll. My tired bones were telling me so, and by the time I'd read the paper and finished my breakfast, I'd convinced myself to take a break.

I surprised Mollie when I walked into the door of my law office and announced, "I'm going to take a short trip along the Natchez Trace Parkway."

"You mean you're not here this morning to find more boxes to cart home?" She posed her question while placing stamps on billing envelopes. "That's amazing. Great idea, Mr. Clinton. Maybe then, you'll get your senses back and—"

I stopped her. "Don't mess with it, Mollie. Just be happy for me right now. And, please don't pour me any coffee. I'll pick up some to go from Walker."

I started thumbing through the weekend mail.

"Would you please call Trinity and leave a message that I'll be gone for a couple of days? Say that I'm taking a little vacation and will return Wednesday morning, first thing."

"No problem, Clinton. And I am really glad you're getting some time off. You deserve it." Mollie smiled, as she completed her postal chore.

I'm sure that most Mississippians don't know much about the Trace—a magnificent four-hundred-mile-long highway of exceptional scenery and ten thousand years of North American history. This is a good thing because the best way to enjoy the drive is in solitude. Then, while roaming this unique national park, it's possible to feel as if you're in true wilderness.

"Did you know Native Americans hiked the Trace?" Mollie asked, after learning about my plans.

"Not just the Natives, but 'Kaintucky' settlers roamed it, too, and even future presidents walked the Old Trace. You can still explore parts of the actual ancient foot trail."

"Well aren't you smart. Bill and I've been there too, with the kids, and I read the pamphlet."

I laughed and handed the mail stack back to her, after seeing there wasn't anything requiring my immediate attention.

"Will you be doing any camping or biking?"

"I'll do some walking, then pull off tonight for a motel, probably in Jackson. But I am taking some snacks for lunch so I can eat in nature."

"Well, have fun, and I'll see you in a few days." Mollie waved good-bye as I drove off.

After picking up my fresh coffee from Walker, it took four hours driving U.S. 61 South to get to Natchez, where I entered the park off Liberty Road. Stopping at the first small visitor's station, I asked the attendant for some of her newer brochures before looking for a lunch spot. I'd packed apples, cheese, toasted pecans, and some of Betty's wheat berry bread for this quiet meal, but before starting off, I did a quick read of the folder the park attendant handed me that described the small habitats I'd see on my drive. I took it from her, but knew what to expect, since there was always so much to enjoy when traveling the Trace. Still, I read through the list while leaning up against the car. I was already sensing the freedom of being outdoors in the woods and away from it all.

The attendant waved me off as I drove away. I looked for the best first place to stop and enjoy my treats. It was going to be a great lunch. I'd even brought a small tablecloth along and a bottle of mineral water. I wondered if there were any new spots constructed since I'd been there last with Joe, a couple of years ago.

The park was built back in 1937, but it was still being developed, particularly around Natchez and Jackson. Always there were places to stop on this two-lane highway, small side trips that captured me, like the old Rocky Spring Methodist Church, a cemetery, and several building sites, all nestled between the Parkway and the Old Port Gibson Road. Cypress Swamp was located 122 miles into the trip, and several cascading waterfalls, requiring a short hike, were particular favorites of mine.

Parts of the original trail were still accessible, and I always looked forward to spending time out of my car, walking into the wild. Maybe I would have my picnic at Emerald Mound, the second largest Native American ceremonial mound in the country, just west of the Trace and north of Natchez. It offered a unique look at the ingenuity and industry of native culture with its two smaller mounds rising from the top of the main one. Hiking up to the top promised a view above the treetops. It would take only a five minute detour from the main Trace highway to reach this spot, which had been built by depositing earth along the sides of a natural hill, reshaping it and creating an enormous artificial plateau.

Although I could go on and on about the wonders of the Natchez Trace, it was Joe who really loved this quiet place, each time discovering something new. Often we would stop at the remote science stations, where Joe diligently would question the professors and students about their projects as they worked out in the open.

Because most of Mississippi is heavily forested except for the Delta, which was cleared for cotton cultivation in the nineteenth century, seeing the lush foliage along this park highway is gratifying. Each stop, with picnic tables, hiking, and horseback trails—even swimming holes— always made the trip good for an instant restoration of the soul.

Leaving my car to hike the winding trail meant seeing and hearing the easy-to-access waterfalls while enjoying the small forest creatures skittering about. In the summer, we'd discovered Yellow-billed Cuckoos, Eastern Phoebes, and a Wood Thrush or Kentucky Warbler. Winter months meant Brown Creepers, Yellow-bellied Sapsuckers, and small ducks swimming in the ponds. The Trace was a place where I could think or even shut off my mind and just enjoy the silence, interrupted only by sounds of wildlife creatures.

"Be sure and hike to Fall Hollow for me," Mollie suggested.

I'd planned to do just that, remembering how to find the particular path, the one with a set of wooden bridges crossing the small creeks just before their water begins tumbling down. I'd planned to drive nearly all of this park, from Natchez to Tupelo, allowing me to cross four ecosystems, something I'd wanted to do since Joe had died. He knew the Trace better than I. He'd read every brochure and purchased giant, colorful coffee table books about it. We would drive along, enjoying each moment, as "Professor" Joe recited what he'd most recently learned, afterward adding his own scientific two bits.

Joe could sound utterly ridiculous, sometimes breaking up the delightful silence of the road trip with his racing mouth.

"Hey, Clint, does ontogeny recapitulate phylogeny? Or is it the other way around? I can't ever remember, but I was just wondering and thought you might know. I should remember this from my biology classes, but I've forgotten."

"Hey, Joe," I'd volley back, "Has anyone ever explained that your phylogeny needs a hard nooooogggieee?"

And I'd hit him so hard in the upper arm with my middle knuckle, he'd fake a scream. Then we'd stop at another Trace habitat where I'd hope that no scientists would be hanging around to get Joe going again.

We had taken this drive every so often, watching the trees change each season and noticing color differences from the first forests of oak-beech in the far south, through oak-pine mixes covering the vast middle section. The colorful show ended near Tennessee with oak-hickory dominating in the north. As these memories flooded through my mind and settled in my heart, I finally had to pull the car over and stop.

I found myself thinking long and hard about Joe, for the first time since I lost him, and what our life had been together, and what it could have been. After Joe finished law school we were supposed to grow old together, dying in each other's arms. We'd been closest during the worst times, the years of bewilderment and sorrow—the times of counting coup in the 60s, of who was being severely beaten and murdered, and who was staying alive. These were years that required love to keep our young souls from dying. But this did not happen, and I never understood why we didn't maintain our life together in full, and I don't think he really did, either.

I knew he had other partners, and so did I. But it worked for us, and I assumed that Tara wasn't smart enough to pick up on everything that was happening. I was probably wrong, now that I think about it.

After getting the phone call about Joe's death from Tara, I had done what I'd needed to do that day: drove to Montgomery, met with Tara, and found Joe's body in that damned freezer. I'd tried to learn more about his death. If I only could know what happened to Joe, maybe it would help. But nothing was going to bring him back to me.

Tears gathered in my eyes, and I could feel small muscles twitching in my face. I leaned back in the seat of my car and put my head against the rest, taking a deep breath, releasing it slowly from my mouth. More tears welled up; I could not hold them back, nor the sobs. I cried and stopped, cried more, and then broke down. It needed to happen. I had put off grieving for too long.

After a few moments, the crying resolved for a while, I left my car and walked along a deep trail that looked much like the place where we'd made love one fall day. The memories were overwhelming. We had walked into these woods together, embraced, and then lost ourselves on the forest floor, afterward holding each other tight, It had seemed we would be together for the rest of our lives. So why did everything have to change? Who took Joe from me? I found no answers that day—I really hadn't expected any.

CHAPTER TWENTY-SIX

I got back to Clarksdale late Tuesday night. The rest of the trip was peaceful, and I'd enjoyed my deep memories of Joe, but never cried about him again. Once I opened the door to my home, everything inside looked brighter and better than before. I had gained fresh perspective and was in the right mood to hit the boxes, once again. The fires encircling Clarksdale had disappeared, and I could breathe more easily. My dull headache went away, and I went back to sifting, reading, taking notes, and generally looking for anything unique, strange, or familiar—clues to solve who may have killed Joe, and why.

I resolved to locate Kimble. This man with possible ties to the U.S. intelligence community, and to right-wing militia groups like the Minutemen, the Klan, and organized crime was now in my cross-hairs. After putting it off for a month, I finally called Dan Bell at NYU. I had to know how to find Kimble—or the man who helped Joe track him.

"I've been thinking about what you told me about Joe's meeting with Kimble," I started out, "But first I have to tell you about Joe's death. He didn't commit suicide, Dan. He was murdered. Only you and two other friends know the truth."

Dan was silent for a moment. "I presumed the coroner ruled suicide and that you agreed."

"There was no coroner. I went to the funeral home, looked in the prep room, and found Joe's unautopsied body. He'd been tortured. I don't know exactly how he was killed."

I quickly went through the rest of the story, telling Dan about the bruises and broken fingers. "There was nothing I could do, except look for answers. Try to find out who did this to Joe and why."

Dan waited a moment to respond.

"I didn't know Joe very well, but from what you'd always said about him, suicide made no sense to me. Considering what he'd been working on, anything could have happened in this clandestine world of crime and assassinations. But I don't think we should talk on the phone any more about this. You know—PRISM."

Dan was referring to a mass electronic surveillance data mining program secretly operated by the United States National Security Agency or NSA since 2007. I caught his drift.

"Okay. But can you arrange a meeting for me with the same guy Joe talked to? The one who helped him find him?"

I was purposely vague, figuring Dan understood who I was talking about.

"Are you sure this is a good idea, Clint?"

"What choice do I have?"

"Okay. Give me some time." Dan's phone clicked off.

While I waited for Dan to call back, I returned to work, sorting through another small batch of Joe's notes. Tipping back in my computer chair, I remembered the day he'd dropped them by my office on his way home from Tennessee. He was heading back to Montgomery, after interviewing the family whose house was taken over by the intruders, who may have been an assassination planning team. I had found the rest of these notes.

Joe accompanied their son on a visit to Memphis, where the family lived in a small home. Once they could afford it, they had moved away from the log cabin. After some coaxing from their son, the mother and father spoke with Joe, who took thorough notes during the conversation. He confirmed that they'd been strong-armed from their cabin by a group of white thugs three months before Dr. King's assassination.

"They barged into our home with no notice, scared us, and made us leave," the husband told Joe. "Only gave us ten minutes to clear out!"

To keep family members from being hurt, the father promised his family would not talk about what happened. The heavies had counted on the family's inability to get help from white law enforcement, knowing that no one would take such a complaint seriously from a poor, black family—not in the 1960s.

The family reclaimed their house three months later, learning from a relative that it had become vacant. They found the walls covered with diagrams and maps, Joe's notes read: "Diagrams that looked like escape routes, son reports. No documents saved. Father says he tore down everything and threw away."

According to the notes, the thugs never returned to bother or threaten the family.

"Mother reported they never saw them again, but house was wrecked. Beer bottles, chicken bones on floor. Old newspapers, cigarette butts everywhere. Surprised they didn't burn down the house, mother said."

I remembered more about the day Joe dropped off these notes at my office. He'd also given me a newly declassified document, a report of an interview with the FBI in which Kimble claimed he'd flown the two snipers into Memphis to shoot Dr. King. Their rifles were identical to Ray's, Kimble had claimed. Kimble also insisted that Ray didn't do it, that he was a patsy. The FBI agent had carefully printed Kimble's statement in this report.

Investigators from the House Select Committee on the Assassinations, formed in the late 1970s, gathered as evidence a black and white photo of Kimble, taken in Montreal. Joe had a copy. Yet, the final HSCA report denied any evidence of a Ray-Kimble association, leaving the photo out of their report. Crafty Joe! I wonder how he'd gotten his hands on this photograph.

Garrison wrote in his memoir that Kimble divulged that a year before JFK's assassination he'd flown to Montreal with David Ferrie. They'd been on Minutemen business, as Kimble called it. This right-wing group, named after a heroic Revolutionary War militia, was linked by the FBI and Garrison to neo-Nazi and Ku Klux Klan groups. Members saw themselves as well-trained, highly mobile, rapidly deployed forces. I am sure the real militia would be embarrassed to be associated with this organization.

Kimble promised Garrison's investigators he would gather further information from these right-wing groups and report back, I had learned. But he never returned to New Orleans. Never delivered the promised information. Again, I found myself asking questions about this strange man: Why had Kimble stayed away from New Orleans? Who was he, and who controlled him? Was Kimble still alive?

As I was contemplating Kimble, my eyes rested on a handwritten note located on the left side of the FBI report I'd pulled from Joe's files. I turned the paper sideways to read one word that Joe carefully had printed out: C U E N C A. The word meant nothing to me. But just as I was about to move on, something clicked in my head: Dan had mentioned a South American city by this name. This was where he'd taught at a small university. This is where he'd run into Levison. Why had Joe written this city's name on the side of an FBI document—one relating to Kimble, of all people?

CHAPTER TWENTY-SEVEN

It was 9:00 p.m. I had worked a long day and was tired. As I left the church and locked the door behind me, I saw him standing against his car across the street and down a block from me. Dark pants, light grey jacket and smoking a cigarette—I had never seen him before. He opened his car door and eased into the front seat, when he saw me leave the church. Then he picked up and began to read a newspaper from the car seat, but I saw him peer over the top and then look down again.

Maybe I was being overly suspicious. I decided not to pay this much attention. But then, it happened again—the next night—same guy.

I'd put off thinking about Joe's strange handwritten reference to Cuenca, for a couple of weeks. I was busy with church and my law practice. I believed if I kept looking for more clues in Joe's files, I'd eventually discover why he had jotted down this word. But I wasn't overly concerned.

It didn't take long for Cuenca to pop up once again, however. I got a call from Mollie late one afternoon, about a week later.

"You'd better sit down, Mr. Clinton." Her voice sounded mischievous.

"And why is that?"

"Well, you're just not going to believe who I heard from this morning—who sent me some juicy email."

"So, I'm waiting. Who was it?"

Mollie loved drama. She didn't tell me right away who the email was from; that would have been too easy. I was supposed to guess! I drummed my fingers on the table, but I was the first to break.

"Okay, okay. YOU called ME on the phone, so who is it? Who sent you a message on the Internet that has you so wound up?"

"Why, it was Missy Tara Means!" Mollie dragged out Tara's name for as long as she could. "Our new friend from Cuenca, Ecuador! Ever hear of the place, Clint? I'll bet you haven't!"

I didn't close my mouth until my stomach dropped, which was right after hearing Tara Means and Cuenca, Ecuador, in the same breath. What could Mollie be talking about? It made no sense. Why would Tara, who despite her glamor was a homebody, be sending email from a foreign country? She'd never traveled anywhere outside of the United States in her life. The last I knew, she'd moved back home with her parents. I hadn't heard from her since our visit in Montgomery. But now, Missy Tara had emailed Mollie? From Ecuador? This couldn't be right.

"What are you telling me, Mollie?" I had taken a couple of deep breaths before rebounding. "To my knowledge, Tara's rarely left the Deep South, and I know she doesn't speak Spanish. She hardly speaks anything but suthrin."

Mollie clearly was enjoying my reactions.

"Well, I just got this big, fat email from Blondie that said she misses me—and you, too! She wants us to know she's fine, and that she is very happy in her new Ecuadorian home. She's got a penthouse in a high-rise. She says cabs only cost $3—"

"Hold it." I cut Mollie short. "Did she say why she is in South America? How and when she got there? Is she coming back home?" I wanted the basics.

"I have no idea about any of this, Clint. She carried on and on about Cuenca—said it's really cheap to live there, and she likes going out to restaurants. She's met some other Americans who play bridge together on Tuesdays. She's learning some Spanish, and she travels around the Andes by bus to little villages. And she's even found a guy!"

Why would Tara have moved to this equatorial country? Had she read something about cheap living in South America? Did she have friends who'd already moved there? Had some crook sold her a timeshare? I honestly had no idea why Joe's widow would suddenly show up thousands of miles away, but I felt strongly that something wasn't right. It was entirely possible that Tara, so far away from home, might be in trouble.

When Mollie finally quit talking, I asked her to come over to the church.

"Listen, I need you to forward Tara's email to me. Then lock up the office for the afternoon because I'm going to need your full and undivided attention."

"Is there something wrong, Clint? Did I say something that upset you?"

I kept my voice steady, trying to sound casual.

"No, not at all. But I need to see Tara's email, and we need to talk."

"Okay. Will do. I'll be right over. I just hope you're okay, and I haven't made you angry."

"No problem, Mollie. I want to see what she sent, and we have to talk about it."

Ten minutes later, Mollie walked in, shut the door, and sat down without saying a word. She had been right about the email being big and fat, with lots of gossipy stuff, but I'd managed to read it all before Mollie arrived. However, nothing answered my questions—why was Tara there and when she had arrived.

Besides Tara living in Cuenca, Ecuador—and that was enough for concern considering Joe's reference to this place in his notes—there was something in Tara's email that didn't hit me right. One sentence, one Mollie must not have noticed, caught my eye. It looked like Tara was trying to tell us more, or was at least unsettled over something.

"Did you see this, Mollie? The part about her boyfriend's maid? She never leaves Tara alone and even goes everywhere with her. Tara tries to make a joke of this, but it doesn't sound right. You know how Tara likes her privacy."

Mollie agreed. "You're right, Clinton. She likes her 'alone' time. Do you think Tara's trying to tell us something? Why wouldn't she just tell that maid to bugger off?"

I didn't have an answer, but I knew we had to check this out further. At first, I considered calling Tara on the phone. Talk with her a bit and see if she would confide in me if there was a problem. But I changed my mind.

"Someone has to talk to Tara face-to-face. I don't think sending back an email and asking her if she is all right is wise. I'm not sure I trust a telephone call, either. If things aren't okay, she can't be totally open or honest if we contact her in this way."

While Mollie and I were thinking about Tara, my phone rang, and I answered it. Silence, and then a click.

"That's strange. No one was on the line. Same thing happened yesterday."

I waited for a moment, took a deep breath while deciding what next to say. I'd told Mollie I would be more truthful and forthcoming; the time had come to honor my agreement.

"Something else isn't right, Mollie. That anonymous call to start with, and I'm pretty sure I'm being watched."

Mollie took some time to respond. "What do you mean? What are you going to do?"

"Call the FBI," I whispered. We both laughed.

But then I told her about Joe's references in his notes to this South American city.

"I have no idea what Joe was trying to say. But this unnerves me, that Tara suddenly shows up in the same place. It's not right."

It dawned on me that we would have to go into Ecuador and find Tara—which would be tricky since she'd given no specific address or way to contact her. We needed to learn what was going on and maybe bring her home if she was in trouble. I owed this to Joe. But "we" really meant Mollie. If I were to go there, and if someone is watching or spying on me, my leaving the country would draw attention and maybe put in danger Mollie, and Tara—or even me.

I watched Mollie reflect on what I'd just said about being watched and receiving the hang-up calls. I'd known her for so many years and trusted her judgment, her ability to assess what went on around her, and her basic survival instincts. I knew that she would have to make this trip alone. But how would I convince her?

I talked more about the strange man who'd been hanging around the church, telling Mollie that I had also seen him parked near my home.

"Can you describe him?" she asked.

"I haven't gotten a very good look, Mollie, but he's tall and on the thin side. He wears jeans and a dark hoodie. I can't really see his face, but I think he has a long nose. When I went outdoors to try and talk to him, he turned and half-ran, half-walked away. I don't like what I'm feeling about him. I didn't recognize him, and I can't explain anything else about him, except I wonder if he's making these anonymous phone calls, too."

When I was finished, and without saying a word, Mollie stood from her chair, walked over and gave me a hug. Then she picked up her purse and sweater and prepared to leave.

"It's getting late. Bill needs his dinner. I'm going home now, Clinton. I know we can come up with a plan tomorrow."

I felt a sense of urgency. That we shouldn't end the day without deciding what to do.

"You must go find Tara in Ecuador. I can't be the one to do this. There's a strong possibility of danger to you and Tara if I go there and am followed. You won't draw attention if you leave, but I will. You speak Spanish, and I don't. You've got to go to Cuenca, Mollie. You have to find Tara, and if there is a problem, convince her to come back to Mississippi."

Mollie dropped her belongings back on the chair.

"I understand, Clinton. I agree. My passport is in order. And you know how I love adventure," she said, "and, I suppose you want me to go tomorrow. Right?"

I didn't give her an immediate answer. I knew that I was thinking on the fly, and perhaps I would come up with a better idea by the next morning. But I also knew this probably wasn't going to happen.

Mollie assured me that my thinking was straight.

"I hear you Clint. We need to check on Tara. You've already had your vacation—driving to the Trace. Now it's my turn!"

"What will you tell Bill?"

Of course I already knew the answer.

"The truth. I always tell Bill the truth," Mollie said.

CHAPTER TWENTY-EIGHT

Dining alone isn't as bad as you might think. It has its benefits. You don't have to make phony conversation with dinner guests, and you can pick your own music. If you don't like the food, you can toss it and fix something different—or you can always find a restaurant and start over again.

I fixed myself a small dinner that evening. Poured a glass of dark red wine I'd picked up at the Old Rebels Winery in Natchez and then took the first bite of my meal, deciding it was quite good. This activity improved my current state of mind.

I worried about Tara. She was a big talker—never could keep a secret. If she'd started gossiping with her new friends in Ecuador about Joe and what happened to him, someone might hear the story and report it back to someone else. Who knows who that someone might be! I knew I was more suspicious than usual, but I'd moved into this headspace after seeing the stranger leaning against his car, watching me from outside the church. And especially after I heard that Tara was in South America. Actually, when I thought about it, I had a lot of reasons to be concerned. Whoever was out there—and whoever might have their eyes on Tara—could be anyone from a neo-Nazi jerk with militia or Klan ties, to a rogue military intelligence agent, or even a CIA asset.

Hearing Tara's story, such a person could deduce quickly that Joe was a person who had gathered secrets on the assassination of Dr. King and/or President Kennedy. Information he should not have had. Since any of those organizations could have ties to these murders, Tara's loose comments could get back to someone who, in turn, might believe that she knew inconvenient secrets—and boom! Even if Tara knew nothing, she could be killed in a flash.

I tried to relax while finishing my wine and taking slow bites of my pasta. Perhaps I was overreacting. But so many questions popped into my mind, questions that deserved answers. I had a choice. I could try learning more on my own, or Mollie could go to Ecuador and persuade Tara to come home. We'd figure out the details once she and Tara returned.

By the time I'd finished my dinner, I knew exactly what had to be done. I logged onto the Internet and purchased Mollie's airline ticket. She'd given me her passport number to use. Pretty simple, really: she could enter and stay in Ecuador for up to ninety days without a visa. I'd left the return open, and she could use her office credit card to purchase Tara's airfare. I routed her out of Jackson the following day with stops in Dallas and Miami before reaching Guayaquil, Ecuador's largest city. She would arrive there around 10:00 p.m., too late to travel through the Andes. I booked her into the Hilton and arranged for a hotel shuttle and a private driver to take her to Cuenca.

After doing some quick homework, I learned that Guayaquil was not a particularly safe place for single women travelers, not unlike most port cities in developing nations. Well-dressed tourists are targets.

I'd need to tell her to keep her clothing plain and inconspicuous and not to trust any cabs except for those hailed by official porters or, in this case, officially representing her hotel. The private driver would pick her up late the next morning for the three to four-hour drive through the Andes to Cuenca. In Cuenca, I rented Mollie a short-term condo in the gringo section of the city.

If anyone stood out like a *gringa*, it would be Tara, so I knew it wouldn't take Mollie more than a few days to track her down.

We met as planned for breakfast, where I went through all the trip details.

"I'm told that you need to carry lots of one and five dollar bills on you—twenties can be hard to cash."

For a moment, I switched topics. "Was Bill okay with this?"

Mollie nodded yes. "But you owe him dinner and a full explanation while I'm gone. You got that?"

I'd dug out my money belt for her to use, planning to pick up cash at the bank. She was on all my business card accounts so she was okay for money. Ecuador uses U.S. currency, which made it even easier. I even remembered to tell her that Ecuador was on Eastern Standard Time.

"You'll need to drive to Jackson tonight," I continued, "to catch tomorrow's flight to Dallas."

The serious part of the conversation came next, a topic I wanted to avoid, but knew I couldn't skip.

"Remember my friend, Dr. Dan Bell, the NYU history professor? Here's his phone number and email address. I signed you up with a special number, and you can call directly to the U.S. from this cell phone."

She gave me a look—unspoken questions in her eyes.

"Dan knows about Joe," I said, "so don't worry about what you tell him. I have a good hunch that he may even know more than I do about who killed Joe, or is in the process of trying to find out what happened. He's too much of a sleuth to leave this alone. If something goes wrong, and you can't reach me, or if something happens to me, Dan is the person to call."

"But Clint," she interrupted, and I could tell that she was scared. I shushed her, putting my finger to her lips, and kept talking.

"We have to be prepared for anything, Mollie. Dan has a level head, and knows South America better than the two of us. You can trust him if something goes wrong."

I gave her a quick pep talk. "You're one of the smartest, most creative people I know, and I wouldn't suggest that you do this, if I thought that you couldn't handle it.

Our eyes connected.

"Look. I know you will do fine. It's a cosmopolitan city. And even though I know I'm being watched, nothing has happened to me since Joe's death. I just want to be cautious. We need to focus on getting Tara out of Ecuador, and then we can talk about everything else, later—like why in the hell she went there in the first place."

Mollie rolled her eyes up, and we both laughed.

"She shouldn't be that hard to find," I said. "I think she will be living in one of the apartment buildings around your condo. Look for the tallest, widest one in Cuenca and start there; you know how she loves phallic symbols."

Mollie broke. Her laugh eased the tension.

You will do just fine."

And then she really laughed.

"Dammit Clinton, that's what my mother said when she dropped me off at college when I was seventeen! You will do just fine!"

We both laughed at Mollie's joke, but I had to get serious, again. There was a lot more to talk over.

"If they're busy watching me, they aren't going to follow you when you leave the country. But I honestly don't know what you're getting into, and you'll need to watch out. If something happens to me, and you hear

SUSAN KLOPFER

about it on this trip, you can't let that stop you. You will have to keep going and find Tara."

I had to say something to bring Mollie back up; she was looking upset.

"Look at me, Mollie. Right here." I caught her attention, pointed to my eyes, and then hers with two fingers—an old trick, but effective. "Dan's a very smart man; he knows South America and speaks the language fluently. He will help you decide what to do if you run into a problem, and I am not here to help."

This was hard to talk about, but I had to keep going.

"Just remember. You're going there to find Blondie and tell her a story of some kind to get her butt back home. That's all. Think positive, Mollie! A quick in and out!"

She was starting to look more confident. I changed the topic to her trip schedule, adding it would be hot in coastal Guayaquil, and much cooler in Cuenca, with its high altitude.

"It's nearly 8,500 feet. You'll want to take a jacket. You'll need jeans, some dark slacks, a couple of light tops, a sweater, one dressier outfit, and a pair of beat-up walking shoes to blend in. Oh, probably some nicer shoes, too. People wear darker colors, Dan says. Black, olive, brown. Don't dress like you're going to Cancun!"

Mollie gave me a look of amazement.

"Only a gay guy would come up with such complete clothing requirements for a short trip," Mollie interrupted. "But this really helps, Clinton." she said, as I continued going over the final details. Then Mollie left to do last-minute errands while I walked over to the bank.

152

CHAPTER TWENTY-NINE

Thursday afternoon.

I picked up the cash Mollie would need. The bank was prepared for her trip to Ecuador and assured me that she would be able to withdraw funds from most ATM machines. I would remind her that she was listed as a co-owner on the account.

"Sometimes the machines get grumpy in foreign countries, but tell her to keep trying or call us if there's still a problem. We can always do a direct transfer to a larger bank," the bank president promised.

We met again at the office in the early afternoon before she left for the Jackson-Medgar Wiley Evers International Airport, again going over her plans.

"You have a good trip, now, you ha'ir, Miss Mollie," I told her, after we shared a cup of fresh coffee together, before she left. I'd brewed it myself in advance of her arrival, saving her the worry and protecting my stomach from acid reflux.

I had seen pictures on the Internet of an iguana park in downtown Guayaquil, and told her about it. "You might want to take that place in, for fun, before you return home," I suggested. She gave me a funny look, picked up her purse, and walked out to the car, all packed and ready to go. We hugged, and I watched as she drove off, waving good-bye, when she turned back and smiled.

It was going to be a busy day for me, starting within the hour. I'd arranged for my troubled client, Mike, who owed me money, to help me with construction on the new home I was building at the edge of town. He was to meet me at the office at two, and we'd go to the building site to get some work done.

I'd helped my dad and grandpa build the house I'd inherited when my parents died. I was currently living there, and it would be hard to leave. There were so many memories. We'd constructed it from the two sharecropper shacks our families lived in for their entire lives. I remembered the day we hauled the houses into Clarksdale from the old plantation, each one on a flatbed. We joined them together and built a common roof. This family home had meant a lot to me; there was love in it. I wasn't even sure if I wanted to demolish it or leave it standing in their memory when I moved into my new place. My sister already had a home and didn't want to move. But I believed my father and grandfather's spirits would follow me wherever I went, even when the new home was completed, and ready for my occupancy.

"*Yo*, Mr. Clint. I'm fired up and ready to go!"

I didn't have to look up from my paperwork to know who was standing in front of my desk. I gave him a quick glance, seeing right away that his back pants pockets were resting half-way down his ass, with his white underwear showing—he called it sagging. I had to stifle a laugh. Mike was constantly in trouble and each incident was worse than before. I'd seriously warned him recently that Parchman prison wasn't so very far down the road from Clarksdale. Would he ever grow up? I had my doubts.

Mike expected the world owed him. And here I was, doing him a big favor, letting him work off his last legal bill instead of paying it outright. Still, I had no idea that he would try to kill me!

Around seven that night, after Mike shot me and left me bleeding on my stairway, taking money and driving off in my car, the stranger came. He found me, put a gun to my head, and coldly pulled the trigger, just as my grandfather's hand extended out from the circling winds above. Our fingers touching, Grandpa pulled me into the gentle whirlwind, and I was never afraid for a moment. Death is exactly what he said it would be so many years ago, when telling me stories as we sat on the porch of our family home. The Mississippi River quietly flowing by. I went into the light, never knowing where I'd end up. But, finally, I regained some version of consciousness and watched all the activity that followed.

I watched Mollie get the call from her husband telling her I was dead. She had reached Dallas at eleven in the morning and answered her cell phone on the first ring, looking surprised to hear its sound.

"Mollie, Clinton has been murdered. We don't know what happened yet, who killed him, or why," her husband gently told her.

I saw her catch her breath. But she shoved away her emotion and behaved exactly as I would expect.

"How did you hear this?" Her voice showed strength.

"Betty called me at work. She asked me to pick up James at school and to check Clinton's office."

James was my only nephew. We were close, and this would be devastating to him.

Mollie quietly found a vacant couch, sat down, then continued speaking to her husband.

"Look, Bill, you can't tell anyone how to contact me. Don't give this phone number to anyone. I will come home as soon as I find Tara. Please kiss the kids for me again, and tell James we are here for him, too. I love you. This should not take long!"

"I love you, too Mollie, and I understand why you must continue this trip. There's something else I need to tell you. When I ran down to Clinton's office, to see if everything was locked up, there were two men inside wearing dark suits. One man was working at Clint's computer, and the other man was tipping over boxes and tearing through papers. I shouted at them to stop, but they pulled out guns and forced me to leave. Clint's rifles were gone from the corners of his office. I couldn't check inside his house. There's still crime tape all around his yard."

"You did good," Mollie assured him. "Remember to protect this phone number. I will come home with Tara, once I find her."

I knew Mollie would not go home early. She and her husband were made of grit. Once we boarded the Miami-bound flight, she settled in, drank a glass of wine, and slept until the plane landed on this next to final stop. I hovered beside her and wanted to hold her hand to comfort her. I watched as she selected Luciano Pavarotti on the music channel and put on her earphones, embracing the haunting music.

"I am not afraid," the great tenor sang, and I followed along, whispering these words over and over and over into her ear, hoping she would pick up my presence.

PART III

CHAPTER THIRTY

We landed in Miami. I followed Mollie to a small bar in the noisy terminal. She sat down and ordered a glass of dark red wine, which she nursed during two-hour layover. I hoped she would call Dr. Bell at NYU. She had only spoken to him twice before, when he'd called me at work. She didn't know him by face, but I'd entered his phone number and class schedule into her cell phone before she left Clarksdale.

She glanced up to a report on the overhead news monitor about a Chilean couple arrested for torturing and killing their infant child. She quickly looked away from the television news, focusing on people as they rushed by the bar to catch their flights, waiting for her drink to be served.

Soon the waitress brought her wine. Mollie took a sip, then set it down. She pulled out her cell and dialed. In two rings, Dan answered. After a quick introduction, she told him I'd been murdered and why she was headed for Ecuador.

Dan, always a good listener, interrupted her only once, with a short question of clarification. When she finished, I heard his warm and steady voice kick in. I hoped she would trust him to help her, and I hoped he quickly would gain her confidence. He asked if anything strange happened to me in the past few days or weeks. She told him I'd been followed.

"This started happening only two days before Clinton was killed," she said.

"Do you have any idea why Tara is in Cuenca?"

"Not really. But Clinton felt we needed to bring her back home. It looked like she was being watched."

"Well, I can understand why you need to go ahead with this plan." Dan's voice tightened. "These murders have to be related. Either Clint or Joe stumbled upon something critical to the Kennedy or King assassinations, I am sure. But let's not focus on that possibility, right now. You and Tara must get back home—safe."

Dan had not shared specifics with Mollie, and this didn't surprise me. I was sure he didn't want to scare her. He gave her some quick advice about the rest of her trip to Cuenca.

"Look, Mollie. I have no idea what you're walking into, but it could be dangerous. Both you and Tara could encounter trouble before this is over, if you don't get in and get out fast. That's the key—get in, then get out as quick as you can."

I could not have agreed more. Dan followed his advice with a quick history lesson.

"U.S. visitors to South America sometimes experience problems based on misunderstandings that go back many years. You can still bump into a neo-Nazi or militant racist, so be careful. There were several marches in the city a few years ago, and some buildings have been tagged with Nazi symbols. Don't go anywhere alone at night. Some of these white supremacist fools are dead serious, and their actions can be lethal.

"Ever heard Clinton talk about a man named Boris Weisfeiler?"

"No, Dan. Should I remember him?"

"Likely not. When I was teaching at Penn State back in 1985, a professor on faculty was kidnapped while he was hiking and camping alone in the Southern Andes. After several years of hounding Chile's government, his sister learned he had been taken to a Nazi-run holdover terror camp called Colonia Dignidad. She believes he was killed. The Chilean government was unwilling to do anything to help her find her brother or give her answers to his disappearance. Until very recently, Chile would not even admit the place was still dangerous. But now trials are going on in Santiago and it could be tense, even in Ecuador."

Mollie listened to Dan. I could tell that she took his words seriously.

"By the way," she asked. "Should I worry about what I say to you on the phone? You know, the government records everything we say—NSA."

Dan laughed. "Well here's my philosophy. They may record everything. That doesn't mean they listen to every recording. Anyway, the more people who know what I think, the safer I am. I don't believe in keeping secrets. Now back to this story. I mention it, Mollie, because you could run into some bad characters in South America. We have our own problems in the U.S. regarding secrecy, but so do these governments. You really need to be cautious. I cannot say this enough. Regarding Boris, I plan to be in Chile in two weeks to try and help Olga talk to officials, so we might meet, but I hope to hell that you are out of Ecuador and back home with Tara before I arrive."

As Dan spoke of Weisfeiler, I noticed Mollie began scanning the airport bar, looking for anyone who seemed out of place. I found this a good sign! She was understanding Dan's warnings.

"I've never heard of Nazi camps in Chile, Dan. How did this Dignidad place ever get started? Does anything go on there, now?" She peppered him with her questions, before looking down at her watch to check on her connection to Guayaquil. She had enough time before her next flight to hear his answer.

"The colony was first started by a German preacher," he explained, "and used by the Augusto Pinochet government for killing and torturing political prisoners. Pinochet was dictator of Chile from 1973 until 1990, after he assumed power in the overthrow of the popular government. This ended civilian rule."

"I think that I remember reading something about that, Dan. Wasn't the U.S. involved, sort of?"

"You've got to go back to 1973, to the Chile coup d'état that overthrew Salvador Allende's Unidad Popular government and ended civilian rule. This came about with material help from the U.S. government, I'm sorry to say. To make matters worse, Colonia Dignidad was used during some of those years as a CIA training facility."

It looked to me like Dan was giving Mollie a quick but effective history lesson.

"Horrible things went on there—and occasionally still do. But, I don't want to keep you from missing your flight. Just be damned careful who you make friends with while in Ecuador."

I was concerned, too, about Mollie getting to her plane on time. It wouldn't be easy to rebook all of her plans. But he seemed to have more to tell her.

"One more thing, Mollie, when Clint and I talked not so long ago, he was fishing for information about a man named Kimble, that's Jules Rocco Kimble, a mysterious Klansman and CIA asset, possibly linked to the Minutemen and the assassinations of both Dr. King and John Kennedy."

"He's not in Cuenca, this Kimble, is he?" Mollie nervously asked.

I was curious what Dan might be talking about and hovered in close.

"Clint was never able to put his hands on Kimble's location or status since the guy left prison in Oklahoma, but possibly Joe learned where Kimble was and may have talked to Kimble recently. I'm feeling uncomfortable about Kimble, especially after hearing Clinton was killed. I'm guessing that Kimble might be involved."

"Are you saying this Kimble guy could be in South America, Dan? That he could be a problem? How would I even recognize him?"

"Anything is possible. I have no idea if he is even still alive, let alone where he might be, or even what he looks like. But I need to warn you of this possibility. I will go back through some old files today and see if I can find any photographs. Give me your email, and I'll send them to you. Look, I strongly doubt that you will run into the guy. I just want to give you a head's up. Okay? My chief concern is helping you find Tara and getting home. If Kimble is still alive, he would be in his mid-70s. That's all I can say, for now."

This was smart of Dan. Kimble could have ended up in South America as a prisoner or even a guard at Dignidad since the CIA had been hanging out there. It goes both ways when you work for The Company. Dan closed his conversation with Mollie.

"Be cautious of who approaches you. Don't trust just anyone who you meet. Just—"

"I know! Get in, find Tara, and get out. And stay the hell out of Chile."

"You've got it, Mollie. Call me when you get settled in Cuenca, and let me know how it is going."

I heard digital silence on each end of their cell phones as Dan and Mollie clicked off. I imagined Mollie as Alice looking up from the rabbit hole, as she began her curiouser-and-curiouser trip to the Southern Hemisphere.

CHAPTER THIRTY-ONE

Although Mollie would take a private car into Cuenca from Guayaquil the day after she'd landed, I wasn't sure how I'd deal with the four-hour winding and bumpy trip over the Andes in my present state. I went to Cuenca ahead of her.

I wandered around the central park, getting a feel for the city, when I noticed a couple of ladies who didn't look local by the way they were dressed. A little lonely by now and seeking company, I moved in closer to share their space.

From their conversation I picked up that Sara Mercury, the older of the two, was a freelance blogger, not entirely by choice. She'd moved to this city of a half million people hoping to re-kickstart her writing career, she was telling her journalist friend, Kate Hall, who wanted to know why had she left her reporting job at The Dallas Morning News so quickly.

"Oh, the 30-something-year-old kid-editor said I was too obsessed with JFK's assassination, and that most readers didn't care about it anymore. So he got rid of me."

"What a louse," I quickly thought, assuming that Sara must have been an outstanding reporter, since she'd worked the presidential assassination story for years. She emoted passion when explaining this to her friend, and she looked pretty cool for someone probably close to sixty-five or so.

"He didn't care about my valuable experiences or what I've been through in life—the multiple assassinations, Vietnam, women's and gay rights movements, Grey Panthers, you know what I mean. He told me to pick up my final check in two weeks. The newspaper threw in a nice bonus after I agreed to leave with no drama."

"Harsh," Kate said to Sara, shaking her head. "Absolutely ridiculous."

I wanted to go back to Texas and haunt that little creep who'd fired Sara. My guess was he'd never read a book in his entire short life on the assassinations, or even a summary of the Warren Commission Report, or much of anything else.

"Anyone who believes it, simply hasn't read it," said a well-known Dallas attorney, the author of four books on the topic. And I'd always agreed with Mark Lane, my favorite JFK conspiracist.

Sara checked her watch. "We've got to go. Sue starts playing at seven thirty."

I didn't have a clue about who Sue was, but decided to tag along. I liked these women; they'd succeeded in a hard-hitting profession, and Sara showed grit, hanging in there and covering the assassination, even after others gave up and moved on. She could have projected deep depression after getting eighty-sixed, dressing like a depressed loser, but she didn't. Her hair was lightened, and she wore long dangling earrings and an exotic outfit that probably made her feel good.

Kate, the owner of a professional writing and editing business, had retired as editor from a major Minneapolis newspaper. She looked smart in a flashy Italian jacket and a pair of slim black French pants.

I followed along the few blocks to the Cuenca Jazz Club, learning this was the last night to hear a world-famous saxophonist before she returned to New York City. The ladies and I shared a table; I felt a strong connection, even if they didn't know I was there. Just to be a true Southern gentleman, I sniff-tested their Chilean wine selection, pronouncing it "a fine scent that combines honey and wildflowers, with a prolonged grape fruity aftertaste." Of course, they couldn't hear a word of this.

"It doesn't get better than this," Sara whispered to her friend, as "Sweet" Sue Terry wailed away on her soprano sax. With her left hand, Sue seductively shook a small percussive African instrument parallel to her body, while blowing haunting notes, supporting and fingering her saxophone with her right hand—each arm working independently in complicated counter rhythms. I was pretty sure she was playing from heaven, so I moved in closer and wave-tested my theory. Sue winked back.

"Look at that, Kate. Just listen to that girl. How does she do it?"

"I really don't know. I think it is impossible. But I love her dreads, so androgynous! You don't suppose she's uh—?"

"Doubt it." Sara pointed over to Sweet Sue's cute husband standing beside her and playing his alto sax. But I'm pretty sure I heard Kate mutter, "Damn."

Later, I followed my new friends back to the park where they returned to the benches and talked mostly about Sara's move to Cuenca and her new life as an expat. A big-time agent in New York had encouraged her to keep him in mind, Sara was saying, if she ever came up with a riveting story about JFK's assassination.

"He WILL represent my story to international news services. I plan to uncover something big this year for the fiftieth anniversary. It's still not too late," she told Kate.

Sara admitted she hadn't scored anything big enough yet for a major news publication. Her eyes spelled frustration. Her voice dropped to a near-whisper.

"I did hear a juicy rumor from a retired University of Cuenca professor about the plot to kill Kennedy. There were secret meetings here in South America. And a professional assassin, who once tried to kill Charles de Gaulle, was hired to murder our president. The professor heard this from a famous Argentinian journalist. I plan to go visit that writer, real soon."

"Do you really trust this stranger as a news source?" Kate politely asked Sara, while listening to her friend's plans.

"I know that I'll have to flesh it out myself, Kate. I have started saving money to travel to Pinamar on the Atlantic coast, where that reporter lives, for an interview. I could probably write an exclusive for my old Texas newspaper's op-ed page."

"Do you think the kid-editor will buy it?"

Sara shrugged her shoulders. She got up from the park bench and walked a couple of steps away, before turning around and addressing Kate. And changed the topic. Maybe she felt Kate was criticizing her. So she decided to talk about something else. It's always hard to discuss personal matters that others find suspect. I'd learned this myself when following cold cases and the assassinations.

"The expats—foreigners—we all hang out together." Sara's voice re-energized.

About this time, a horse and buggy clip-clopped by on the cobblestone, making it harder for me to pick up on what she was saying. But I did hear mention of a Navy officer Sara had met at an expat singles group. This "Jay" worked at the embassy in Quito, making him either an intelligence agent or a guard, like most military attachés, I presumed.

"Jay says he will help me find a publishing venue. He believes the U.S. Mafia killed JFK all by themselves with no help from anyone else—CIA rogues, FBI, Ku Klux Klan, military intelligence, military industrial complex, Corsicans, whatever. But I still don't think anyone acted alone. I am sure Jay is wrong."

I agreed with Sara. Thinking Oswald did it alone was about as dumb as accepting Bill O'Reilly's insistence that President Johnson did it, while Lady Bird planted wildflowers and fought billboards.

"I think it takes a village to pull off a sophisticated assassination like this, don't you, Kate?" Sara looked over at her good friend, who was smoking another cigarette.

Kate looked grim. She was younger than Sara, I was sure, and probably had a story behind her.

"Oh, yeah. Sure," she finally answered, standing up from the park bench, sweeping her dark blonde hair from her eyes, while snubbing out her cigarette butt with the toe of her left shoe.

Both women looked tired. It was late, and the altitude was probably affecting them, at least Sara, since Dallas is only a little over four hundred feet above sea level and Cuenca is at least eight thousand feet higher.

"You make some good points Sara. By the way, not to change the subject"—but she did—"Did you hear the CIA is about to get internationally blasted, again?"

"No, tell me more." Sara looked attentive to what Kate—who always kept her ear to the ground for news—had to say. Actually, I was surprised that Sara didn't know about Colonia Dignidad, the place in Chile that I guessed Kate was referencing. There had been recent, limited news coverage about the torture camp there, but the stories hadn't received attention in the U.S.

She told Sara about rumors that the CIA held back secret documents showing their early involvement in this Chilean post-Nazi death camp. She added detailed background on the horrible place.

"It makes a great new story," Kate said. "Maybe you could write something about that place, since you're living down here, now. I wish I had the time to do it myself, but I'm too busy with my clients."

Sara's cheeks drew color. She seemed to be warming up to Kate's suggestion of a promising writing project.

And then it came to me: a solution for solving this mess with Tara. I knew that if Sara and Kate, or even just one of them alone, ever got hooked up with Mollie, they could find Joe's widow in two seconds flat. Both had the tenacity to turn over every rock in Cuenca until they found Tara. They were forceful enough to get her on a plane headed home.

It was too bad that Kate was going back to Minnesota so soon, but Sara could do this alone. She always could consult with Kate by phone or email, if needed. I began to see Mollie, Tara, and I standing together at the Jackson-Evers airport, arms linked and smiling, postured like the Monkees band as they walked on stage, with their funny criss-cross step. Even if I was only a shadow on the tarmac!

CHAPTER THIRTY-TWO

After my night out in Cuenca, floating around the city with Sara and Kate, I felt guilty for abandoning Mollie. So I returned to Guayaquil to accompany her back to the colonial city. After she finished her breakfast in the sunlit restaurant, I watched her rise and head for the front door of the hotel lobby, looking for her driver. But her eyes caught a stunning oil painting, and she set down her luggage to walk over and take a closer look.

The artist had painted tan, brown, and gold—nearly skeletal—upper torsos of an alien-like man and woman. The female was leaning her raw-boned head to the left, resting on the male's angular shoulder.

Mollie tipped her head, trying to capture the artist's perspective.

"You like this painting?" a tall man with high cheek bones and a long, narrow nose, stopped to ask Mollie. I watched his eyes land on her.

"It is stunning. But I have to admit, I don't know the artist," Mollie answered.

"Oswaldo Guayasamín. He dedicated his life to our people," the man said.

His focused stare stayed with Mollie as she drew herself into the art. Clearly she was affected by its magic, forgetting that her driver was waiting. Could I use this powerful painting to tap into Mollie's spirit, to make contact? To let her know that I was at her side? Would she be able to feel my presence? I asked myself these questions and wanted to try.

In the Mississippi Delta, we call it hoodoo, when trying to wake up the spirits. That's what Grandpa Willie said the day I caught him whirling and chanting rituals in the tool shed. I'd tugged at his coveralls to make him stop until he finally dropped to the dirt floor. Then sitting next to me, he explained what he'd been doing.

"I'm putting myself in balance, Clinton. It's our heritage that comes from our African and Native American roots. And some of that European blood that got mixed in."

Later, I asked my mother about this.

"Hoodoo was our people's medicine and religion they brought across the ocean. Grandpa still believes in it," she told me, with no hesitation, "and I can't say always I don't agree. Rev. Alan says hoodoo is devil worship, but I know some people in the Bible used it. It is not Voodoo! Grandpa doesn't hurt anybody. Just don't eat his potions unless you ask me first. And you'd better not try hoodoo yourself."

Well, of course I tried it— the next day. What kid wouldn't?

"Helps make my life better, Clinton," Grandpa said when he caught me dizzy from turning circles. "Anything that you do is the plan of God, and you'll get what's coming to you. It comes down to your own spiritual power and what you believe to be accessible," he preached.

Grandpa gave me a small charm when I graduated from high school a few years later. A tiny alligator tooth sewn into a small hand-stitched leather pouch that held a pinch of his homemade potions, grated from Delta roots, berries, and vines.

"This is your mojo, Grandson. Remember always to carry it with you."

Now I wondered. Could I wake a living spirit— Mollie— through hoodoo? Didn't have my pouch on me, and honestly Hoodoo hadn't done much for me as a kid. But could it create synchronicity with the living side, now that I was dead? I swirled around Mollie, calling out her name, trying with all my might to attract her soul with this magic. Demanded she feel my presence! Petitioned the gods that she know I was near!

Suddenly, my little mojo bag jettisoned through the lobby door from out of nowhere. It swirled across the top of the room, back and forth, twirling and sprinkling colorful charms that sparkled and gleamed as bright as the sunlight falling on her hair. One ray hit the painting, shooting out a spectrum of lights that bounced off the back wall and then were sucked in by the stranger, like they'd entered a black hole. I thought for a moment that Mollie shivered. Her eyes flashed and darted. She dropped her arms to her side, and I swear I saw her lips move. Was she chanting? I moved in, still maintaining my quiet presence —as if I had a choice. I had to remind myself that Grandpa's hoodoo worked in its own time frame, since I wasn't really sure about what had just happened. And didn't have any idea of what to expect in the next moment.

The stranger had recovered from his hit and was asking Mollie if it was hard for her to pull away from the painting. I didn't trust him. His smile looked forced. And I still wondered about that disappearing light ray!

"I have to admit it is not easy to escape," Mollie was answering him.

"Let me share a secret about Guayasamín. He was a crusader of *imaginismo*." The stranger drew out each syllable of this Spanish word, explaining the concept to her. "People should be careful of approaching his paintings, because they are not easy to withdraw from," he warned.

Maybe Mollie didn't hear what he'd said, because she leaned in closer, slowly tracing her finger in the air, mapping the wide eyes of the man and woman, repeating her circles several times before standing down.

I was close enough to whisper into her ear, "I'll be beside you. We'll find Tara and bring her home."

Momentarily, my legal assistant looked confused. I think she heard me, but then Mollie walked away, to pick up her suitcase. When she turned to say good-bye to the stranger, he had already left the room. I was sorry I hadn't kept my eyes on him, since I would have liked to know just how in the holy hell he'd escaped.

Mollie gained speed in her walk to the door, now signaling for the driver to help her with her luggage and into the car. As the van pulled out, Mollie looked straight ahead while the driver shot through the busy Guayaquil traffic. That morning we journeyed high into the vortex of the Andean cloud forest, before dropping down to Cuenca, three hours later.

CHAPTER THIRTY-THREE

The car rolled to a stop in front of a ten-floor red brick condo building located on the west side of Cuenca. The apartments, nestled into the surrounding hills, overlooked the Tomebamba River, a part of the Amazon River watershed and one of the city's four urban streams. Punctuated with boulders aerating the water as it flowed and bubbled through the city, sounds of the fast-moving water coming off the mountains increased as Mollie opened the car door and stepped onto the pavement.

Moments before arriving, people of all ages started appearing along the river's plush greenways. Behind the tinted windows, we'd spotted hikers, youngsters playing soccer, and other people using exercise equipment or walking their dogs as they bonded with the smell of eucalyptus in the air.

"What's happening down there?"

Mollie pointed to a dozen men and women standing in the rushing water. Brigades of children passed heavy baskets of clothes up and down the grassy banks to them as they scrubbed laundry on the huge rocks, rinsing it in the river.

"They're washing their clothes," the driver smiled. "Many indigenous people still use the river in this way. It's what they do together as a family, and it's practical since it saves on the cost of water, a washing machine, dryer, and electricity. They've been doing it this way for hundreds of years, so don't worry."

Laid out on the grassy riverbanks were bright clothes and bedding, drying in the direct sun. Overhead, thick dark clouds threatened to spill rain. How hard it would be to do one's laundry this way, I was thinking. The swirling waters looked frigid, even for a person wearing rubber boots. But it was a memorable sight, especially watching the women who labored in their colorful, knee-length velvet skirts, hand-embroidered white blouses, woven shawls, and black-banded, white Panama hats. The men were not dressed as flashy, but at least some wore the traditional hats.

Once inside the condo building, Mollie tried looking up a couple of Spanish phrases before approaching the front desk clerk to check in. Standing in the main lobby, near a grand bouquet of yellow roses, green fern, and baby's breath, she was consulting her pocket dictionary when an attractive and familiar-looking woman approached her.

"Buenas tardes. Can I help you with a Spanish word or two?" The woman smiled kindly and extended her hand. "You must be new to our condos. I'm Sara Mercury, and I live here. And you are?"

Sara! Oh, my God, it was Sara! The journalist who I'd sat with the night before at the Jazz Club with her friend, Kate. The fired-up JFK conspiracy reporter! She was standing right there, talking to Mollie, who must have decided that she looked safe, because Mollie introduced herself and returned the smile. Sara guessed she was from Mississippi by her accent and the two hit it off immediately.

"You must read minds. I just got in from Guayaquil and, honestly, it is the first time I've spoken much Spanish. Haven't used it since high school," Mollie rushed out her words.

"You'll do fine. People here like helping anyone who tries speaking Spanish. They are flattered that you make the attempt. The region's accent is easy to understand—

it's slower than in other parts of the country; it is musical—almost lyrical." Sara looked down at Mollie's bags, set next to the flowers. "So you are brand new to our city?"

"Oh, yes. I don't know where anything is, including my condo unit."

"Well, come on, and I'll help you check in at the desk."

With Sara's help, Mollie quickly got her key and directions to her unit.

"I am sure you are tired. Why don't we do an early dinner together? This way you won't get too stressed looking for a restaurant," Sara suggested.

"That sounds great."

"I will meet you at five-thirty in the lobby, by the flowers."

The elevator door opened, and Mollie left Sara, waving good-bye. "Adios!"

"We say ciao, here. Very Italiano," Sara called out. "Oh—almost forgot to tell you about—" Before Sara got out her last words, the elevator door closed, and Mollie had to figure out for herself that the fifth floor was really the sixth! As we rode the elevator up to her floor, I was in awe. The universe had brought these two powerful women together. Maybe this would be a quick in-and-out after all, as Dan and I both hoped. All I could do was watch and pray.

After unpacking her suitcase, Mollie rested before returning to the lobby to meet Sara for their dinner date. The cab took them to a restaurant across the street from a massive brick cathedral that was near a central park.

"Such a charming place. How did you discover it?"

Before Sara could answer, a nattily dressed, older Ecuadorian man sporting a gold-colored Panama hat and wearing a long-sleeved white shirt and a blue chef's apron tied over his khakis approached their table. He rested his forearm on the back of Sara's chair.

"Hello girls. Who's the new lady, Sara? Another gringa writer from the States? I sure miss that Katy—is she ever coming back?"

The gentleman removed his hat, swept his hand through his pepper-gray hair, and then placed the hat back on his head and smiled.

"Mollie, meet Don Colón. Colón, please behave, and meet Mollie. She's from Mississippi." The chef kissed the side of Mollie's cheek with a quick peck.

"So you're a newbie to Cuenca? Are you here for permanent residency or just a visit? You a journalist, like Sara?"

I noticed how quickly this Latino man collected personal data. Mollie appeared drawn to him; I was thinking that I liked him, too. Hopefully, she would go ahead and confide in both Colón and Sara, since they seemed like good people. Do it now, Mollie! Tell them why we're here! I wanted to shout.

"I'm here only for a short visit, but the more I see of Cuenca, the more I like it." Mollie's voice grew serious. "I am in Cuenca, actually, to find an old friend I've lost."

Had Mollie read my mind?

"I know for certain that my friend is somewhere here in Cuenca, but I don't have her address. I need to find her for important personal reasons. I need to track her down, without violating her privacy. I can't just go out on the Internet and start asking if anyone has seen her. I hope you can understand the need for keeping this discreet."

Colón was nodding as Mollie spoke, and Sara watched her eyes.

"What's her name?" Sara asked. "I might know her, since I have lots of gringo friends. My bridge club has a dozen members, and my dinner club has close to thirty."

"Her name is Tara Means." Mollie pronounced Tara's name slowly.

"I haven't heard that name around here. What does she look like?"

"Tall, white, skinny, very attractive, long blond curly hair—dresses expensively and speaks with a soft Southern accent—not so thick, like mine."

Mollie was giving a good list of Tara's traits, better than I could have coughed up.

"She's personable, polite, and easy to talk with. She likes to go out a lot—you know—to concerts and restaurants."

"We need to find this lady for you," Colón said quietly, as Mollie finished her description.

Sara asked a few more questions. "How old is Tara? Does she smoke? Have a car? Like men?"

"She's in her late fifties and looks ten years younger than she really is. No, she doesn't smoke, but she likes wine and has a beautiful smile. She probably uses cabs a lot, because she doesn't drive. Most men fall for her fast, and she likes handsome men."

"Is she married?" Colón drew in closer to Mollie, waiting for her answer.

"Her husband died a couple of years ago."

His expression changed to a feigned look of sorrow.

"Oh, that poor lady. I could make her feel so much better."

I was sure that he could.

Colón straightened up and retied the chef's apron around his slim waist.

"You know, I think I might have met her."

"You're lying," Sara asserted. But Mollie looked like she was hanging onto his words and appeared to believe him.

"You really think that you might know her, Señor Colón?"

"Oh, honey, Just call me Colón," he grinned.

His eyes were kind, and I even found myself hoping that he could help. He probably knew most expat and Ecuadorian women in Cuenca because of his unique social intelligence and bilingual abilities, at least this was my assessment. I wondered how many languages he spoke besides Spanish and English—he seemed so worldly. I was sure he'd help track down Tara. I crossed my fingers and kept listening.

"There's a pretty blond lady who has been in here for lunch a couple of times, Mollie. She's about the age you gave and speaks with a charming accent. Maybe a week ago she was in here having lunch with an older man, say in his mid-seventies—quite a lot older than me."

Colón preened.

"She was well dressed, and a real looker, so I do remember her. I was surprised she couldn't catch a young man, like me."

His tail feathers had spread like a peacock. This ability to see auras was something I'd gained since I was dead.

It was sounding like Colón had spotted Tara, all right. The problem would be tracking her down in this enthralling city. Strolling around, I had been taken away by the numerous gardens tucked in the interior of many structures and narrow cobblestone roads. It was not going to be easy finding her, hidden in all of this, but Sara said she was ready and willing to take on the challenge.

"Mollie, your search for Tara is intriguing, and I love intrigue. I'm pretty damned good at finding people, too. It's an old-school journalism skill that I have. So let's find your friend together. I'm ready and willing to go to work!"

I wanted to hug Sara and give her a kiss. And not one of those goofy little cheek pecks, either. But Colón would have to do my lady-kissing for me in Ecuador; I was sure he'd be happy to oblige.

"When will we start?" Mollie asked.

"Tomorrow morning we'll start with Gringolandia. Did you bring a picture of Tara with you?"

Mollie reached into her purse and pulled out an old wedding photo of Tara she'd found in my desk before leaving Mississippi. Joe had sent it to me when they were married.

"Tara is quite a bit older than this picture, but you can still get an idea," she said, handing it over to Sara. I detected sarcasm in Mollie's voice when she hit the word older.

Colón took a quick peek over Sara's shoulder.

"Yes. That's definitely the lady, the one who was here."

"Good. Now we know who she is. I'll take you around to all the Gringolandia apartments. It sounds like this is where she'd be living," Sara said. "I'll pick you up tomorrow morning at nine sharp."

I could tell that Mollie was happy over such quick progress.

"Sara, I can't leave this restaurant without Colón's recipe for the lime salad we just had." Mollie staring directly at Chef Colón.

"Oh, honey. It's a secret. I don't give out recipes, except for the few I demonstrate in my weekly cooking class. Come by Sunday afternoon and that's what I'll specially prepare—lime salad just for you."

He winked, smiled, and winked again. I didn't notice if Mollie returned the same, but it wouldn't have surprised me. She could be quite a flirt!

"Put me down for Sunday classes," Mollie told him, as she and Sara got up to leave. Sara paid the bill; it wasn't very much and I could see why Cuenca had nearly three thousand American expats —the low cost of living and its beauty.

"My treat. Welcome to Cuenca, Mollie," Sara told her.

"Bye, darlings." Colón pecked each woman on the cheek. I had to admire the guy. He had stamina.

"Remember to call me if you need anything. If you find Tara, you can bring her to the cooking class, too!"

I really wanted to leave Ecuador and head back to Mississippi with Tara in hand before Sunday's class! Mollie would have to take a rain check if they found Tara, and I was sure that Colón, with his natural imaginismo, easily could find a replacement student, or even two or three or four, without trying.

Later that night, Mollie called Dan to report her progress. Dan agreed that her new friends sounded like a small army coming to Tara's rescue.

"Be careful, Mollie. Don't freely spread Tara's photo around. Be discreet. That's my only advice, and good luck tomorrow."

CHAPTER THIRTY-FOUR

As a defense lawyer who's been on the receiving side of the media—good and bad—I have developed a few ideas about what describes a skilled journalist. Rooting for the underdog comes at the top of my list, and this is followed by the instinctive ability to piss off important people. If you need a quick ride somewhere, any real journalist's car looks like they've lived in it for a month, with pop bottles, foam coffee cups, and hamburger wrappers covering the car seats and catsup pasted to the floor. Besides collecting and writing news stories, a decent journalist knows how to tweet and post on social media, but that's secondary. It's the personality characteristics that count.

If Sara had a car, it would be a dump. I knew she was a real journalist, after listening to her talk with Kate—also a real journalist—at the Jazz Club, and then with Mollie at Colón's restaurant. I sensed in her a passion for solving crimes. When she hooked up with Mollie and promised to bring her full set of journalism skills to the table, for the first time since we'd landed in Ecuador, I knew we would quickly locate Joe's widow.

As promised, Sara came to pick up Mollie. First, they sat at the table for morning coffee.

"I'm sorry it's instant. That's all I could find at the market."

"You'll have to come over to my place for coffee next time," Sara told her. "I use special beans."

I could tell Sara was excited over a Cuenca girl-hunt, but recognized that Mollie was hesitant in sharing details like exactly who Tara was, what was going on in her life, when she left the U.S. (exactly where she left from), and why Mollie was so desperate to find her (and secretive). I had a hunch Mollie feared Sara might write a news feature story about all of this—how Tara was a missing widow of a dead lawyer—and about the search. But it turned out Sara already had considered this possibility and decided better, even taking the initiative to talk to Mollie about possible complications.

"I understand how you might feel about me," Sara led off. "Don't worry. I'm not writing any stories about your search for Tara. I am sure that you have good reason to keep this quiet, and I'll respect you. I'm more interested in trying to find a JFK assassination link to South America. That's the big story I'm working on these days, Mollie. You are a good person, and I just want to help you, if I can."

This seemed to put Mollie at ease. She quickly washed up their coffee cups so they could leave the condo and start the search for Tara.

"Be sure and lock your door."

Mollie already had the key in her hand. The plan was to walk into the lobby of each gringo apartment or condo building and seek out the manager. Show him or her Tara's photo and watch for reactions. Ecuador has no complicated privacy laws, so they didn't anticipate running into managers unwilling to talk about their occupants. But for the first three hours, no one admitted seeing Tara's face.

Sara was persistent, but aggressive. Combined with Mollie's patience and charm, they made a great investigative team. Finally, at 12:32 p.m., they found Tara. It was that easy. And I couldn't believe where it happened. In their own building. Unbelievable! Just as they were returning for a quick lunch, while waiting for the elevator to Sara's floor, Molly spotted Tara walking into the building with a stern-looking Ecuadorian woman at her side. Mollie nudged Sara. Tara realized what was happening and responded with the look of a deer blinded by headlights.

"It is okay, Tara." Mollie stayed calm as she walked up to Joe's widow and took her hand. Sara held back, giving the two women breathing space.

"I'm surprised to see you, Miss Mollie. I am sorry if I look shocked."

The dark woman accompanying Tara acted suspicious, keeping her eyes on Tara, who spoke to her in a slow, disjointed Spanish.

"Lena, this is my friend Mollie, from the United States."

Tara switched back to English, introducing Mollie to Lena—her "boyfriend's cleaning lady."

Mollie shook hands with Lena, then quickly embraced Tara, who still looked uncomfortable.

"What are you doing here in Ecuador, Mollie?" Tara's voice was both friendly and suspicious. I watched Lena who had her eyes on Mollie, likely wondering who she was.

"I'm here for a quick holiday," Mollie told Tara. "I've known Sara for years and came to visit her. Isn't it lucky that we ran into you?"

Mollie's explanation appeared to work for Lena, who gave a quick, nervous smile and backed off, leading me to believe Lena understood some English. Still not mentioning the email, Mollie instead invited Tara to lunch.

"There's a cute place across the street where we can have almuerzo or lunch for three dollars."

Sara quickly jumped in—a true tag team effort. She crossed over to Tara's left side and took her arm, while Mollie grabbed Tara's right arm. "Ciao, Lena."

Mollie waved off the small woman as they marched Tara out the lobby door.

"She'll be back later on, so don't you worry—no problema!" Sara called over her shoulder, pointing to the tienda across the street with her index finger.

Lena looked confused as Tara feebly waved good-bye to Lena while mouthing, "Don't worry. I'll be back," in her slow Spanish.

I watched Lena take a seat in a large stuffed chair in the front lobby and pick up a magazine. Then I headed across the street to the small grocery. There were a couple of outside tables complete with umbrellas and chairs, so Lena could keep Tara in her direct line of sight.

It was a close shave crossing the street for Mollie and Sara. Cuenca's traffic light system, purchased from a German corporation, was poorly synchronized for cars and foot traffic. Even though a green light flashed for pedestrians in the crosswalk, Sara held Mollie back.

"We'll have to wait for the right moment and run. I usually watch for locals and stay in the pack," she half-shouted above the traffic noise. "I use them as human shields!"

They watched as cars whizzed by. Then Sara shouted, "GO!" when a hole appeared in the traffic—at the same time a couple of tough-looking guys started to cross the street. At the other side, Sara ran over and grabbed a table. Tara was starting to look relaxed and even giggled before Mollie got serious.

"I don't understand the email I got from you a couple of days ago, Tara. You know that's why I'm here. I had to make sure you were okay, but you never sent your phone number or address. Luckily, my new friend, Sara, helped me find you."

Sara gave Mollie and Tara time to talk. She lit a cigarette, offering one to Tara, who turned her down.

"The almuerzo for all of us, por favor," Sara turned and said to the young man who'd walked over from the counter.

"It's a kind of a blue plate special. Okay for you?" Mollie and Tara nodded in approval.

"It's usually a meat, some rice and beans, a small salad and vegetable, like potatoes. I know, extra carbs! That's Cuenca!"

The lunch arrived in five minutes with a tall glass of fresh papaya juice and, later, a fried banana, for dessert. Once they finished, Sara announced she was going for a short walk, to smoke another cigarette. I wished she wouldn't smoke. If I could ever make contact with her, I would try to convince her to stop.

Mollie didn't have much time to get Tara's attention. Thankfully, Lena hadn't budged from her chair across the street.

"Okay Tara, we don't have time to kid around. First, what's with that woman over there—your warden?" Mollie nodded towards Lena.

"Oh, she's my boyfriend's cleaning lady. He lent her to me while he's in the States."

"Lent her to you? Tara, have you noticed that she doesn't let you out of her sight?"

"Well, she's insecure."

"You're in trouble, aren't you? You're being watched. Right?"

"You could say she's possessive, I guess. I am really surprised to see you, Mollie. And I am so glad that you got my email."

Tara had quickly changed the topic. She was afraid, I was convinced. Would she let Mollie know what was going on? I doubted it. Mollie would have to gain Tara's confidence and then work quickly. That's exactly what I watched her do.

"Tara, some very bad things have happened at home. I can't tell you what they are, here in public. You will have to ditch Lena tonight, and we will talk alone. When's your boyfriend coming back to Cuenca?"

"He left three days ago, Mollie. It was really quick. He got a phone call from some man and had to leave for the U.S. Said it was personal. Lena and I are driving to the Guayaquil airport to pick him up late Sunday night. We'll get back in Cuenca around two the next morning."

This gave Mollie at least two days to get Tara out of the country before the boyfriend returned.

Sara came back from her smoke break and took over the conversation.

"Remember Mollie, I have that dental appointment in twenty minutes. I know you wanted to go with me and have him look at your tooth, so let's walk Tara back over to the condo. You can meet up with her later tonight. Okay?"

Mollie picked up Sara's cue, told Tara what to say to Lena to get away for a later meeting where they could freely talk.

"Tell Warden Lena that I'm here for a couple of days. That I'll be leaving Saturday, before your boyfriend gets back. Just say we're old school friends, and we are going to have dinner together. Say we won't leave the condo. Okay, Tara?"

Mollie grabbed Tara's hand and squeezed it tight.

"We're going to help you get home, back to Alabama, or to your mother and father, Tara. Don't worry."

At the mention of her parents, Tara's face tensed. "I don't have any problems to sort out, Missy Mollie, and I don't need any help from my family or you," she stammered.

Who was she afraid of? Mollie didn't stop long enough to try and find out.

"Look. I will come back and join you for dinner. Six tonight, Tara, your place. There's more we have to talk about. Bad things that you need to know. So keep Lena the hell away. Promise?"

Tara nodded a tentative yes. "Everyone's okay, aren't they?"

"We'll talk about it tonight." Mollie firmly closed the discussion.

The three crossed back over to the condo building where Tara picked up Lena and headed to her penthouse condo. Tara turned at the elevator door and waved good-bye, with a puzzled look on her face.

"Come on, Mollie, let's get out of here! Vamanos!"

Sara and Mollie returned to the street, where Sara hailed a cab and instructed the driver to head for Colón's restaurant. Once inside, Sara walked out back to the parking lot to smoke a cigarette while Mollie ordered a glass of red wine.

"Find her?" Colón asked Sara as he brushed by to wait on another table. She gave him a thumbs up and kept walking to the back. He returned to his kitchen, getting involved in his dinner prep. Once Sara returned to the table, Mollie opened up.

"I know that I can trust you, Sara, and you deserve to hear why I had to find Tara so quickly, and get her home. You have no earthly idea how much you've helped me today, so listen up. Here's why I came to Cuenca."

CHAPTER THIRTY-FIVE

Tara's eyes were moist. Mollie had just halted an intense conversation moments earlier to view the sunset from her picture window. It was dusk, and the yellow ball of light disappeared from behind the mountains. The sky lit up with a combination of colors—yellow, orange, and crimson, but it was over quickly; the sun never actually sets on the horizon in Cuenca.

"There's a big difference for sundown watchers here. It's beautiful, and the painted skies are gorgeous, but it's not the same as home. When you're so near the equator, it doesn't last more than a few seconds," Tara was saying.

Meeting Mollie at her door earlier in the evening, Tara asked to hear the bad news first before they sat down to dinner, and Mollie complied. My murder greatly upset her.

"I don't know very much, Tara," Mollie concluded. "Only that I got a call from my husband when I was in the Dallas airport, and he said Clinton was dead. He was shot at home, the night before. His car was taken and some of his money. They're saying that one of his clients, a kid with a bad attitude, did it. But that's all I know, and I must get back home to take care of things."

"Clinton is really dead?" Tara broke down and sobbed. I found her reaction unusually touching. "I always liked Clinton. He was like a brother to Joe."

I accepted Tara's words as an apology. I admit feeling momentary guilt over being on the down-low with Joe, something we'd hidden or tried to hide, from her. As I watched Mollie wait for Tara to dry her eyes, I wondered if she would be able to convince Tara to leave Ecuador and fly home? Or if there would be a confrontation?

Tara's tears changed to sniffles, and she dabbed at her eyes with a lace handkerchief. I was curious how Mollie would proceed, but out of the blue, and without Mollie having to pry, Tara started talking about what really took place in Montgomery when she heard about Joe's death.

"I was home, waiting for Joe," Tara began. "He'd been coming home late quite a lot, and I didn't usually trust he was telling me the truth about where he'd been. Sometimes he'd call and say he was working late, but I knew he was lying. He'd be in a bar. He'd try to muffle the sounds behind him, but I could hear it all going on in the background, and I knew he was playing around behind my back."

Maybe I was finally going to hear the truth from Tara. So far, her story sounded plausible.

"I didn't think this night would be any different," she continued. "That he'd eventually come home and make some weak excuse before coming to bed. He hadn't touched me for months." She sniffed, taking a moment to blot her eyes and compose herself.

Mollie nodded encouragingly as Tara spoke. She didn't interrupt with natural prompts like "go ahead" or "and then what happened?" Mollie simply let Tara talk. And it worked. Very little of Tara's story surprised me. A conservatively dressed man had presented himself at her front door that evening, flashing an official badge and asking for permission to come inside her home.

"He looked important, Mollie. He was wearing a trench coat. His shoes were shined, his suit was pressed, and I know his badge wasn't phony."

With her long arms crossed in front of her chest, Tara started rubbing her upper arms slowly, while giving her story. Her already-pale skin was looking blotchy.

"Where's your coat closet, Tara?" Mollie jumped up. "I'll get you a sweater."

Tara stopped the arm rubbing long enough to point to a door near the entrance. Mollie picked out a long-sleeved mohair sweater, walked over, and placed it around Tara's shoulders, keeping her eyes on Tara's face as she sat back down.

"I let him in the house, Mollie. He leaned forward on the edge of the sofa with the fingers of each hand touching, you know, doing that pyramid thing, and he looked me in the eyes and said that Joe was dead. I couldn't speak at first, but his face was so kind. He explained that Joe killed himself. I didn't even know that Joe worked for the FBI, but this man said Joe was a very good special agent for years. That sometimes when people are under a lot of stress, like Joe, they don't make good decisions."

When I heard FBI, I knew right away Tara had been snookered.

"He said they'd been watching Joe for the last year and knew he was being inappropriate, but I didn't think he was one of those men who chases boys," Tara continued. 'This man, you know the agent, said he was surprised, too. But he said it would be so embarrassing if it got out what Joe did. He promised me he would make sure this didn't get into the news—for Joe's sake and mine. He was assigned to watch Joe and had followed him to the park. Noises came from the restroom, and when he looked inside, Joe was zipping up his pants, and a boy ran out. He was about fourteen. The agent said Joe was scared when he got caught and took off running. He said he lost Joe at first, but later he found Joe dead, hanging from a tree by his belt."

What a load of bullcrap! Whoever this man was, this phony agent, had fed Tara lies that she was gullible enough to swallow. Joe would never touch a child. He never worked for the FBI. But I could understand Tara getting caught off guard and being made to feel so vulnerable or embarrassed that she would believe anything he told her.

Mollie got up from her chair, looking for a box of tissue, as Tara kept talking. I found myself believing Tara's story. This version—not what she'd first laid on me in Montgomery. Her gestures matched her words. She wasn't wearing that frozen smile, the one I'd encountered the first time she tried telling me about what happened to Joe. She wasn't twisting her hair, either.

More came out, as Tara admitted the agent scripted exactly what she was to say to me. And what she reported he'd told her to say matched what she'd said to me back then, when we had first spoken on the phone in Clarksdale and she dropped the bomb. The man told her what to say when I visited her in Montgomery. It was he who'd decided I couldn't see Joe's body, not Tara. But she hadn't viewed Joe's corpse either, as it turned out.

"The whole thing was a lie, Mollie. That man said they would take care of everything, even make sure I got Joe's pension that month if I didn't cause trouble. He said Joe's actions would have sent him to prison if they'd arrested him, and it was better that he killed himself, because he would have been murdered inside the walls—for sure."

Better that Joe kill himself? I grew even more disgusted as Tara continued telling Mollie what took place in Montgomery.

"This would have been a horrible embarrassment to the Bureau, he told me. Kind of like the problems Catholics are having with their priests. As a good wife, he said I needed to help them sweep up the mess before the media got hold of it. It was best for the country, and I wouldn't get Joe's pension—any of it—if I didn't do exactly as he said. That's what he told me, I swear Mollie."

Tara stopped to blow her nose and drink a sip of hot tea before she told the rest of her story.

"So I called up Clint and said that Joe killed himself. I believed this was true. And I told him that he couldn't see the body. I had to say this, Mollie. That agent said if Clint or any of Joe's friends inspected his body, they might try to get an official autopsy done, and this would slow everything down, and Joe's story would get into the news media. He said the Bureau would handle all of the mess only if I cooperated. He said they would work discretely with the funeral home and the local police to take care of all the paperwork. I wouldn't have to do a thing."

On that last sentence, I heard a little of Tara's usual smugness creep in.

Mollie, who'd been listening quietly, started pushing for details.

"Slow down, Tara. This agent—you say that he mentioned Clinton's name?" This was her first direct question, and I hovered in closer, wanting to hear exactly how my name had come up in the conversation between Tara and this bogus agent—whoever he was.

"Yes. He said to call Clinton—he seemed to know who Clint was—and say that Joe killed himself—hanged himself in the garage—four days earlier. He said this would put pressure on Clint not to ask questions, if he felt sorry for me. Clint would think it was best if I'd get the funeral over with. At least that's what the agent thought. He sure didn't know Clint very well, did he?" Tara stopped for a moment, and smiled at Mollie.

But Mollie pressed on, ignoring Tara's small joke. "Did you tell him anything specific about Clinton, Tara? Like where he lived?"

"No. I didn't argue. I just wanted this all to go away, Mollie. Wasn't any of this true about Joe? You don't think that I caused—"

Mollie interrupted Tara before she could complete her question. I was sure Mollie wanted to keep Tara from blaming herself for my murder and having a meltdown. It was too important to get out the rest of Tara's story out before she figured that she'd been used by whomever was behind Joe's and my murders.

"I never saw Joe again, never saw his body." Tara started to softly cry. "That man promised me Joe would be cremated, and I would get his ashes to scatter, but they never came in the mail like he said they would. I was afraid to ask where they were because I didn't want to make things worse." Tara looked into her lap and fidgeted with her handkerchief.

"Tell me how you got to Cuenca?" Mollie walked over to hand Tara a fresh tissue. I was glad she was able to keep Tara talking. I wanted to hear all of her story, and maybe I could figure out who this creep was and why he or an associate killed Joe, and probably me. If Molly would just ask Tara for his physical description, but she didn't—not yet.

"He arranged everything for my trip to Cuenca, my passport and my tickets. He even had a nice woman lawyer—her name was Grace—meet me at the airport and give me all of my important papers. Even a little plastic card with my picture. He said I'd be lots safer here in Cuenca than in Montgomery, and I wouldn't have to explain anything to Joe's friends or clients. He arranged for the newspaper obituary and made sure that Joe's secretary knew what to tell his clients and friends.

"I didn't know I was in danger, Mollie, but he said I was. Said it would be best for me to get out of the country. I like Cuenca. I've made lots of new friends, here."

Tara had finally stopped crying, starting to became animated when talking about her new expat life.

I noticed that Mollie held back any personal or negative remarks. I guessed she shared my reaction, when Tara whined about missing her bridge club partners if she had to leave Cuenca. They usually met at some private home, she told Mollie. Maybe this was fair. Joe hadn't treated her very well, and I hadn't been nice myself. She went on.

"I get money deposited every month from Joe's survivor benefits." Tara's voice picked up volume and speed. "The Bureau makes sure. I only had to promise not to tell anyone about what happened. The agent was serious when he told me this part, so I believed him, and you are the only person I've ever told this to, uh, except for Frank."

"Frank? Who is Frank?" Mollie looked concerned as she pressed Tara for an answer.

"You know, Frank. My boyfriend. You haven't met him yet. I told you he's in the States, but he will be back in Ecuador Sunday night."

"Where did you meet Frank?" Mollie closed in on Tara. I wanted to hear this, too.

Tara said she'd met Frank at a small coffee shop and bakery, a panaderia next door to her condo.

"I was trying to understand how much I owed for three rolls, and he stepped up to the counter and showed me exactly what to pay; he speaks perfect Spanish. You know they use the same money we do in the U.S., but they speak Spanish here. So I was confused. I knew when he stepped in and helped me that he was a real gentleman."

So Frank had set it up to meet Tara, making it look accidental.

"We started dating after that. Frank dresses really nice. He has great taste in wine and music—we have a symphony in Cuenca where he takes me to the concerts and treats me like a lady. He still does some part-time work. He goes to different countries when they call him. But mostly he is retired. He wants to spend the rest of his life in peace and quiet, he told me. So he chose Cuenca."

Mollie moved in closer. "Exactly what did you tell Frank about Joe? You had to say something, so when did you say it?"

"It was only last week that I talked about my past. We'd gone up in the mountains to Chordeleg. It's a little town —smaller than Clarksdale—close to here, where they sell special silver jewelry. Oh, it's so beautiful, Mollie. I've never seen anything like it! Their silver jewelry is all twisted and woven into beautiful designs. They call it filigrana, and—"

I was certain that Mollie was getting disgusted each time Tara flew off on a tangent. I saw her foot tapping on the floor! But she maintained a cool front, while trying to move Tara quickly along in the story.

I had been finding it interesting that Tara told this Frank, whoever Frank is, about Joe's death. Tara sends Molly a chatty email, and someone starts following me. Meanwhile, Frank gets a call and leaves for the U.S., and I wind up dead. I went back to listening as Mollie completed an amazingly good job of extracting still more information from Tara.

"Tell me more about Chordeleg. You seemed to like this village." Mollie was careful not to push too hard.

"Well, Frank wanted to buy me a piece of jewelry. He said he was getting serious, and it was so sweet, Mollie, I wish you could have seen his face. So, you know, I didn't think it would be fair to accept an intimate gift without telling Frank about my past—about Joe."

"So you told Frank about Joe's suicide? The FBI agent?"

Good questions, Mollie! Now just ask her what Frank looks like. Get some physical details, I thought.

"You told Frank about Clint's funeral? Your move to Cuenca, and who paid for it?

Tara continued nodding in agreement as Mollie expanded her list, her eyes welling up with tears, until she half-whispered, "You don't suppose this had anything to do with Clinton's murder, do you, Mollie?"

Mollie let Tara's question pass. She was going for everything that she could get.

"All I know is that we must get back to Mississippi as fast as I can buy your air ticket, Tara. Frank might be a nice guy, but you don't really know him. He could have good intentions or evil purposes, but we can't afford to hang around here and find out which. Hey, if it turns out he's a nice guy, you can always come back to Cuenca."

I believed Mollie convinced Tara to return home. It was looking this way, since Tara offered no objections.

"You have to promise me you will do exactly what I say and not tell Frank anything about our talk tonight if he calls or texts you before we leave. Okay, Tara? Oh, by the way, how did Frank respond when you told him all this about Joe?"

A look of warmth came to Tara's face.

"Oh, he was so sweet. He said he was sorry that I had to go through so much. He wanted to know if anyone in the States was helping me, and I said no—except for the FBI. He told me that Clint sounded like a fine man, and that he'd like to meet him some day. He asked where Clint lived, and I told him about Clint's house—how he'd built it with his father and grandfather. Both of us have been through a lot in our recent lives, Mollie. Frank's first wife died of Alzheimer's disease. He was trapped in Chile taking care of her, and that's why he moved to Ecuador when she died. He needed to get away from his old life and meet new people."

"Where is he from, Tara?"

"The South, like us. He grew up in Tupelo, and then lived in New Orleans for a while. But he's been making his life in South America for years. His company moved him to Chile a long time ago, around 1975. That's why he speaks good Spanish. I think he lived in Canada, too. And in New York!"

Mollie straightened her spine before taking a deep breath.

"Do I really have to go home, Mollie?" Tara started back whining. "I've told you everything. When Frank comes back, he promised me a trip to Chile." She pronounced it like chilly.

"Frank says the Southern Andes are so beautiful this time of the year. He told me about this beautiful little German village outside of Santiago, Chile, where the people are so nice. He used to work there."

I watched Molly stare out the picture window of Tara's penthouse, looking straight into the dark Cuenca sky where the sunset had earlier spread its colors. She rose from her chair and slowly walked to the bathroom, opened and shut the door behind her. I heard her retch.

CHAPTER THIRTY-SIX

Mollie trusted Sara. She shared everything Tara had revealed over dinner, including Tara's encounter with the phony FBI agent who'd lied about Joe's death.

"Disgusting, and believable," Sara asserted, after hearing Mollie's recap. "Now I understand why Tara was so vulnerable, and why she ended up in Cuenca. That fako pulled a number on her. I agree with you—whether it was that phony or his associate, the same person who killed Joe must have murdered Clinton, too.'

Mollie was listening to Sara's monologue, while looking for international flights on the Internet. "Should we leave from Guayaquil or Quito?"

"Listen. We'll go together and pick up the flight tickets in the morning. I'm sure you will be able to leave by Saturday evening—if there are still two seats available. It's easier to depart from Guayaquil, even though Quito has the new airport. It is closer, less crowded, and no more expensive. But I'll help you get out of here from either location. I want to see you back home safe and sound."

Mollie closed her laptop and turned to face Sara.

"Not a doubt. That phony jerk or one of his partners killed Clinton and Joe. And you're right, Tara's story was chilling. But Sara, I have to let my mind rest, at least for tonight, or I won't get any sleep, and I will be too tired to finish this project in the morning."

Mollie went into the kitchen and brought out a bottle of Cuban rum in one hand and a couple of glasses in the other.

"Hey, I picked up this brand earlier today. We can't buy it in the U.S. since we're still feuding with Cuba, but I hear it is good stuff. Care for some? I have a couple of cokes in the kitchen and lime to squeeze on top—if you'll get them for us.

"Honestly, I can't imagine a better time than right now to open that bottle!" Sara jumped up from her chair to get the items. "Hey! I'm going to miss you when you go back home, Mollie. Mississippi is so far away," she called over her shoulder. "We'll have to chat online to keep up with the news."

"I'll have a tough time going back, too. I like what I see of Ecuador, but my family needs me. Will you come and visit me in the Delta? I think you'd find the place interesting—well, different!"

Mollie sat on the couch with her rum in hand. I thought I heard her sigh; she'd looked frazzled since her long talk with Tara.

"Guess I'll have to consider your invitation. I've never been in the deep South." Sara took a swallow of her drink and walked over to the window to stare at the city's soft lights. "It's beautiful here at night. No big flashing neon stuff to get in the way. Cuencanos call their city tranquil, and I see why."

She turned back to her new friend.

"It really has been fun, you and I working together. It didn't take long to figure out how to blend our skills. I can almost read your mind, well maybe sometimes. I believe in fate, Mollie. Nothing happens by accident. Do you suppose we were meant to work together?"

Mollie nodded her head. "So, what will you be working on, once Tara and I get out of here? The JFK assassination?"

"Don't think so, unless I run into something unique, and make that soon! I'm afraid the fiftieth anniversary has passed me by. I had hoped to find something relevant in South America that would inform international readers, but now that Colonia Dignidad is heating up, this could be a good possibility for me. The trial opens soon in Santiago, and I need to start collecting background details before—"

Mollie did a double take and then waved her hand at Sara, stopping her mid sentence.

"Wait! I can help you with that! One of Clinton's friends, a history professor from NYU, personally knew a math professor from Penn State who was killed at that horrible place. At least he disappeared there, years ago."

Sara looked interested. "Tell me more."

"He is coming to Santiago soon, maybe next week, to help the man's sister. She is the major reason why the trial is happening in the first place—and why Chile finally did something to clean up their mess. That's what the professor told me, and I'm sure I can get you an interview with Dr. Dan Bell. He's a famous lawyer and historian from New York University. Would that help you, Sara?"

"You could do this for me? I would be grateful to you forever. So how do I get hold of him? This Dr. Bell?"

Listening to Sara and Mollie talk about Dan and Chile, I realized how little I actually knew about the colony, only what I'd been told by Dan a while back. But I was about to learn more.

Mollie settled into her chair, took another sip of her drink, and started telling Sara what she knew about Dan, and the information he'd passed on about Colonia Dignidad. But soon Sara took over; as it turned out, she had done her homework and knew much about the horror of Dignidad. We listened as she wove a complicated, but fascinating, account.

"The colony is set in a highly remote part of Chile about four hours south of Santiago—that's about 4,800 miles south of Cuenca. So I can't simply jump in a car and make the drive. I'll have to fly into Santiago first and then hire a driver to get there. I became excited about this after viewing a recent short documentary, filmed by reporters on a government-escorted visit to the colony. In the early 1960s, a German evangelist built what was to be a utopia, but you know how those plans can go south. Its members first were contained and tortured by the leader and his guards, then later all colony members were forced to help the Pinochet regime perform its foulest deeds— even the children."

Sara caught my attention, and I noticed that Molly wasn't nodding off to sleep, like she had warned could happen before Sara started talking. Suddenly a loud shriek punctuated the air. Mollie jumped from her chair, and walked over to look out the window. She said she saw a helmeted man on a beat-up bike cycle by, blowing his steel whistle. He was wearing an official-looking uniform.

"What's that about," Mollie asked. Sara acted like the commotion was funny!

"Oh, don't worry. That's only the night security guard. He comes around every half hour or so and blows his whistle. If a stranger is hanging around the neighborhood, the noise is supposed to scare them off. At least that's the theory."

"I guess I was too tired to hear him whistle the first night I was here." Mollie slouched back in her soft chair and waited for Sara to continue with her story.

"So, maybe this place, Colonia Dignidad, started out with good intentions?"

"Well, I can tell you where it ended up— and it is the grimmest, the worst, story of human torture I've ever heard in my life. Possibly worse than some of the atrocities that occurred in Nazi Germany's concentration camps," Sara responded.

In her seriousness and passion, Sara reminded me of the late award-winning newscaster Edward R. Murrow, the one journalist I'd always admired—probably my only mass media hero. I saw that she'd lit a cigarette. Smoking was allowed in the condo, but I remained worried about her addiction, wondering if she knew that Murrow died of lung cancer. Would Murrow have reported on Colonia Dignidad? So few journalists have reported from this strange place. He probably never heard of it, but maybe the colony's story would offer a needed professional boost for Sara to get back into journalism. She deserved a break!

As Sara described the physical layout of this Andes torture colony, I began to see in my own mind "land that stretched across seventy square miles, rising gently from irrigated farmland to low, forested hills, against a backdrop of snowcapped mountains." The picture she painted sounded like a heavenly place, and yet for some unknown dark reasons, the colony had morphed into a living hell. For decades, its sole connection to the outside world had been a long dirt road winding through tree farms and agricultural fields, cut off by a guarded gate.

Few outsiders ever were allowed inside while its reclusive leader, a man named Paul Schaefer—no relation to the talented band leader—remained in power. Years before coming to Chile, Schaefer had tried to join the elite Nazi SS corps, but was rejected for health and mental reasons. He'd spent the war as a nurse in occupied France, then became a popular evangelical preacher. A couple of decades after the war ended, he was invited to Chile by the Chilean ambassador.

Where are all the people who were tortured and survived? Would zombies be wandering the grounds? Mollie must have been on my wavelength, because she asked Sara if anyone still lived there, now that it had been turned into a tourist venue by the Chilean government.

According to Dan, Amnesty International and the governments of Chile, Germany, and France finally investigated the colony. Former colonos, as members were called, testified to its horror, and Chile finally pulled the plug. Its few escapees revealed evidence of terrible crimes: child molestation, forced labor, weapons trafficking, money laundering, kidnapping, physical and mental torture and murder.

As it turned out, Sara had done quite a bit of research on the colony. I hoped that she and Dan would get together and share; she had enough now to write an award-winning story. She continued telling how Pinochet's military junta seized power in Chile, and Schafer allowed Colonia Dignidad to serve as a torture and execution center for the disposal of enemies of the state. Later, the CIA used these same grounds as a training site. I remembered Dan telling me this, when we were strategizing generally on how he could get his hands on more declassified CIA documents.

A clinical psychologist and a psychiatrist recently visited colony members and their children, Sara told us.

"They all looked and acted like robots or zombies. Some tried to interact in a normal way, but in an interview with a Santiago reporter, the psychologist said that they all were haunted. She felt uncomfortable, yet profoundly sorry at the same time for what they'd been through. Some of the younger people have apologized for their own past involvement in horrific crimes of torture and talked to her about trying to make amends of some kind. But the older members would have none of that."

Was I surprised at Sara's statement about the lack of apologies? Hardly. Whether Colonia Dignidad or the Delta, it is hard to get criminals to say they are sorry and really mean it. I'd discovered this when we never could get honest Truth and Reconciliation projects organized in Mississippi.

I was curious about what finally happened to Schafer and Dignidad. Did he ever admit the truth or apologize? It turned out he spent a few years behind bars before passing on to hell. The colony's ruling council kept things going for a while, but eventually the whole place fell apart, as colony members kept torturing each other, even without Schaefer's presence.

Sara continued sharing what she had learned, well into the night. She said that colony leaders eventually cooperated with the investigators. They showed hidden files on the Pinochet years and led them to underground bunkers, weapon caches, and mass graves. Later, they found vast numbers and types of weapons, from machine guns to rocket launchers, surface-to-surface air missiles, and more. Who'd provided these weapons of destruction? What war profiteering corporations' name plates would show up on the equipment? I doubted there would ever be answers to my questions.

The colony's gates are open today, and traffic passes freely through the community, with visitors welcome from around the world. Sara definitely was planning to visit the place within the next couple of weeks, and I imagined what it would be like going there for a class reunion or a family get-together, since it was now a tourist spot. Would you have a picnic on top of an old bunker? Next to a torture chamber? With zombies hanging around?

A hiking trail has been set up to pass through the colony, and many of the surviving men, women, and their children, are trying to live a normal life, according to Sara. Would she feel okay walking down that trail? I wasn't sure if I would want to go there.

Mollie was yawning, but still awake, as Sara came to the end of her lengthy ad hoc presentation. In early spring 2005, she told us, Schaefer was caught and arrested in Argentina by a SWAT team, then extradited to Chile where he was placed in a maximum security prison in Santiago. One year later, he was filmed standing in front of a judge, convicted of child molestation and sentenced to twenty years in prison. He later received an additional seven-year sentence for weapons violations, plus three for torture. He died in 2010 at the age of eighty-nine.

A nurse told Sara that he was a crotchety old asshole when he finally passed on. At least he'd experienced some form of punishment. However, he didn't suffer in any way close to the extent he had inflicted on others.

Sara took a deep breath when she finished with her story.

"I've left out a lot of details of torture, especially what was done to innocent children. If you want me to—"

"Oh, please don't. Thank you. What you've told me is sufficient." Mollie sat up in her chair. "I truly appreciate your restraint."

She rose for a glass of water, looking tired and in need of sleep. They had decided earlier to meet for breakfast at Colón's, then visit a travel agency to buy the plane tickets. Of course I'd be hovering nearby. So, what could go wrong with this?

CHAPTER THIRTY-SEVEN

Sara returned to her condo, and Mollie went to bed. It had been a long night. Early in the morning hours, I heard a screeching, grinding noise coming from Sara's condo, one floor above Mollie's unit and directly across the hall. I'd been troubled all night, thinking about the horrors of Colonia Dignidad, and this interruption gave me reason to focus on something else. I floated up to Sara's to check out the racket.

I guessed like most writers I've known, Sara did her best work in the hours well before dawn breaks. I wasn't surprised to find her in the kitchen wearing fluffy pink slippers and a matching robe, brewing a cup of fresh coffee. I sure wished I still had a sense of smell! In fact, I'd noticed my senses were starting to weaken since I'd arrived in South America. Was this a sign of something?

In the living room, I saw her papers scattered around her laptop and knew she'd been working most of the night. But the grinding noise was coming from Sara's sophisticated coffee-making system and the ritual she was performing. She'd had already scooped the small coffee gems into the top of her grinder by the time I arrived and set it to fine. I watched as she ground the beans for forty-five seconds. Then gave them a second lethal blast, an extra fifteen seconds of crushing death.

"We kill to live," shot through my mind as Sara ground down the beans. My favorite anthropologist, Joseph Campbell, made a memorable and pragmatic statement about killing to live years ago in a lecture I'd attended on campus, and I recalled his words just as the beans released their final puff of aroma. He'd said the only justification one has for harvesting food sources, the necessity to kill live plants and animals, is to sustain our own human life. Yet, would some people live to kill? Does killing sustain them, in some strange way? I remember Campbell shushing away a student who tried twisting his statement, as such. But now I was forced to wonder if this oppositional undergraduate was more aware of life's cruelties than Campbell? Less isolated, perhaps?

My attention drifted back to Sara, who now was securing a specially waxed filter into place onto the bottom of an open glass container. She poured in the fresh grounds and reached over to flip on her stainless steel electric water heating kettle to raise the water temperature, continuing her complicated sacrament.

I knew this entire ceremony by heart. I had become tired of drinking Mollie's weak-warm coffee, so tired I'd ordered a system similar to Sara's and learned how to use it at home, not wanting to hurt Mollie's feelings. After re-pouring her drink into the prewarmed coffee glass, Sara left the kitchen, taking her drink back to her desk. She powered up the computer.

A couple hours after finishing her coffee, and getting some solid writing done, Mollie came knocking at Sara's door.

"I can't sleep, so I thought I'd come up to your condo. I figured you'd be awake, since you're a writer," Mollie joked. "I know it's only four thirty or so, but the cop blowing his whistle under my bedroom window every thirty minutes, plus my anxiety over getting Tara safely out of Ecuador, are making me nervous and keeping me awake."

"Understandable. Come on in." Sara opened the door for Mollie to enter, then shut and locked it behind her. "Have a seat. How about some coffee?" Sara looked pleased to have company, providing another opportunity to fire up the grinder.

"Oh, I'd love it. But please don't go to any trouble." Once more, Sara returned to her rites, as Mollie closely watched.

"Damn, that's hard to do." Mollie drew her eyebrows slightly downward and together, and tightened her lips. I could tell that she was worried, after watching Sara work so diligently to make her special brew just for her.

"When I get back to the States, I am going to send you a regular coffee machine, Sara. You just dump in the coffee. It's already ground up. You pour in some warm water and plug it into the wall. Okay?"

Sara glanced over at Mollie and grinned at her well-intended offer.

"You don't have to use that Cuban stuff, either," Mollie carried on. "I'll even send you some instant from Mississippi. I get it at the little grocery store near my house."

I finally had to laugh! If Sara only knew how dreadful Mollie made coffee, she would have choked up, too. But Sara politely changed topics. Sitting on the sofa and balancing her freshly poured cup of coffee on her lap, Mollie again was telling Sara that she appreciated her help and compassion.

"I hate leaving Cuenca so quickly, because I've enjoyed meeting you, Sara. Maybe you can come and visit us someday in Mississippi."

"Wha' that would be real nah's, Miss Mollie" Sara said, faking a Southern accent, and not very well!

"I'm serious Sara; you are always welcome to my home. My life is going to change, now that Clinton is dead. I wish you could have known him. He was such a gentleman. Always spoke eloquently, very careful of his diction. He did wonderful things for many people. He worked quietly behind the civil rights movement for so many years, getting very little credit. I think some people ignored him because he was gay. This was something not well understood at the time—even now."

Sara listened, watching Mollie's tears began to spill. Everything had happened so quickly—the sudden decision to search for Tara, the fast trip to the airport, and then my murder. Sara rose to walk over and give Mollie a hug, holding on to her and letting her sob. I knew that she could sense Mollie's pain.

It hurt me to watch, "Please hold her." I did my best to send out this message. I hated seeing Mollie cry and loved her so much, even more now that she was working so hard to save Tara.

"I really don't know what to make of it," Mollie told Sara, after she'd wiped away her tears, "except that I want to find who killed him and why. Clinton survived for over two years after Joe's murder, and then this happened to him, so fast."

CHAPTER THIRTY-EIGHT

A couple of hours later that morning.

"I don't think you and Tara should go out together to buy flight tickets. It might draw attraction if you're seen together." I overheard Dan talking to Mollie on the telephone. She'd called him before leaving for breakfast to report she'd found Tara. I understood his reluctance, now that he had heard from Mollie why Tara had moved to Ecuador, and how Tara was conned into believing Joe killed himself. Dan was suspicious. So was Mollie, and so was I.

Knowing Dan, he would factor in Ecuador's political atmosphere, especially in Guayaquil, the country's largest and most populous city, that buzzed with U.S. intelligence personnel. There was reason for this, at least in the eyes of the U.S. government and major U.S media, after Ecuador's president, a bright PhD economist who'd been trained in the States, gave asylum to the founder of an embarrassing Internet website. WikiLeaks regularly posted secret U.S. policies and activity reports—many of them extremely unflattering on its site.

President Barack Obama was unhappy with President Rafael Correa's decision to protect Julian Paul Assange, an Australian editor and founder of WikiLeaks. Some said Correa's action had nothing to do with protecting Assange's right to a fair trial or freedom of the press, but had more to do with regional and local politics in the

Western Hemisphere. Editors of Guayaquil's major newspaper insisted the CIA already had spent $87 million in Ecuador for additional agents to destabilize the government, not only because of Assange, but as part of regular, ongoing activity in South America. Correa confirmed this, publicly stating his life was in danger and that he likely would be killed by the CIA. Correa cited reports of a plot to "destabilize the region" emphasizing "strong U.S. influence in Latin America."

Then Edward Snowden appeared on the international scene, with his National Security Administration or NSA leaks. At first, Ecuador showed interest in sheltering this whistle-blower who'd been employed by a U.S. government contractor. In this atmosphere of political posturing, I was certain Dan also was considering the presence of rogue intelligence agents in the seaport city, some who'd been part of assassination witness cleanup crews for the past fifty years, since the JFK assassination. These were unscrupulous men and women who worked for hire, without question, for any government or private corporation, as long as they were paid.

My thinking might sound paranoid, but from what I had uncovered in my own secret document collection, some of these people who'd caused problems for witnesses and researchers of the JFK, MLK, and RFK assassinations over the past fifty years were still alive, maybe continuing their cover-up work. Some of them easily could be operating in Ecuador, given the current political atmosphere.

It still bothered me, the link between Kimble, Joe, and Ecuador. Where was Kimble? Still working for the Company? Or the FBI? Keeping investigators like Joe and me quiet? Anything was possible!

It made sense to me that Dan saw Tara, as Joe's widow, to be a potential target. She probably didn't know a damned thing about the assassinations, civil rights cold cases, Kimble, or any of what Joe and I had worked on, before we were killed.

"You've done great so far, Mollie," I heard Dan saying. Mollie had caught him on his way to morning classes at NYU. He didn't have much time to visit, but praised her for her success.

"I can't believe how quickly you found Tara and got her to agree to go home. Now it's important to keep her quiet and invisible before getting on that plane. We don't know what we are up against in Ecuador. When you hit the ground in the U.S., we'll figure out what to do next."

Mollie ended the call just as Tara was knocking on her door.

"Where's Sara?" she asked, walking into the room and doing a quick scan.

"She'll meet us later. She had a couple of errands to run first, so she'll find us at the restaurant," Mollie bluffed. "How did you escape Lena? I thought she'd be with you this morning."

Lena's absence would be one less problem for Mollie.

"She wanted to help her mother do laundry this morning, and I told her to go ahead. I said I was having breakfast with you and would come back later and help her work, if I can. She doesn't expect to see me for a couple of hours. She'll probably have everything done, but maybe I can put some of her wet stuff in my clothes dryer." Tara explained.

Mollie was putting the final touches on her makeup, but taking more time than usual to keep Tara in her condo until the cab arrived. She'd arranged for the doorman to call when it was time to come down.

"I'm so sorry I have to go back home to the States," Tara started in. "I was thinking about this all last night, and I couldn't sleep. I've been having so much fun here in Cuenca." She massaged her long fingers, examining her manicure, while talking to Mollie. "I'll need to say good-bye to my boyfriend when he comes over later tonight, of course. Maybe he can visit me in Mississippi. What do you think, Mollie?"

I watched Mollie slowly turn from the mirror and walk from the bathroom. She waited before asking Tara to explain what she'd said about Frank coming home. I wanted to hear this, too!

"I thought you said Frank was flying into Guayaquil Sunday night and would be rolling into Cuenca around two Monday morning."

Tara had an answer that surprised Mollie.

"Oops. I forgot. He phoned last night. Said he finished his business sooner that he'd planned and was leaving at midnight. He'll be in Guayaquil a day early—well, really early this morning—and he said not to worry. He'll take a taxi to Cuenca from the airport. Lena and I don't have to go over to the airport and get him. He's going to surprise me! That will be so yummy," she giggled.

About then, a cab pulled up in front of the condo building, and the doorman called Mollie's phone. She quietly said they would be right down.

"Don Colón Restaurante, por favor," Mollie told the driver. It took ten minutes going down Calle Sucre turning right on Benigno Malo. I noticed an Art Deco building on the corner near the restaurant, with scaffolding in place; sure looked like a good place for someone to do surveillance. But I didn't see anyone nearby. When we got to Colón's, Mollie handed the driver three dollar coins and thanked him. She and Tara quickly walked across the cobblestone street to enter the restaurant.

Chef Colón walked out from the kitchen to greet Mollie and Tara.

"You found your lady! See, I said you would."

Colón gave them both a quick kiss and grinned. "Just the two of you this morning?"

"No, we're waiting for Sara," Tara answered, looking annoyed.

Colón laughed and gestured for them to choose a table, then walked back over to his service station to pick up coffee and juice. Once he delivered their drinks, Colón took an empty chair beside Mollie. He was probably the most-used, informal expat psychotherapist in town.

Sara arrived ten minutes later, wearing a three-piece olive-colored business suit, a tan briefcase strapped over one shoulder, and carrying a Cuenca newspaper under her arm.

"Nice outfit," Tara muttered, as Sara took a seat.

"Very ny'ees," Colón offered, slipping in an extra syllable, while looking Sara up and down.

"Wonderful seamstresses here in Cuenca. Show them anything, and they'll make a replica," Sara told her friends, blowing off Colón's stare.

Mollie turned toward Tara, giving her a stern look. "Did you forget to comb your hair or put on makeup this morning? You sure look messy." Mollie was feigning—this seasoned prankster.

Tara put down her coffee cup to pat her face and head with both hands. Her eyes scanned the walls for a mirror to see what Mollie was talking about. When she couldn't spot one, she jumped up.

"Up that way," Colón said, pointing to the upstairs restrooms.

"Take your time, honey," he called after her, obviously figuring that Mollie wanted Tara gone, so that she could talk behind her back. And he loved gossip! As Tara climbed the stairs to find a mirror and repair her hairdo and face, Mollie pulled Sara and Colón into a quick huddle.

"Listen, I need your help getting Tara away from her condo today, while Sara and I pick up the plane tickets," she told Colón.

"You look upset, Mollie. What's wrong," Sara asked. Colón looked over at Mollie, taking his eyes off Sara for the moment.

"Tara just happened to tell me that Frank is arriving in Guayaquil—in about fifteen hours! He phoned her last night from Miami and said that he'd finished early with his work—whatever that was—and will catch a plane TONIGHT. He should get into Guayaquil at about ten and will take a taxi to get back to Cuenca."

Sara looked stunned. "You aren't kidding me?"

"That would get this Frank-person into Cuenca at about two tomorrow morning or possibly sooner," Colón calmly calculated. He furrowed his eyebrows to look concerned, even if he didn't know why.

"Dan is worried," Mollie continued, "because there are secret CIA and military intelligence agents all over Ecuador, and he thinks we could have trouble at the airport getting Tara out if we run into a rogue agent, or someone else up to no good. So, it's best to keep her from being seen anywhere in public. When we arrive in Guayaquil, it should be no more than two hours before the plane lifts off. Even then, we'll have to be careful."

Mollie glanced over at Colón and stopped to explain what she'd been talking about.

"Dan is a professor who's been helping me find Tara, all along. He was an old friend of my boss, Clinton Moore. Tara's husband was murdered because of what he knew about some important crimes. Then my boss was murdered last week. I know this sounds awfully complicated and messy, but—"

"It is okay. I used to live in Florida. I know how ugly things can get. I just want to help you, if I can," Colón said to Mollie. "Seriously, you're a nice lady, and I want to make sure you're all right."

"Dan says to keep a low profile," Mollie went on, her words guarded, and watching Colón's response. "We'll probably be okay. But we've got to get Tara on a flight that leaves earlier this evening—before Frank's plane gets into Guayaquil."

Colón leaned in toward Mollie and gently placed his hand on her arm, looking into her dark eyes.

"She'll have to leave after this Frank-person arrives. There are only two flights a day out of Guayaquil for Miami, 7:00 a.m. and 11:40 p.m. I know this because I fly there every few months to see my kids."

Mollie looked trapped, but Colón kept talking, never letting go of her arm.

"Don't worry, Mollie, it will work. I'll help you keep Tara out of sight for the rest of the day while you buy the tickets. Don't worry. You will have time to catch your flight—"

"If we can get tickets for tonight on such short notice," Mollie blurted out.

"Oh, don't worry about that." Colón pulled his cell phone from his suit coat pocket. "I have friends." He winked at her, then started to dial.

I watched Colón take command and was not surprised that we'd found him—or that he'd found us, however the universe works. Nothing happens by chance. Everything seemed destined to work out. Tara would safely get home, and Mollie, too. I had to believe this would all fall into place.

"Let me know when you'll have them, all right?" Colón finished talking on the phone, tucking his cell phone away.

"I'll need passports—yours and Blondie's." He nodded over to Mollie.

"Don't worry. I have mine, and I took Tara's last night from her dresser drawer when I was at her condo."

Mollie pulled the small blue booklets from her purse and handed them to Colón.

"Real quick, before Tara gets back from fixing her hair," Colón continued. "My girlfriend and I will take Blondie to Sigsig for the day. It's a small village outside of Cuenca that's up in the Andes. We'll meet up with you back here—with the tickets. But don't come back here until seven tonight. Hey, you two will have a whole day to go to the spa or the mall—or both!"

Colón rubbed his hands together and grinned. Then his expression turned serious.

"And you will have plenty of time to get to the Guayaquil airport, tonight. You'll have to drive there, since there are no evening flights on Saturday from Cuenca. I know a place where you can stay when you arrive; it's an apartment five minutes away from the international terminal. And I'll have someone watching out for Frank. He will call you after Frank leaves the airport and all is clear. So we're set?"

Colón hit the table with the palm of his hand and flashed a wicked grin. His brown eyes twinkled as he leaned in toward Mollie. "I could have a very special taxi pick up Frank when he lands in Guayaquil, if you'd like, Mollie."

Mollie slightly shook her head, indicating no.

"Just remember, I offered." Colón laughed.

"Don't look worried. It's going to be all right, ladies." He was reassuring Mollie when Tara appeared at the top of the steps. Colón quickly whispered. "Sigsig's not far from here. About an hour away. They hand weave Panama hats there, and we'll make a fun shopping day of it. Tara will never know what we're up to. My cook can handle the restaurant while I'm gone."

"Good plan," Mollie whispered back.

"It's a sure winner," Sara leaned over and murmured to Mollie.

Tara returned to the table, with her hair freshly combed. "Look better?" she asked, swinging her blond hair left to right.

"Most definitely," Mollie answered, smiling over at Sara and Colón.

CHAPTER THIRTY-NINE

There was no problem convincing Tara to go shopping. Colón's clever plan to spend money on hand woven hats "like Angelina Jolie wears" won handily over drying Lena's cold, wet clothes back at the condo.

"How did you know I love Panama hats? I'll take some back home for my friends," Tara marveled as she, Colón, and his girlfriend sped out of Cuenca in his red sports convertible, top down, and headed southwest into the nearby Andes.

It already was turning into a bright sunny day, and the blue sky over Cuenca was filling with puffy white cumulus clouds. In Sigsig, the altitude would reach 8,800 feet above sea level. Colón knew the weather could turn at any moment and had brought light jackets and umbrellas along, just in case. I wondered if he'd thought to bring a gun, too.

Sara and Mollie quickly flagged down a cab and took off for Cuenca's biggest shopping mall while I returned to Tara's condo, figuring that Frank might arrive earlier than he'd announced, just to surprise Tara. I was picturing him either as a horny old goat, who wanted to get back to his girlfriend ASAP, or something worse. If Frank turned out to be a problem, I would have to divert him from finding her, although I wasn't sure how. And then I heard his voice.

"Where's Tara Means?" A tall, slim man with an angular face and thin nose had walked into the condo building demanding this information from the desk clerk. I'd been hanging around the lobby for an hour, hoping this would not happen.

"I tried ringing her unit, but no one answers," he said in perfect Spanish.

I took a closer look at this older man. His body was well-toned and his hair was short—steel gray. Just as Tara had described Frank to Mollie. So it had to be him. As Frank stood there, waiting for his answer, I picked up on something else about him that nagged me, information that Tara hadn't shared. He looked too damned familiar. I wasn't sure why I felt so suspicious, until I got up real close in his face and noticed his well-defined pointed nose and high cheekbones. And then I saw those two crazy-ass, differently colored eyes, and it hit me fast.

Tara's Frank was the man who'd killed me. Last week in Clarksdale. And he probably killed Joe. It was strangely electrifying to come face-to-face with my assassin. But I had to get past this. I knew that Tara was in danger.

Now that I was dead, I could see energy fields clearly, and the cloud circling Frank was black. I had to keep him away from Joe's widow. I watched as he tried to browbeat information from the older desk clerk.

"We don't check people in and out of our condominiums," the clerk was nervously telling him. "This is not a hotel, you know."

"Did you see her leave?"

"Yes. With her friend."

"You mean Lena?"

"No. Lena's out there." The clerk pointed out the back window, toward the Tomebamba River where Lena was standing ankle deep in the cold water, washing laundry with her mother and extended family. I followed Frank as he bounded down to the river.

"Lena," he shouted, waving his arms and yelling above the roar of white water crashing over huge boulders. "Where's Tara?"

"It is okay, Señor Frank." Lena looked up to smile.

There! I got my final confirmation! Lena addressed him as Frank!

"She's with her best friend. You know, Mollie, the black lady who came to visit her from Mississippi. They went to breakfast. She's coming back this afternoon to help me with the laundry."

"So, I couldn't even leave the country for five frigging days without everything falling apart," Frank mumbled, turning to stomp up the embankment. He circled back, catching Lena as she returned to her work.

"You screwed up Lena. You're fired! I told you to keep Tara in your immediate sight at all times! That's what I paid you to do!"

Leaving the woman standing in the river holding wet laundry and looking stunned, Frank rushed back to the building to question the desk clerk, once more.

"Look. This is an emergency. I must find Tara Means because there's been a death in her family. I have to get her back to the U.S.," he lied.

"Think hard—do you have any idea where she might have gone with that other woman? The black one?"

"Well, we can ask the doorman. He might have heard her tell the cab driver where to take them."

Frank walked behind the desk and yanked the clerk by his upper arm, pulling him across the room and pushing him out the front door. "Ask him," Frank pointed to the doorman.

"Uh, Jerry. Where did Tara and her friend go this morning?"

"Don Colón —You know, that restaurant downtown," the doorman quickly answered the desk clerk, eyeing Frank's firm hand on his arm.

"Open that door," Frank barked, pointing to a parked yellow cab, and then sliding into the back seat of a taxi that had pulled up for a waiting customer. Before the surprised woman could complain, the cab pulled out with Frank and me.

CHAPTER FORTY

Frank's cab headed to Colón's restaurant, a ten-minute taxi ride into the heart of downtown Cuenca. "Where's your boss?" he shouted to the cook, after bolting into the restaurant's kitchen.

"He's off for the day."

"So, where'd he go?"

The cook stopped slicing tomatoes to look over and answer Frank. "He said not to tell anyone."

"I have something really important to tell him."

The cook wiped his hands on a fresh towel. He studied Frank's face before answering. Frank flashed a warm smile, and the cook relaxed.

"In that case, he wouldn't mind me telling you, I'm pretty sure. He took his girlfriend and another lady up to Sigsig. They went hat shopping."

"Of course. He was expecting me to go with them, but I was running late. Where's this Sigsig? Very far from here?"

Once Frank had pried the directions to the small town where Colón planned to spend the day, I watched him hail another yellow cab, instructing the driver to head into the Andes. I got there first, to see Tara, Colón, and his girl walking through the hat factory, where Tara was going nuts. I could hear her voice from down the street!

"I want this one, and that one, and this one—how am I going to get them all on the plane?" she giggled. Tara was holding onto three straw hats of different colors. She could see they wouldn't fit in the overhead luggage; but, of course, she had no idea that Mollie planned to leave all of her belongings in Cuenca. Tara would never see her condo again. The plan was for her to be whisked away to Guayaquil by car that evening, then returned to Mississippi. There would be no stopping off for suitcases or saying good-byes to expat friends. Mollie wanted to take no chances in having the trip to Guayaquil interrupted.

"How about some lunch? I know a great place—a small café down the road where they serve a traditional lunch that you can tell your friends about, back in the States." Tara nodded her head, and they took off in Colón's car.

"You are such a good driver," Tara told Colón, as he swerved to avoid a flock of geese being guided down the road by an old woman, swinging a cane.

"Worked on a racing team when I was young," Colón smiled, expertly maneuvering his car on the dirt and loose gravel road.

Once inside the café, the three took a table and ordered the daily special.

"What a fun place," Tara was saying, as she leaned across her soup bowl to ask Colón a question about Panama hats. She'd left all three of her purchases in the car and turned around occasionally to make sure they weren't being stolen.

As they began eating the fresh mountain stream trout, rice, and avocado salad they'd been served, Tara asked how Panama hats got their name.

"If they're made in Ecuador, why aren't they called that," she puzzled, between bites.

I'd always loved the mystery of these hats and learned how years ago they were shipped to Panama before traveling to their final destinations. Colón, I noticed, wore a superfine, pumpkin fedora, probably a Montecristi Cuenta that easily set him back $3,000.

Grandpa Willie had worn a Panama made of white straw with a black ribbon circling the base of the crown, but paid $25—a lot of money back then.

"Why are some hats $10 and others hundreds of dollars,?" Tara asked.

"It's the weave," Grandpa had explained. "Count the number of rows of weave in one inch horizontally. Then count the number of rows of weave in one inch vertically. Multiply the two numbers, say 13 by 13, to get the score."

We'd counted his weaves together back then, and Grandpa's hat scored only 169, meaning it wasn't really so great. While a hat like Colón sported, a superfine hat made on Ecuador's coast, looked to be a 600.

The 900 or more weaves takes months to create and can cost $75,000! The Sigsig version of the Panama is not of that quality, but both are made from the same fibers of the carludovica palm.

"That's your Angelina Jolie hat," Colón chided Tara, reaching over to pull her new hat from her head and give it a fling across the room. While listening to his hat lesson, I kept my vision on the road winding up to Sigsig, expecting to see Frank. Sure enough, it didn't take much longer for the yellow taxi driver to enter through the village's unique wood-carved, colorfully painted entry gate.

Tara saw Frank first, sticking his head out from the cab window, as she was finishing up her lunch. She jumped up from the table and from the café, waving. Colón's response was fast. He followed her out and grabbed her around the waist.

"Come with me, my Pretty," he snapped, carrying her out to his car, tossing her into the back seat. Colón's girlfriend caught the drift, followed him, and jumped in the front seat.

About to be in the car race of his life, Colón peeled his red convertible around, and with a screech of tires, headed back to Cuenca. Would he be able to outmaneuver Frank's cabbie? I wasn't so sure. But Frank was in a less powerful car, and he must have read the tea leaves. He reached over and opened the taxi door to push the cabbie from the driver's seat onto the gravel. Frank took over the wheel to do a one-eighty, then hit the accelerator hard to catch up with Colón.

Colón was picking up speed as he drove by Sigsig's imposing brick clock tower, which was anchored next to a Catholic elementary school. Children in blue-checked uniforms stood on the pavement, watching the cars race by.

"What are you doing, Colón?"

Tara screamed from the backseat. "I want to talk to Frank!" Her new Panama hats flew from the car seat— and off her head—as she tried to sit upright.

"Wait! Stop! I lost my hat!" she shouted, waving her arms.

"I'm making sure you're safe, Tara. So get back down in the seat and hush up!" Colón yelled at her, while keeping his eyes focused straight ahead.

Both cars blew through town and were reeling on the open road, one known for its sharp turn every fifty to sixty feet. Colón now was traveling at a speed of nearly eighty miles an hour, with Frank still on his tail. On this paved, narrow, winding downhill grade, I was certain this car race would be short and swift, with one of the drivers hitting either a loaded farm truck, a herd of crossing sheep, or an indigenous person carrying textile goods on his or her back.

The drive from Sigsig to Cuenca was never meant to be a road rally. The small highway served as a daily route for bringing the Panama hats and other handcrafted goods down to the Cuenca markets. Drivers typically took extra caution as they rounded each narrow curve.

"Please do something, Grandpa," I whispered, having no idea of any action I could take at the moment to save

Colón and his passengers. I didn't know if Grandpa could hear me—if he was even hanging around.

Colón saw it first and quickly swerved around the huge boulder in his path. He deftly took the right curve that came up. The giant rock must have rolled down the hillside and planted itself in the middle of the highway while we all were up in Sigsig, since it wasn't there on my way up.

Either Frank's older taxi didn't have the same steering radius as Colón's new car, or Frank didn't see the sixty-ton rock in the road soon enough. I watched as the man who'd killed Joe and me, and who was after Tara, tried to drive around it. Coming upon the sharp right turn, he had a narrow strip to pass between the boulder and the left edge of the road. There was enough physical space to make it to the other side of this rock, but Frank got too close, and the right side of his cab glanced the big rock, with just enough force to send it flying over the edge of road, in a country where guard rails are mostly unheard of.

I watched as Frank's car sailed over the edge, a foot or so out from the cliff, far enough to not hit on the side while crashing down to the bottom of a ninety-foot canyon—with enough time to tumble once before landing flat on its roof. The car crashed into the quiet trout stream, touching down on a three-foot jagged rock. I watched as the bottom of the car collapsed. Steam came up from the radiator, but there was no fire. No giant explosion like in the movies.

The crash sound was horrible and quick. I instantly knew that Frank could not walk away from this mess; I was sure he'd turned into a pancake or waffle. Looking up to the main road, I saw Colón stop his car and step out, peering over the edge of the cliff. Tara remained in the back seat, looking stunned.

"Go help Frank!" she commanded.

"There's no use in trying, Tara," Colón announced, while getting back into the driver's seat. "I'd never make it down that cliff. I'll call for an ambulance and report the wreck from Cuenca, but Frank is dead. Count on it!"

Under his breath, I swear I heard him mutter, "And frankly, Tara, I don't give a damn!"

As Colón drove away, I stayed behind and watched as portentous dark storm clouds gathered above the wreckage. The center of one cloud opened, displaying a small jagged space that began to grow into the shape of a mushroom cloud. Even if I never had been successful in using hoodoo, Grandpa told me how it works, about its strange magic that taps into the forces of nature.

"Talk to the mountains, to the streams and sky," he would say. "Thank the spirits for their gifts, and don't be afraid to ask for what you want."

I looked closely into this cloud that was opening up and saw a hideous face-like image emerge from the dark center, hanging directly over the top of the inverted taxi.

I quietly started chanting like Grandpa had taught me: "From the blue sky above and the golden globe of sun, to the green Earth below, I seek answers."

I asked for the spirit of Frank to emerge from this cloud and talk to me. Before Frank's spirit moved on, I had to learn who'd murdered me and Joe, and why. As a trail of vapor crossed over the face of this threatening cloud, it grew more distinct and I could see Frank's angular features emerging, his sharp yellowish nose and weird two-colored eyes staring down at me.

"Why me, Frank?" I shouted up to this spirit-creature in the cloud. "Why Joe? Why kill us both? What did we ever do to you?"

I forced myself to be quiet, hoping for a response, and then a scratchy-sounding voice came from somewhere, perhaps from inside of me.

"You both caused this mess. You wouldn't accept the answers you were given. You expanded the field of questions. You left the narrow range that the assassination planners carefully constructed, and you widened it. One lone shooter for each assassination. No one else involved. This was the intended message for the public, including both of you, and nothing more."

And for this, Joe and I were killed? And hundreds of others? I listened, as he continued.

"You have to understand, the added debate about a narrower set of issues was the plan. Did Oswald go to Mexico? Did he get off all the shots? Was he carrying curtain rods? Did Martin Luther King cheat on his wife? Was he a communist? These were the questions fed to the media. It was never supposed to go any further. Not questions like: Who benefited from expanding the Vietnam War? Whose money was behind the assassinations? You both should have known better!"

How did they ever think they could enforce this ridiculous stance? I really wondered.

"The planners knew they could depend on the compromised media to keep the details under cover. Most reporters and lawyers kept out of it. But both of you, like too many others we've had to dispose of, kept pushing the limits. And you all had to go."

So there was my answer. The assassination planners had depended on ignorance, fear, and/or submissiveness to suppress the most important questions. But people like Joe and me, we were making this too damned hard to maintain. We were getting in the way.

Frank's spirit started to lose its steam. All of a sudden, the expansive hole in this voluminous dark cloud pulled inward and lifted off the canyon floor in one big huff. I learned nothing more from this aberration. But Grandpa's hoodoo had worked—I was 99.9 percent sure. At least I had answers, but where they would take me? I had no idea.

CHAPTER FORTY-ONE

"Ready for more?"

"As much as ever," Sara answered Jay, her military friend from the U.S. Embassy in Quito, before sitting back down in a comfortable stuffed chair, her notepad beside her, and one leg resting over the arm.

"Care for a glass of wine? I have some good stuff from Chile." She offered to open a bottle, starting to move from her comfortable position.

"Don't get up. I'm okay for now."

It was their second break. The evening had been mentally exhausting. I'd been fascinated as Jay revealed the documents he'd collected over the years on President Kennedy's assassination. He'd surprised Sara at the door with his papers and photographs, ready to share what he'd been hiding and holding inside him.

"I want to sleep nights. I'm so damned emotionally tired of hanging on to all of this stuff, and I know it will help you with your career. If we hurry, you can probably still get a story filed before the end of the year—before the fiftieth JFK assassination anniversary ends."

Sara looked stunned. Her friend was standing at her door, holding a large box in his hands. She had not asked this favor of him. At least I'd never heard her request secrets to which he likely had access. Data that he had no right to share.

"Well, what can I say, but come on in. I'm buying the drinks," she laughed, after he'd quietly explained why he was standing at her front door late at night with his box.

"Of course, I have more that I could show you. But I figured you wanted me to follow some rules—so, here's what I can substantiate," he explained, setting the heavy carton down on her dining room table.

"So let's get started," she said. He smiled as he pulled out the first document.

"You wouldn't know this, but old Lyndon B. Johnson knew it was coming, and he actually ducked the bullets before they came flying."

"What are you talking about?" Sara asked.

"There is good evidence LBJ was directly involved or knew what was coming, since he was seen ducking down in his car thirty to forty seconds before the first shots were ever fired, even before the car turned onto Houston Street. The vice president had to know bullets would be flying and laid low until the shots finally went off. Of course, Governor John Connally got stuck riding with JFK, and look what happened to him!"

Jay had begun to look more relaxed about sharing his papers. He got up from his chair, walked into the kitchen, and opened the refrigerator door.

"All this is beginning to make me hungry. Care if I finish this cold pizza," he asked Sara.

"Go for it," she called across the room.

He went back to the file box, pizza in hand.

"Then there's this photograph I just happen to have." The embassy attaché handed Sara a worn black and white photo. "It's Congressman Albert Thomas winking at a smiling LBJ," he pointed out. "See how JFK's grieving widow is standing next to Johnson, as he is being sworn in as President on Air Force One? The longtime Democratic congressman from Houston, who's grinning, was later responsible for bringing the Johnson Space Center to his city."

"Where did you even get this photo?" Sara asked.

"Oh, I have friends in high places," he answered, at first, but then set the rules for the rest of the night. "Look, don't ask me questions like that. Then you can't give answers, if I get caught."

Jay continued. "I'm sure you know about the meeting the night before the assassination, when Johnson met with Dallas tycoons, FBI key players, and organized crime kingpins? Now that was one party!"

Sara interrupted him. "I have a friend who lives in Lubbock, and her mother's housekeeper talked to her about that meeting! The housekeeper said she overheard a bigwig who brought the assassination party up while she was cleaning his house. He and his friends were laughing about it while she was dusting."

"I hadn't heard that story before," Jay responded. But he had gathered information on Johnson's mistress, Madeleine Duncan Brown, who years later, after Johnson's death, told a magazine reporter how LBJ had emerged from an earlier conference to tell her that after tomorrow, the Kennedy's would never embarrass him again.

"We have our own Navy intelligence briefings with her. LBJ's girlfriend was talking to other journalists, so we decided to ask her about this, too," Jay said, handing Sara still more papers. She quickly started going through them.

"Of course, it was no secret that JFK and Johnson despised each other, and that LBJ hated Bobby Kennedy even more," Sara was saying. "The world of the Kennedys was an elite place, and Johnson did not fit in—didn't belong. I understand the brothers had been preparing to dump him before the next election, and he knew it."

"They also had information on LBJ that could put him in prison, along with J. Edgar Hoover; Hoover was also on the assassination party guest list. When we talked to Madeleine Brown, she said the group at this meeting included not only Jack Ruby—known for his call girls, drugs, gambling fixes, and even contract killings—but also Clyde Tolson, who was Hoover's intimate friend and FBI associate director, and John J. McCloy—"

"Back up. You must be kidding me."

Jay stopped, as if he'd expected her to make the connection. "So you think McCloy is interesting? You know his background?"

Sara reminded me of Joe; she could recite people's names and backgrounds at the drop of a hat.

"John Jay McCloy was a lawyer and banker who served as the Assistant Secretary of War during World War II. I've often wondered about his possible involvement. He was president of the World Bank and a U.S. High Commissioner for Germany. Became a prominent U.S. presidential advisor and served on the Warren Commission. And he was there, you're telling me? At the party held the night before JFK was killed?"

"Sure was, Sara," Jay said. "We've established a list of everyone who went to that get-together, and here are the authenticating documents, your highness."

"Oh, shut up and hand me the damned papers."

Jay's eyes were twinkling. "The Warren Commission should have investigated its own members. With both former CIA Director Allen Dulles and McCloy in the same room, the night before JFK was killed, there never was a chance of the Commission getting anywhere, except for covering it all up.

"I remember hearing that Chief Justice Earl Warren cried in Johnson's office when he was badgered to head the Commission. LBJ had dirt on him; he couldn't refuse. Now, I can see why he was in tears. You do know that Dulles's deputy director, Charles Cabell, was brother to Earle Cabell—who happened to be the mayor of Dallas when Kennedy was killed there?"

This surprised me! Sara sounded surprised, too, as she jumped in.

"No wonder the American public gets confused," she said. "Most realize Oswald didn't do this alone. But they still have no idea that all of it was an honest-to-God coup d'état. I remember hearing that Johnson was about to go to prison before JFK was killed. That this was another reason he went along with the plan, even if he didn't come up with it himself. LBJ didn't plan it. Am I right?"

She walked into the kitchen, opened the refrigerator, and pulled out a bottle of wine, waiting for Jay to answer.

"Well, Sara, Madeleine Brown told us that a number of people were set to testify against Johnson for indictment proceedings that related to illegal kickbacks he'd received from agriculture programs before the assassination. But some witnesses were set up in homosexual scandals or were found dead. Johnson probably would have gone to prison. The Kennedys would have rid themselves of him, had JFK not been killed."

I had to wonder if something like this had happened to Joe, considering the park bathroom scene the agent had described to Tara, and the way Joe reportedly died versus the truth. Sara already had asked Jay if he was afraid of being killed for giving out the ONI information, and he'd talked around her question. But now Jay was telling her about an FBI agent named Regis Kennedy, no relation to the president, who helped seize the film and home movies made by various families on the day of the JFK assassination.

"Regis Kennedy was subpoenaed by the House Select Committee on Assassinations to testify about what happened to all this evidence. On the day he was to appear, he was found dead at home."

I had wondered about informants on that compromised committee. Apparently, so did Sara, who was now talking about "over two hundred key witnesses" to JFK's assassination who could have testified to what happened, had they not died under mysterious circumstances or been obviously murdered.

"I've seen their names on the Internet. I know this statistician, Richard Charnin, who develops analytical software and worked in the aerospace industry. He tracks these names, Jay. Charnin contacted me once, right before I left the Dallas News—displeased over some move about to come out. We agreed it would be a propaganda piece which would obscure the facts and perpetuate the fifty-year-old lie. All the Parkland doctors said JFK was shot from the front—in the throat and at the right side of the head. Oswald was just a patsy. It is inexcusable for Hollywood to perpetuate the BIG LIE. Charnin knew about a real Parkland doctor. No Hollywood BS. Said if they presented Oswald as a Lone Nut, the director's reputation could be tarnished forever. I tried to get my editor to let me interview Charnin further and write a feature, but of course he wouldn't. The next week, I was fired."

Sara had gone off on a tangent—a fascinating one—but I was interested in Charnin's list and the statistical analysis he'd completed on dead material witnesses. Sara suggested she had read some recent articles criticizing Charnin's list.

"I want to be fair about this, Jay."

Was she trying to persuade him to believe that he would not be a target for sharing the secret information he'd gathered from the Office of Naval Intelligence?

"Sure, Sara. There is nothing solid behind Charnin's list. Tell this to—"

Then Jay reeled off dozens of names I'd never heard of. These were people who had met untimely deaths when called to testify before various assassination-related committees. Sara was quiet, listening as he read the names, looking down at her socks, stretching her feet and legs, maybe feeling a little guilty.

"Okay then, Jay. Let's get to the point of why you are here. Answer this question. Who in the hell shot President Kennedy, and why?"

I had been waiting to hear this.

"I am sure it was the same hit men the CIA planned to use against Castro, including two of the Watergate burglars, E. Howard Hunt and Frank Sturgis. They were brought into Dealey Plaza that day and were actually caught by Dallas police officers who were conducting a search of the area behind the grassy knoll."

Sara interrupted. "How do you really know this—that Oswald didn't fire these shots, alone? Or that other international shooters weren't in Dallas, too? Because I think there was a South American connection."

"Here's a good study," Jay said, handing Sara a set of fresh documents he'd dug from the bottom of his box. "You know the House Assassinations Committee agreed there was a shot from the grassy knoll. That was their key finding in this congressional investigation that concluded in 1978, replacing the flawed Warren Commission report. They said JFK's murder was 'probably the result of a conspiracy' and that it did not involve the governments of Cuba or the Soviet Union. They also decided that a shot from the grassy knoll meant that two gunmen must have fired at the president within a split-second sequence. Lee Harvey Oswald, accused of firing three shots at Kennedy from a perch at the Texas School Book Depository, could not have been in two places at once."

Jay looked tired. But he didn't waver.

"In other words, our own government later contradicted the heart of the Warren Commission Report. But back to the grassy knoll," Jay went on. "Many witnesses heard gunshots and saw smoke just after the shots rang out. In the area were several railroad boxcars and some witnesses reported men running from the fence behind the knoll toward the boxcars, where three men were found. And we know who they were."

"Who was the third man," Sara moved closer to Jay, filling his wine glass.

Who WAS the third man? It was an important question, and I waited to hear Jay's answer.

"The three tramps as they came to be known, were arrested right after JFK was killed, but they were never booked, photographed, or fingerprinted and were released," Jay began, building up to answer our question, I guess.

"As the police led them through Dealey Plaza, several press photographers fortunately snapped their pictures, and when talk started that the CIA might have been involved, these photographs received quite a bit of publicity through some of the media—the few reporters who really did seek truth.

"Of course, two of the 'tramps' looked an awful lot like the burglars Hunt and Sturgis, who both worked for the CIA. We believe the third tramp is someone often referred to as Raoul," Jay said.

Raoul! I knew that name. He was the Martin Luther King assassination suspect; his photo was briefly circulated by the police after King was killed, then it was quickly pulled. The focus moved to James Earl Ray who later claimed he was set up by a man with this name.

Then Jules Rocco Kimble told British reporters that HE was Raoul. The only man with ties to both assassinations, and as far as I knew, the man who both Joe and I had been looking for, who Joe might have found in witness protection, before we were each killed.

The human pancake floating in the trout stream, outside of Sigsig—that used to be Raoul—his body by now had washed away into the Amazon basin, after his dark spirit drifted off into the storm clouds.

If Frank was Raoul, Tara and Mollie would never have to worry about that evil monster again. And I knew who killed Joe and me—I still wasn't sure why. But I had all the time in the universe to figure it out.

EPILOGUE

June 2014

I'd listened in on several practice sessions of James and the Head Bangin' Delta Blues band and had to admit it was not good. The kids, led by my sixteen-year-old nephew, were loud and once in a while, a riff sneaked through. While not always in tune, they probably had enough songs in their repertoire to do a live gig after three-hour practices most Saturday, for the past six months. They believed so.

"Big party, dudes. My Uncle Clinton's place. You know, the construction site of his new house that never got finished. The lady next door wanted to buy it up and plant flowers, but my mom said no. She wants to build Uncle Clint's house in his honor. And I think that's cool. We have the lot for our fall blues festival! Mom promised!"

I heard James telling his band members to bring their instruments to my vacant lot this weekend—to see what they sounded like playing "all out."

If everyone agreed they sounded good—and surely they would—Clarksdale's first hardcore blues festival would take place Saturday, September 27. When I heard the date, after a moment, I had to rub my phantom hands together and laugh. I remembered that Lucy Bingham Moore and the Clarksdale Culture Club had planned their Fall Event to take place at Lucy's house, next door to my lot, on the same day. If Missy Lucy was worried about my weeds and rusted iron gate, wait until she heard James' head-banging blues band! All out!

I'll just bet old Lucy's going to have one big hissy fit when those blues festival posters go up around town!

If you enjoyed reading The Plan, please leave a positive review. You are also invited to visit www.ebooksfromsusan.com where you can contact me by email. I have posted a bibliography there, as well.

Thanks, Susan Klopfer

ACKNOWLEDGEMENTS

In writing The Plan, I appreciate the valuable help received from my mother Betty Orr, a wonderful writer who is always my inspiration, and from my husband Fred who has greatly helped me along the way, offering special words and creative ideas. He is terrific with analogies! He always takes the time to stop and listen, answer questions, and show his support. I also appreciate help from the Cuenca Writer's In Transition Group, whose members gave me critiques along the way. I could not have written this book without their help.

To my development editor, Frances, I owe much. She got me going! Also wonderfully encouraging and helpful has been my copy editor, Geri Jeter. Her advice and help were excellent.

Also, I want to acknowledge and thank those people of the Mississippi Delta who shared their stories and their time early in my Delta "career." Help and encouragement also came from dedicated JFK researcher John Bevilaqua. He is tireless in his efforts to uncover the truth about JFK's assassination. Also thanks goes to Judyth Vary Baker for her interest and help. She is a brave woman. Thanks also to Richard Charnin who shared his fascinating statistics on dead potential material witnesses.

Still another great person, who asks to remain anonymous, helped me enormously with technical information when it came to describing death and car crashes, He knows who he is! Others have helped along the way, and I appreciate them all, so much. Even if they are not named, their interest and assistance has been critical.

In The Plan, you will find several names of real people, heroes who played vital roles in the modern civil rights movement. This book, however, is historical fiction. Many other names, characters, businesses, organizations, places, events, and incidents either come from my imagination or are used fictitiously. Any resemblance to actual persons, living or dead, events, or locales is entirely coincidental.

Susan Klopfer
Cuenca, Ecuador
October 2013

Susan Klopfer lives in Cuenca, Ecuador, with her husband Fred and their cat, Popsicle. They enjoy wandering South America, and she looks forward to their upcoming visit to Santiago, Chile, as she works on a sequel to The Plan. She is a former acquisitions and development editor for Prentice Hall Computer Books, and she has won journalism awards for investigative and government reporting. Susan became interested in Mississippi civil rights history, while living with her psychologist husband on the grounds of Parchman Penitentiary. They are the parents of Barry Klopfer, a New Mexico lawyer

www.ingramcontent.com/pod-product-compliance
Lightning Source LLC
Chambersburg PA
CBHW070054260626
47160CB00004B/1201